CHEDDA BOYZ

C.J. HUDSON

Life Changing Books in conjunction with Power Play Media
Published by Life Changing Books
P.O. Box 423 Brandywine, MD 20613

Library of Congress Cataloging-in-Publication Data;

www.lifechangingbooks.net
13 Digit: 978-1934230756
10 Digit: 1-934230758

Dedication

This book is dedicated to the memory of Camryn Murphy Speight. Born 3/18/09. Ascended to heaven 6/30/09. You will always have a place in daddy's heart. I love you Camie.

Acknowledgements/Thank You's

Where do I start? At the top of course. First of all, I would like to thank my Lord and savior Jesus Christ for the Strength, patience, vision, and wisdom to complete my first novel. Philippians 4:13 is a verse I live by daily.

To my wife, Margo Murphy Speight: I thank God every day for placing such a special lady in my life. I didn't think it was possible to find someone that I have so much in common with. Having your support means more to me than you will ever know. I truly know what it means now to marry your best friend. She also proofreads my book, with red pen in hand!(lol)

To my mother, Joanna Speight Willis:You instilled in me the stubbornness and drive to do things when everyone else said that I couldn't. The life lessons that I have learned from you will stay with me forever. To my father, John Henry Hudson:You're the strongest man that I've ever known. Even though illness has robbed you of your health, you will always be an inspiration to me. I always tell people that if they've never met you, then they have truly missed out.

To Tressa, Leslie, Nakea, Natasha and the whole LCB family for giving me a chance to shine. I look forward to working with you now and in the future.

To all the LCB authors: Azarel, Tiphani, J-Tremble, Capone, Miss KP, Carla Pennington, VegasClarke, Mike Warren, Tonya Ridley, Ericka Williams, Jackie D, Danette Majette and any other LCB Author that I may have forgotten. Thanks for all you guys support.

To Twenty First Street Editing and Kisha Green. Y'all gave me my first ever interviews as an Author, so I want to thank you both.

To Kwan: Man it ain't enough ways to thank you dawg. I wouldn't have even known about Life Changing Books had it not been for you. Your advice has been invaluable to me. You answered all my questions and never complained. (at least not to me) Now, if I could just get you to jump on the Browns and Cavs bandwagon, you'll be straight. I feel honored and humbled that you would even consider my suggestion for a name to your novel, let alone accept it. Thanks for everything man.

To all the bookstores that is housing my book: I feel honored and privileged that you would let my story onto your shelves.

To the Street Lit authors who have inspired me to step up my game: Kwan, T-Styles, Quentin Carter, Azarel, Capone, J-Tremble, Tiphani and all others whose names escape me at this time: Every time I read any of you all's material, it only served to inspire me more.

To my brother, Justin A. Willis. Yo' you need to start back drawing kid. Graphic design is your future. God doesn't give everyone the talent to draw so don't waste what he gave you.
To Christopher Deonte Lilly. My son. My main man. No matter what, I'll always love you.

To Aaron Lee Murphy. You're my son too. Ain't no steps on you. You're on your way to becoming a very, very successful person. Keep up the good work and remember the excellent teachings that your mother has given to you.

To my sister, Sharima. You've had my back from day one. If it wasn't for you teaching me some things about the computer, I woulda been assed out.

To my sister, Tamika: Even though I don't see you a lot, you know I got mad love for you sis.

To my Aunt, Earnestine Taylor: The big tee. The understanding Tee. The one person in the world I can talk to when I can't talk to anybody else. Your wisdom and advice has gotten me through so much in life. For that I am eternally grateful.

To my Aunt, Christine Cottingham: The little Tee. The down ass Tee. The Keep it Real Tee.

To my first cousins: Leslie, Michael, Nettie, Earnie, Samantha, Tim, Nita, Caroline, Maurice, and Jay(R.I.P). Come on now. Y'all all know that Big 'Hann had greatness in him. (lol)

To my second cousins: Man it's Way too many of y'all to name. I'll get y'all on my next joint.

To my in-laws: Melvin and Marilyn Murphy. All I can do is laugh. I've never met a married couple as much fun as you two.

To my sister-in-laws: Monica: You're one of the few people I know of that truly has a forgiving spirit. Don't ever change.

To Mo-Mo: Even though I don't see as much as I see the other s-n-l's, I always enjoy your company.

To Melissa: Lord have mercy.What is it to say? If it wasn't for you, fun wouldn't have a definition.

To the brother-in-laws: Anthony "A-Jacks" Jackson: Thanks for all the help with my truck dawg (lol).Yep, it's finally happening.

To Jason "J-Boogie" Howard: Thanks for all the computer help man.

To Brain "Laid back-B" Kinney: A special shout out goes to you dawg. Out of 21 people that I asked to read my first two manuscripts, you were the ONLY one to read them both and give me feedback.

To my "Fletcher brothers," Maurice, Coby, Ant, and Jack: We go back thirty years plus. Ain't no way I was gon' forget y'all.

To my boy, Derek "D-Nice" Wheeler: Whether you know it or not, you have always been an inspiration to me. Do yo' thang D.

To Reginald Williams: From Rite aid to VA, the friendship continues. Don't worry man. I won't tell nobody that you're a millionaire (lol).

To Paul Morton: Come on man. Did you honestly think I would forget you? Don't worry. I ain't forgot about yo' hundred (lol)

I have too many FB friends to name, but two in particular that I would like to thank are Kendra Littleton and Lisa Tyrell Perry. You two ladies have helped me network endlessly and I really appreciate it

To anyone that I forgot to mention: I'll get you on the next go-round.

Peace,

The Keyboard Assassin is outta here!!

Chapter 1

"What the fuck?" Big Mo jumped up from the couch and ran to his window, grabbing his hammer along the way. He didn't know what the commotion going on in front of the house was all about, but he wasn't for the bullshit. Pulling the curtains back slowly, he looked out the window, smiled, and just shook his head. CeCe, his future sister in law and a Chedda Boys affiliate was cussing out yet another muthafucka trying to get into her pants.

"Nigga get yo' bitch ass away from me!" she yelled. "I ain't got time to be fuckin' wit yo' broke ass!"

Insulted and embarrassed, the young thug tried to save face.

"Broke? Bitch I ain't neva broke," he said, pulling out a wad of cash.

CeCe looked at the money and then back at the young thug and laughed in his face.

"First of all, punk ass nigga, I don't see no bitches around here unless yo' moms is around here somewhere." The young thug looked like he was ready to swing on CeCe until she slipped her hand in her purse and stopped him cold. "Second of all, that chump change you flashing can't even by me a new pair o' shoes. Now beat it."

Big Mo walked back to his custom made eight thousand dollar Hollywood sectional that he'd just copped from Roche Bobois and took a seat. He laughed heartily as the five thousand dollar Bose surround sound system connected to the fifty-five inch

Plasma television echoed in his ears. He wasn't worried about CeCe. She could more than handle her own. Besides, he was missing Sports Center. The High Definition picture on his fifty-five inch Panasonic was as clear as crystal. After setting his black nine millimeter pistol on the couch next to him, he raised his right hand to his mouth and sipped black coffee from a mug that had the phrase keep ya friends close and ya enemies closer written on it.

Big Mo was the leader of the Chedda Boys. A murderous group of weed selling thugs hell bent on locking down the marijuana trade in Cleveland. His five-man crew consisted of his self, his right hand man Bennie, his two crazy ass homeboys Dre and Ty, and CeCe, the only female in the crew. His girl Stacy was an unofficial member of the crew. Each member had a specific job to do. Bennie ran the operation when Mo was out of town. He grew up with Mo and was the one member of the crew who wasn't intimidated by him. On occasion he would tell Mo when he thought he was making a bad decision. Although he had the final say so, Mo respected Bennie for not being afraid to butt heads with him. In his opinion, a crew was only as strong as the second in command.

His homeboys Dre and Ty supplied the muscle. Whenever muthafuckas got out of line or was slow on the dough, Mo would send either Dre or Ty to tighten they asses up. CeCe was what they called a scout. She would go to different clubs and scout out potential weed heads or bigger playas who might want to buy in bulk. She was also Stacy's baby sister. But the most important person of all wasn't even an official member of Big Mo's crew. That distinction went to Cleveland's Chief of Police Brad Murphy, who was on Big Mo's payroll. Cops on the department always wondered how Chief Murphy could afford to drive a Mercedes Benz, but no one had the balls to question him, or Big Mo.

Big Mo's nickname fit him perfectly. Standing six feet six inches tall and weighing around three hundred pounds, his skin tone was dark like a Hershey bar. He had a shiny bald head that he kept oiled up. The diamond studs he wore in each one of his pointed ears shined like Windex on glass. His eyes were always glassy and shined like black pearls. Rap Mogul, Suge Knight came to mind when you saw his well tapered, full grown beard. Staring at the T.V, he let out a hearty laugh as Stewart Scott started talking about LeBron James leaving Cleveland for New York after the 2010 season was over.

"Yeah right," Big Mo said. "He ain't going no damn where. Don't these dumb asses know the rules of the collective bargaining agreement?" he asked no one in particular.

Just then a fine light skinned honey with curly black hair walked in. Her eyes were hazel and her smile revealed a slight overbite. She was what was referred to as a redbone. She was tall, slightly bow legged, and had full luscious lips. She walked up to Mo and kissed him lightly on the cheek.

"CeCe just came in the backdoor so everybody's downstairs baby."

"Yeah, I saw her gangsta ass walking toward the back," Mo said, laughing.

"What's so funny?"

"She was just out front cussing out one o' dem young niggas."

Stacy just shook her head at her hot tempered sister. "You ready to go downstairs and handle this business?" she asked.

He patted the couch inviting his woman to sit down. "Let they asses wait. You know, I been thinkin' baby. Maybe it's time we went on a little vacation."

Stacy's face lit up like a child's on Christmas morning. "Fo' real baby?" she asked, beaming. They hadn't been on a vacation since they'd met three years ago and Stacy was just dying to get away.

"Yeah, I think it's time we kicked back and chilled a little bit. Where you wanna go?"

"Well," she said as she slung her arm around his neck. "I hear the Bahamas is nice this time of year."

"Sheeiit!" he said smiling. "The Bahamas is nice any time of the year."

"When are we going?"

"I tell you what," he said, "gimme anotha two weeks and if everything is still going smoothly, then we can book it."

"Yes!" she replied, as she thrust her fist in the air.

"Ahight," he said as he stood up. "Let's go take care of these niggas. Go upstairs and look in the closet and get that blue Nike duffle bag."

Stacy sat there for a moment, seemingly in a daze. Mo just assumed that she was thinking of all the fun they were going to have in the Bahamas until he saw the grim look on her face.

"Yo Stacey, you ahight?" he asked.

"Huh? Oh yeah, I'm straight. I was just thinking about my mother. She used to always talk about taking me and CeCe to the Bahamas when we were little." She jumped up and threw her arms around Mo, placing her head in his massive chest. "I miss the hell out of her Mo. I can't believe that she just fuckin' up and left us like that." After a few awkwardly silent moments, Stacy took a deep breath, looked up at her man and smiled.

"Ok baby, I'm cool now," she said.

"You sure?" he asked.

She said yes and started walking past him headed toward the stairs. Secretly, she always wondered why Mo never said anything when she talked about her mother.

As she passed by him on her way up the stairs, he slapped her on her ass.

"Hey! Stop that," she said as she swatted at his hand.

"You wasn't sayin' that last night," he replied grabbing his dick.

"That's 'cause I was tryin' to cum," she said as she continued up the stairs. He shook his head and walked to the kitchen.

She didn't know it, but when they got to the Bahamas, he had every intention of asking her to marry him. She'd been down for him for the last three years and he truly loved her. He trusted her almost as much as he trusted his boy Bennie. His smile quickly faded as he thought about the deep dark secret that he was keeping from her. It was the one thing that he refused to discuss. He inhaled deeply and blew out a long thoughtful breath. He would keep this treacherous act in the dark until the day he left the earth.

Big Mo walked through the kitchen and stopped to admire the fruits of his labor. Leaning on the marble island counter in the middle of his spacious 24x20 kitchen, he smiled as he looked at the 36"/30" Viking cook top stove and nodded in satisfaction as he glanced at the 24" stainless dishwasher. Quickly, he grabbed a napkin off the island and walked over to a stainless steel door that opened up to a pantry. He smiled thinking about the hiding spot he'd built inside to stash his emergency cash.

Life was good for Big Mo and he was going to make damn sure it stayed that way. He reached into the refrigerator and grabbed a bottle of Corona. After popping the top off, he walked through the door leading to the basement. He paused just long enough to check the side door and make sure that it was locked. He made his way down the burberry carpeted steps and stopped at the bottom. He stared at his crew for a moment, who continued on about their business oblivious to his presence.

Dre was standing behind CeCe with his arms wrapped around her whispering in her ear. CeCe looked to be annoyed with him, as she was engrossed in a C. J. Hudson novel.

"Nigga will you back the fuck up offa me for a second? Damn, a bitch can't even read fo' yo ass!"

Off to the side, Bennie was checking his Blackberry trying to keep things tight. Ty was also in his own world smoking on a fat blunt and nodding his head to silent music.

All of a sudden Mo yelled at the top of his lungs, "Police! Everybody get the fuck down!"

Dre and Ty dove on the floor like they were Michael Phelps. Bennie flinched, but didn't move. CeCe didn't even flinch. She just kept on reading her novel. Big Mo cracked up seeing the so-called tough guys on the floor.

"Gotdammit Mo," Dre said. "You scared the shit outta me."

Mo laughed. "Man y'all two fall for that shit every time."

"That's a damn shame," Bennie said.

CeCe just looked at Dre and shook her head. Then she looked at Bennie. "And this the nigga I'm fuckin' on a regular basis?"

Stacy came down the steps holding the duffle bag with a big smile on her face. "Don't tell me y'all fell for that shit again?"

"You know it," Bennie stated.

Ty wasn't smiling at all. He didn't think that shit was funny. "Roll one up lil sis," Stacy said as she dropped the bag on the round black marble table. Putting down her book, CeCe reached into her Louis Vuitton purse and pulled out two phillie blunts. *No use only takin' out one,* she thought. CeCe reached into her back right pocket, pulled out a straight razor, and went to work.

When it came to rolling swishers, CeCe was the best. She quickly split the back and emptied the contents into the ashtray in front of her. She smiled in anticipation as she filled the cigar paper with the sticky green gunja.

She flicked her tongue across the paper back and forth until it was damp enough and rolled it up. Moving shit around in her purse, she discovered that she didn't have a lighter.

"Somebody give me a light," she demanded.

"How 'bout a bud light," Dre cracked.

"You know that's real funny Andre. Let's see how funny it is when you wanna fuck tonight." Dre immediately stopped laughing and passed her a lighter.

Ty cracked up laughing. "Damn cuz, I thought Kunta Kintae was whipped, nigga you all fucked up."

"Fuck you nigga," an embarrassed Dre stated. "Get yo' self a woman before you try to talk shit."

"Nigga please," Ty replied. "I got plenty o' bitches." Being that he was 6'1 with bronze colored skin and body builder arms, it wasn't hard to see why the women liked him. His cornrowed French braids were always tight.

CeCe glared at him. Ty held up his hands.

"I wasn't callin' you a bitch CeCe, it was just a figure of speech."

Mo snickered to himself. He knew why Ty clarified himself. CeCe was a bad bitch in more ways than one. She had black shoulder length hair with sandy brown streaks on each side. Her caramel colored skin was as smooth as butter. Whenever she smiled, she showed a perfect set of thirty-twos. Her five foot ten inch frame more than supported her 34 Double D's.

Her light brown eyes were like chestnuts. She also had a

reputation as a hot-tempered assassin. Over the years, her straight razor had dripped many blood types from niggas and hoes fucking with her. Those were the lucky ones. The unlucky ones caught hot biscuits from her nickel-plated three eighty. Dre was her man but she wasn't the type to be abused by anyone. The first and only time he made that mistake, it nearly cost him his life. If Stacy hadn't stopped her, she probably would've blown his brains out.

"Alright," Mo said. "Everybody got they dough?"

Each member of the crew reached down on the floor and picked up a brown paper bag. Simultaneously they all dumped stacks of cash on the table. Bennie, the human calculator computed the stacks in his head as fast as he could before Stacy could begin her job; his guess, eighty thousand.

Meanwhile, Stacy raked all the dead presidents into a garbage bag and walked over to the bar. She took a seat on the bar stool and started counting the money. Mo, in the meantime, opened the Nike bag and dumped out twenty, 5lb bags of marijuana onto the table. Without hesitation, each member grabbed five bags a piece. CeCe grabbed one of Dre's bricks and added it to her pile.

"Hey! What you doin'?" Dre asked.

"I'm through coverin' fo' yo' ass. You owe me this baby boy."

Dre couldn't say shit. He knew she was right. "Yeah ahight then," he said with anger in his voice. She tried to kiss him, but he turned his head.

"Don't take it personal baby," she said. "Its just business." She tried to kiss him again. This time he didn't resist. Bennie shook his head.

"Damn Ce'. You hard as fuck."

Stacy walked over to the table and looked at CeCe. "Uh… CeCe you're over and Dre yo' ass is short."

Big Mo looked at Dre and rolled his eyes. "Man, that gambling shit gon' cost you big time one day. You just betta be glad you got a girl like CeCe on yo' team nigga."

"Whateva! He's short, just take it from my stack," CeCe replied.

"See what I mean," Mo said.

"Thanks baby," Dre said, still looking embarrassed.

"Umm hmm," CeCe said accepting a kiss on the cheek from her lover.

"Alright," Mo stated. "Everybody got they shit?" I got some shit to do so I'm cuttin' this meetin' short. Y'all more than welcome to stay down here and chill. But next week I wanna full report on what's goin' on." He turned to walk up the stairs. "Oh, by the way," he said, turning his head back. "Fat Jack been tryin' to sell weed on the low on Hough. Dre, I think it's time you paid his ass a visit."

"You sure you don't want me to go?" CeCe asked.

"Nah." Mo shook his head. "I don't want him dead…yet."

Chapter 2

Chief of police Brad Murphy sat in a chair in the corner of his bedroom with his pants around his ankles. He had his big black dick in his hand stroking it slowly as Bennie pumped his dick in and out of his wife.

"You enjoyin' ya' self over there baby?" he asked as he continued to jack off.

"Oh, hell yeah! Ooh...oooh...Aahh shit! This feels good!" Her moans of pleasure made the chief squeeze his dick tighter.

"Uhh!...Uhhh!...don't stop!" she begged. As she started to moan, so did Chief Murphy. Seeing his wife bent over in doggie style position taking dick from a young thug turned his kinky ass on.

"Oohh!...Ooohhh!...Fuck the shit outta me you black motherfucker!" Right on que, Bennie started to thrust deeper and deeper into her blond covered pussy. "Oh fuck! Gimme every inch of that nigger dick!"

Brad snickered under his breath. He'd suggested to his wife that if she really wanted to get fucked hard, she should call Benny a nigger. At first she was apprehensive, not knowing how Bennie would react to that. But then he reminded her of what effect it had on their love life. During one of their fuck sessions he had aggravated her into calling him a nigger so he could get a little angry and punish her pink love house. He knew that she had a thing for black men when he met her and as soon as she laid eyes on his black as midnight skin, he knew it was a wrap.

"What the fuck is he gonna do? He ain't gon' do shit but tear your pussy up after that," her husband had told her. Even though she was still a little nervous about it, she agreed to do it.

Chief Murphy's wife, Audrey, was a pussy pain freak. The harder she got fucked the better she liked it. Bennie grabbed her by the back of her long blond hair and yanked her head back.

"Bitch what the fuck you jus'say to me?" he yelled at her. Breathing and sweating heavily, she cut her eyes at her husband. He mouthed the words, "Its ok." After that, she got a little bolder.

"Motherfucker you heard me! Now, either fuck the shit outta me or get the fuck up!"

"Alright bitch! Yo' slutty ass asked for this!"

He grabbed the sides of both her hips and forcefully drove his ten inches into her womb. She gasped out loud as she felt it growing inside of her. "Oh, shit!! That's what the fuck I'm talking about!" Audrey screamed.

He reached down and around her thighs and opened her legs even wider. The more he thought about that nigger comment, the madder he got. He locked his fingers together to get a better grip on her hair and began pulling back with all his force. Now, he was punishing her.

"Aahh!!...Aahhh!!!...Oh my God!! Oh, shit baby, he's fucking the shit outta me!" she shouted to her husband. "Ooohh fuck, I'm 'bout to cum!! AAHHH!! SHIT!!!" Audrey screamed as she exploded in ecstasy.

Hot cum ran down her leg as she continued to moan. Bennie slid his dick out of her and leaned back. Audrey spun around on one knee until his dick was directly in front of her face. She grabbed it with her right hand and put the head of it in her mouth. Bennie moaned with pleasure as she sucked her own cum off the tip of his dick. Then she slid her mouth down on it until it was in the back of her throat. She deep throated him like a pro while Bennie fucked her mouth like it was a pussy.

"Oh, shit baby here it cums Ma!" Bennie yelled as he shot his load down her throat.

She made gulping sounds as she swallowed every last baby

he spit out. At the exact same moment, Chief Murphy was having an orgasm of his own. He absolutely loved to see his wife get screwed by other men. He was always intrigued by the swinger lifestyle but knew that his former wife would have none of that. But Audrey was different. She loved to go to the orgy parties that accompanied the swinger's lifestyle, so when she suggested that they attend one while they were dating, his eyes lit up like a kid in a candy store. They'd been swinging ever since.

"Oh, fuck!" he screamed, as he shot his cum two feet across the floor.

Audrey turned around and laid back on the bed licking her lips, trying to make sure she got every last drop. "Damn Bennie, that shit was good," a smiling Audrey said. She looked over at her husband and blew him a kiss. Bennie looked at Chief Murphy and twisted up his lips.

"What?" the Chief asked.

"Since when the fuck did she start callin' me nigga?" a ticked off but satisfied Bennie questioned.

"That was my idea," the Chief said. "We figured it would make you fuck her harder."

"It worked too," Audrey replied. "My coochie's sore as fuck."

"Good," Bennie spat.

"So, what's up Benjamin? I know you didn't come by here on my off day just to tap some white girl pussy. What do the Chedda Boys want now?" Chief Murphy asked.

"First of all, don't call me Benjamin. Only people I fuck call me that."

"So, does that mean I can call you...?"

"Shut up bitch," Bennie said before Audrey could even finish her sentence.

Chief Murphy frowned at him. "Nigga don't be callin' my hoe a bitch."

Audrey looked from one to the other. "You know what? Fuck both of you." She flipped them the bird and walked out of the room.

"Second of all," Bennie continued. "Don't act like yo' ass

ain't getting' paid fo' yo' muthafuckin services nigga."

"Ok, ok," Murphy said as he held up his hands. "What can I do for y'all?"

"You remember Fat Jack?" Bennie asked.

"Yeah, what about him?"

"Well, his greasy ass is tryin' to take money out a nigga's pocket."

"Ok," Murphy said as he hunched his shoulders. "What do you want me to do about it?"

"Give me his address."

"His address? That's gonna cost."

"We already know…. pull yo' muthafuckin' pants up sicko."

"Oh…yeah." Murphy stood up and pulled his extra large sweat pants up. His stomach hung six inches over his waistline.

Damn this nigga look sloppy, Bennie thought. *No wonder his wife don't wanna fuck his nasty lookin' ass.*

"Like I was sayin'. We already know that."

Bennie reached into his pocket and pulled out a rolled up stack of one hundred dollar bills wrapped in a rubber band. Chief Murphy took one look at the cash and sang like Boyz to Men.

"He stay stay off of east 87th and Superior. You know, right across the street from where they had that real bad fire a few years ago."

"The one that killed the nine people?" Bennie asked.

"Yeah, that's the one."

"No problem," Chief Murphy stated as he stared at the stack of money in Bennie's hand. "I can get that for you."

Bennie tossed the money at Chief Murphy. "You better be glad you're Big Mo's brother," Bennie said as he turned and walked out the door. "Cause I coulda extorted you and got that info for free. I'm out dickhead."

Chapter 3

Sugar sat back, folded her arms, and smiled. Her sister Spice sat beside her stone faced. "What y'all gon' do?" she asked.

The dark skinned, dreadlocked Jamaican sitting across from her looked at his bald headed partner, who lustfully stared at Spice's lips. Then he looked back at Sugar.

"So, dats da bes' yuu can do huh mon?"

"That's all, baby boy," Sugar replied.

Conceding defeat, the drug dealer from upstate New York readjusted his New York Yankees fitted cap and smiled, revealing a mouth full of gold teeth.

"Ok den pretty lady. Yu got yuself a deal."

His partner, an LL Cool J look alike with a bad attitude, shook his head in disgust. He didn't like doing business with out of towners. Sugar then slid a black briefcase across the table while at the same time the fake LL slid a similar one underneath the table. It was so busy in McDonalds that none of the customers knew what was going on. Both parties opened their respective packages and smiled, equally satisfied.

"Looks like we good here homeboy," Sugar said. "Nice doing business with you boys."

Both sisters got up and walked toward the exit. Spice whispered in Sugar's ear, "I bet your bald headed boy is looking at my ass." Sugar shot a quick glance behind her, looked back at Spice, and laughed.

"You right. He is."

"Um…Too bad."

Hopping into the driver's side of her 2009 Silver Range Rover, Sugar reached into the glove compartment, took out a box of Dutch Masters, and handed them to Spice. "Hook that shit up girl."

Spice scrunched up her face. "The fuck makes you think I got weed on me?"

"Bitch please, you know you stay high."

"Whateva." Spice reached into her Dolce and Gabanna purse and pulled out a thick bag of dark green Gunja and a razor. While she was busy rolling up a blunt, her sister was looking over the money again.

"This is what the fuck I'm talkin' 'bout sis! Making this muthafuckin' Chedda!"

Spice nodded her head in agreement as she lit the end of the Dutch. "You almost blew it though with that ugly ass lip gloss you got on," Spice laughed.

"Whateva," Sugar said before glancing down at her blinged out Rolex watch. "We gotta roll. We got a meetin' wit' Gaines in about forty-five minutes. Maybe he has some new information for us."

"I hope so. "Come hell or high water, I'm gon' find out who killed our dad."

Chapter 4

Inspector Michael Gaines of the Cleveland Police Department sat in the IHOP restaurant sipping water and reading the USA Today newspaper. He was one of the few people in the whole city of Cleveland who still had a jherri curl. The five foot eight inch tall, two hundred and forty-five Gaines had a thin salt and peppery mustache. He was so light skinned, that people often wondered if he was a brother man or the other man. Walking with a slight limp due to the fact that he'd been shot in the calf once, he made his way over to the window and peered out into the half empty parking lot. His training as a cop automatically kicked in as he surveyed the entire area. From left to right his eyes swept across the chain of stores in his view.

Electricians, Carpenters, and Painters all scurried about the Home Depot on the nearby corner. Teachers and all other sorts of professional people filed in and out of the Office Max to his right. Gaines shook his head as foot traffic increased greatly when his eyes fell on the next two stores. People were tripping all over themselves for the big blowout sale at Marshalls. Its neighboring store Wal-Mart was always busy. Not seeing anyone he shrugged his shoulders, slid back to the table, and continued to read his paper. A young white waitress with a chubby face and red hair annoyingly asked him if he was ready to order yet.

He shook his head and ignored her angry mumbles. He was a moody man whose only goal in life was the almighty dollar. The only reason he even wanted to be a policeman was so he could shake down and extort all Cleveland drug dealers. He'd gained a few hundred thousand taking payoffs from not only the higher ups in the Cleveland drug trade, but the small time hoods as well. He'd been doing it for five years as he climbed the ranks and had managed to sock away two hundred fifty thousand dollars.

He could have taken much more but figured taking a little at a time was the safest route to go. This job was gonna net him a hundred and fifty grand. He didn't really want to do it, but his greed overpowered his laziness in this particular instance. He had agreed to find the identity of the person who had killed Sugar and Spice's father. His price was seventy-five thousand dollars, but just to make sure he was motivated, they surprised him by telling him they would give him an extra seventy-five g's when the job was done.

He had an idea about who he thought killed Clarence Johnson, but he had no proof. So, instead of building these two ladies hopes up, he would wait until he had it. He looked at his silver band citizen watch and shook his head.

"This is just like women to be late," he said.

He had briefly thought about stretching this thing out to try and get more money out of them, but thought better of it. Besides, he didn't want to appear to be too greedy. He checked his watch again.

"Wow. I really wish that these women would hurry up. I have other things to do tonight

Sugar and Spice pulled into the IHOP parking lot minutes later bumping Jay Z's song *Parking Lot Pimpin'*. They'd just left the Al Paul car wash on Warrensville Center Road, and the Silver Range Rover with smoke gray tinted windows shinned like Mop-N-Glow. The Giovanni rims sparkled in the sun. Due to the fact that they rarely drove it, there wasn't a scratch on the car anywhere. They both hopped out of the car looking like mega-divas.

Sugar had on a pair of seven hundred fifty dollar Dolce and Gabanna skin-tight embellished washed stretch jeans, a two thousand dollar beaded shirt, and a pair of thirteen hundred dollar Chloe lace-up motor ankle boots. Spice stepped high in a pair of beige two thousand dollar Alexander McQueen ankle boots, eight hundred dollar Burberry Brit jeans, and a beige and white Behnaz Sarafopour lightening tunic costing around seven hundred fifty dollars. They waltzed into the restaurant and strolled over to where Inspector Gaines was sitting. He looked up at the two of them with attitude, and then at his watch. Spice responded by pulling her Gucci shades off her face, looking at her watch and shrugging her shoulders. Gaines smiled and shook his head.

"You ate anything yet?" Sugar asked.

"No, as a matter of fact I haven't eaten anything all day," he answered.

"Order whatevea you want. It's on us."

"Thank you," Gaines said. After ten minutes of making small talk with spice the waitress reappeared and he proceeded to order Country fried steak with white gravy, mashed potatoes that he wanted drowned in brown gravy, a Rib eye steak to go, and then had the nerve to order a diet coke. He was a big eater as his robust frame attested and since he wasn't paying for it, he figured fuck it. Both women sat down side by side across from Gaines.

"Are you ladies going to eat something ?" he asked.

"Naw dawg we straight," Spice answered.

"Did you find out anything else?" Sugar interjected.

Spice just stared a hole through him. It was almost as if she was waiting for some bad news so she could go off.

"A little," he said as he flipped open a notebook. "The man who killed your father used to run with a gang called the Cleveland Sopranos. When several members of his gang got locked up or killed, he disbanded the gang and every remaining member went their own way. So far that's all I've been able to come up with but rest assured that I will not rest until I find out what happened to him."

"Damn! You couldn't find out nothin' more than that man?" Spice snapped. "We payin' yo' ass a good chunk o' change to find this muthafucka!"

"I know, but these things take time. It's not like someone's beating down my door with a lot of information. You're going to have to give me a little more time."

"Fuck that!" Spice snarled. "Just do what the fuck we payin' you to do!" She stood up and stormed out of the restaurant.

"Your sister has quite a temper. I know you ladies are spending a lot of money and all but this could get me fired. To be perfectly honest, I'm taking a tremendous chance here."

"I apologize for my sister," a calm Sugar said. "But you need to understand somethin'. Our mom died when we were young. Our father was all we had. He had some problems with drugs but that didn't make us love him any less." Tears seemed to glisten in Sugar's eyes.

"I understand that," Gaines said. "But I'm going to need a little more time."

Sugar sighed and nodded her head. "Thanks for your time. Call us when you get something."

"Will do," Gaines responded. The two shook hands and Sugar walked out leaving Gaines sitting there waiting on his food.

Spice sat in the car fuming. She couldn't believe that this so-called cop hadn't found any new information concerning her father. Even though he'd only been on the case for a couple of months, she was getting antsy. She wanted her father's killer found. She knew that it was going to take time, but she couldn't help it.

She took a deep breath and tried to calm down. She opened the glove compartment and took out the dime bag of weed she had placed in there a week ago. Then she reached into her purse and pulled out a box of Phillie blunts and a straight razor. Smoothly she split the back of the Phillie and dumped the contents into the ashtray and replaced it with the brownish-green weed. After licking the paper and rolling it up, she waved the lighter across it a couple of times. She lit the tip of it and inhaled sharply twice. After holding the smoke in for a few seconds, she slowly exhaled and released the cannabis fumes from her lungs. Thinking back to the day her father died saddened her deeply.

She was the baby girl. The apple of her daddy's eye. She knew her father had a drug problem but in no way did that affect the way she felt about him. In her eyes, he would always be perfect. She took another hit of the blunt and coughed out the smoke. She turned on the engine so she could listen to some music. Being the dominant personality that she was, she didn't listen to the radio too much because she couldn't control what was on it. She liked CD's. She popped in Beyonce's song *Single Ladies* and laughed at the irony. She would never marry her current boyfriend. She felt he was too weak to be anybody's husband. She was so into her thoughts that she didn't hear Sugar open the door.

"What's so funny?" Sugar questioned.

"Nothin', just thinking bout' somethin'. What did Gaines have to say?" she asked suddenly with an evil look.

"Nothin' more than he said while you were in there," Sugar said as she took the blunt her sister was offering. Taking a hit she said, "But you gon' have to calm yo' ass down. It ain't doin' none of us no good for you to be getting' all pissed off and shit."

"I know, It's just so damn frustratin'." Spice made a steeple with her fingers and put them to her lips. "I was just thinkin'. What if he's doggin' this? What if he's just stringin' us along?"

Sugar looked up to the sky as if contemplating this and then shook her head. "I doubt it. Besides, he knows that if we tell him to go to hell, he won't get the rest of his money."

"If he hasn't found out anything else by the next time we talk to him, I think we should up the ante," Spice said.

"Up the ante? Up it to what?" Sugar asked, as her eyes got wider and she held up her hands.

"I don't know. Something that would make this cop speed up his investigation." She thought for a minute. "I say we offer to double his pay to $300,000 dollars."

Sugar raised her eyebrows. "You really wanna give this dirty cop an extra $150,000 dollars?"

Spice looked at her through focused eyes. "No, I don't. But I also don't want our father's killer to go unpunished. Besides, we got plenty of money."

Sugar flashed a wicked smile and slowly shook her head from side to side.

"He won't."

$$$

Inspector Gaines finished his meal and beckoned for the waitress to come over. Smiling at her with crooked coffee stained teeth, he asked for a second cup of java. The waitress walked away rolling her eyes, still pissed off at him for not ordering his food in what she deemed a timely fashion. The corners of his mouth curled up into a sinister smile. Little did Sugar and Spice know, Inspector Gaines was playing both sides of the fence. He flipped opened his cell phone and started punching in numbers.

"What?" an annoyed voice on the other end of the phone asked.

"It's me, Gaines."

"I know who the fuck it is. I'm busy. What the fuck you want?"

"Oh, I apologize for bothering you. I'll call you back when you have more time to talk. Good bye."

Gaines hung up on him without awaiting comment. After about ten minutes, his cell phone rang.

"Hey man, I'm sorry about that. I had company over."

"No problem. Look, the only reason I called you was to tell you that I met with both of them today. I don't know how much longer I can hold them off. The young one's a real hot head. She really irritated me today by yelling at me."

"Don't worry 'bout her. Just keep stallin'," the voice on the other end stated.

"Do we still have a deal?" Gaines inquired.

"Yeah, yeah we still gotta deal."

"Then I'll see you tomorrow?"

"Naw. I'll have my right hand man bring it to you today. I got shit to do tomorrow."

Click.

Chapter 5

Dre and Ty cruised along east 79th Street past Wade Park in a 2004 dark gray Honda Accord on their way to find fat Jack. This asshole was takin' money out of the Chedda Boy's pocket and had to be dealt with accordingly. Dre made a left on Hough and slowed down to about ten miles an hour. Suddenly, Fat jack wobbled out of the corner store carrying a twelve pack of MGD in one hand and a large bag of pork skins in the other.

"Look at that shit," Ty said. "That's why his ass so fat now. How you wanna handle this dawg?"

"Let's just wait and see where this fat muthafucka goes," Dre replied.

Fat Jack hopped into his Red 2007 Chevy Trailblazer and pulled out of the stores parking lot.

"Damn that's a ugly ass truck," Ty cracked. "And he got the nerve to have some rims on that piece of shit." Dre and Ty followed Fat Jack down Hough all the while maintaining two car lengths. Fat Jack was so busy finishing off the bag of Bar-B-Que pork skins that he never even noticed he was being followed. He made a left on 55th and continued on until he got to Cedar. Then he made another left and drove up Cedar. Ty looked at Dre puzzled.

"What the fuck is this stupid muthafucka doin? He just wasted ten minutes goin' all the way around when he coulda just cut across 79th," Ty said.

"You think fat boy know we following him?"

"Hell naw. He ain't that damn smart."

Fat Jack made a right on 85th and Cedar and pulled into the

driveway of a rundown looking single-family house. The grass looked as if it hadn't been cut in weeks and the yellow house needed a severe paint job. The concrete steps were cracking and the fence around the yard was falling down. Dre and Ty pulled to the corner of 85th and stopped watching as Fat Jack huffed and puffed up the steps.

"Wassup?" Ty asked. "You wanna rush this fool or what?"

"Naw cuz. I got a better idea."

Spotting a crackhead walking up the street, Dre called out to her. "Hey home girl. Let me holla at you for a minute."

The woman was rail thin with two teeth missing in the front. She had on dirty jeans, a tee shirt, and a blue scarf was wrapped around her head.

"Wassup playa?" the woman asked.

"Y'all tryin' to get down or what?"

"Yeah," Dre said. "But not like you think sweetheart. You know the dude that lives there?"

"Who? Fat Jack? Yeah, I know his bitch ass. Muthafucka still owe me twenty dollars."

Ty reached into his pocket and pulled out a wad of twenties. The woman's eyes got as big as dinner plates.

"Tell you what," Ty said, "get him to open the door and keep him occupied for few minutes and I'll give you the twenty he owes you plus another eighty."

"How do I know y'all ain't gon' stiff a sista?" the woman asked skeptically.

"Because I'm gon' give you sixty now and I'll leave the other forty in his mailbox."

She looked at him through suspicious eyes. Dre read her mind. "Don't worry sweetheart. We ain't PoPo. That nigga owe us money too and we tryin' to collect."

"Give me ten minutes," the woman replied as she took the three twenty's. Heading off to Fat Jack's, thoughts of getting high were already in the woman's head.

"She gon' be callin' Scotty all night tonight," Ty said. After passing a blunt back and forth between them for about fifteen minutes, Dre looked at his iced out Presidential Rolex and checked the time. "She's been in there long enough," he said. "Let's roll."

Ty reached up under the seat and pulled out two nickel plated pistols. He gave Dre the nine-millimeter and kept the forty five for himself. Stuffing the guns in the small of their backs, they hopped out of the car and walked toward Fat Jack's house. Taking slow, purposeful, steps they eased up on the porch. Ty reached into his pocket and pulled out two twenty dollar bills and put them in the mailbox to complete his part of the bargain. They quietly turned the doorknob and entered the house to the sounds of Fat Jack moaning with pleasure. Creeping through the living room, they made their way down the dingy hallway pass the piss smelling bathroom until they came to the bedroom door.

Ty whispered to Dre, "And this nigga a drug dealer? Look how he livin' dawg."

They carefully pushed opened the door and peeped inside. The way he was getting his head blown, they could've made all kind of noise and he wouldn't have heard them. Fat Jack was moaning like this was the best head that he'd ever had in his life.

"Oh, shit!! Oh, girl don't stop!" he begged. "Oh, fuck I'm 'bout to cum!! Oh, sh...OOWW SHIT!! What the fuck?" Fat Jack fell to the floor as he felt the cold steel of Ty's gun slam against his right temple. The woman started to scream, playing her part to a T.

"Bitch shut the fuck up before we give you some of what this fat muthafucka gon' get. As a matter of fact, get the fuck out," Ty ordered as he winked at her.

The woman hurried out the house with a smirk on her face. Reaching into the mailbox, she grabbed the forty dollars Ty had left for her. Fuck the rolling stones. She was going to be the rock star tonight.

"Get yo punk ass up!" Dre yelled. Fat Jack staggered up and sat on the edge of the bed.

"What the fuck is this all about man?" Fat Jack asked.

"The fuck you doin' tryin' to sell weed down here nigga?" asked Ty. "You know this Big Mo's turf punk."

"Hey man I'm just tryin' to make a muthfuckin' livin' dawg.

"Nigga you call this shit livin'?" a disgusted looking Ty

asked. "This shit is ridiculous. Stand yo' fat ass up punk. Where yo' stash at?"

"Man I don't keep it here."

Ty backhanded Jack. "Nigga stop lying!" Ty screamed.

"Where is it Jack?" Dre questioned.

"Man I swear…"

BLOC!!

"AAAHH Shit!!" Jack screamed as Dre shot him in the leg.

"The next one's goin' in yo' stomach. And the one after that's goin' in yo' head."

"Ok man ok! Over there in the bottom drawer!"

Ty walked over to the dresser and pulled out the bottom drawer. He reached in it and pulled out a large ziplock bag filled with weed.

"Is that all of it?" Dre asked.

"Yeah man, that's it."

"Man this nigga's lyin," Ty said as he pointed the barrel of his gun at Fat Jack's midsection.

"Nah man, I swear that's it!" a terrified Jack screamed.

Ty removed his gun from Jack's stomach and walked over next to Dre. "Turn the fuck around fat boy," Dre said.

"Oh, God y'all gon' kill me ain't y'all?"

"Turn yo' ass around!" Ty yelled.

With his hands trembling and sweat beading up on his forehead, Fat Jack slowly turned around.

"Now," Dre demanded. "Before you even let some dumb shit go through yo' mind, we know this ain't where you stay. We know you stay off of 87th and Superior. We also know your mother stays in that hi-rise apartment building in Indian Hills. So, if I was you, I would think about that before I plan my next move muthafucka. Ya' feel me nigga?"

Petrified, Fat Jack nodded his head.

"Good. 'Cause from this point on, yo ass is closed for business."

The next thing Fat Jack saw was darkness as the butt of Ty's forty-five came down across the back of his head, temporarily turning out his lights.

Chapter 6

Stacy and CeCe sat at a table at Maggiano's restaurant in Beachwood Ohio. They were both dressed to kill. Fellow male patrons couldn't keep their eyes off of them as they sat and sipped their drinks while waiting for the guys to get there. It didn't even matter that some of them were with their women. They were still feenin' to sneak a peek whenever they got the chance.

Stacy looked like money in her red five thousand dollar Akris belted trapezoid dress with three-inch Jimmy Choo pumps. She accessorized it with a two-inch diamond tennis bracelet and a platinum chain with enough ice to give her frostbite. Not to be outdone, CeCe wore a white knee-length Chevron-print mini dress that set her back forty-eight hundred dollars. She set it off with a pair of thirteen hundred dollar Maison Martin Margiela crystal pumps and a diamond encrusted platinum bracelet. Hanging around her neck was also a platinum chain necklace with a diamond filled "C" attached to it.

An impatient Stacy checked her watch for the third time as she continued to sip on her Long Island Ice Tea. "Where the fuck they at?" asked CeCe as she worked on her second Cosmopolitan.

"I don't know but I ain't gon' wait in here all night," Stacy said. "Is Ty supposed to be bringing somebody?"

"Yeah. I jus' hope he don't bring that stuck up bitch that he brought last time. Ty my boy and all, but I wasn't but two seconds off her ass." Stacy just shook her head.

"What?" CeCe asked.

"I'm just tryin' to figure out what she did to make you not like her," Stacy said. "She didn't say two words all night."

"I just don't think she the right woman fo' my boy Ty."

Stacy's radar went up. *Why in the hell does she care about the women Ty messes around with? Dre's her man.* "Ty don't give a fuck about none of them hoes. Why you trippin' off them bitches anyway?"

"I'm just sayin'. He can do better than them tack head bitches he be bringing around."

Stacy stared at her.

"The fuck you lookin' at me like that for bitch."

"Girl if I didn't know better, I would swear you was catchin' feelins' for that nigga Ty."

"What? Girl yo' ass trippin'. Ain't nobody catchin' feelins' fo' that nigga. Have you forgotten that's my man's cousin?"

"Naw I ain't forgot. Just make sure yo' ass don't forget."

Just then Mo, Dre, Ty, and Ty's flavor of the month strolled into the restaurant. All three men were dressed to impress, but nothing like Ty's flavor of the month. She stood close to six feet tall with long shapely legs, and a pair of tits to die for. The black three-inch heels she had on made her resemble Lisa Leslie. She had long jet black hair that hung to the center of her back and mocha colored skin which obviously had Ty mesmerized. The woman smiled as Ty pulled the chair out for her causing Stacy and CeCe to look at each other curiously. They had never seen Ty be that nice to any woman. Mo took a seat next to Stacy and Dre plopped down next to CeCe.

"Well, well looks like the gang's all here!" Mo shouted.

"And who the fuck is this?" Ce Ce interrupted, referring to Ty's date.

"Gloria," the woman spat.

Stacy stared at Mo until she was sure that she had his undivided attention. "I thought this was supposed to be a business meeting," she said, turning her cold stare to Gloria.

"Yeah, I know but since Ty decided to bring a date, let's do that tomorrow. We ain't been out together in a while so let's just enjoy the evening. You know, spend a little money."

Stacy hunched up her shoulders, picked up a menu, and started looking through it.

Ty decided to break the spell on the weird vibe at the table. "Gloria, this is Mo's Girlfriend Stacy and this here is my cuz's girl CeCe."

"Nice to meet you," Gloria said.

"Nice to meet you too," Stacy replied. CeCe didn't say a word. And the snub didn't go unnoticed by Dre.

"Aint you gon' speak CeCe?" Dre asked.

"Huh? Oh, my bad. Wazzup?" CeCe responded.

What the fuck is her problem, Dre thought.

Shrugging it off, he looked at Big Mo and nodded. "I see you looking dapper as usual homeboy. I hope you got ya credit card," Dre teased cause I'ma bout to eat up some shit."

Big Mo burst out laughing. "Nigga you know damn well The Chedda Boyz don't do that credit card shit when we go out. We leave that shit to them broke ass muthafuckas that can't pay on the fuckin' spot," Big Mo said, reaching into his pocket. "This is how the fuck we roll," he said as he took out and displayed a wad of hundreds . Big Mo then scrunched up his face and looked at Ty strangely.

"What?" Ty asked as he looked around trying to figure out what Mo was looking at.

"I see you got some new Cubic Zirconia in ya ear playa," he teased.

"Shiieet nigga, you tripping Mo. This little piece right here set a nigga back twenty G's," he said of the VS clear cut diamond in his left ear.

"But y'all know that ain't shit for a Chedda Boy."

Mo laughed then turned his attention to his woman. "What did you do today Stacy?"

He wanted to see if she was going to lie. He had already peeped the Nordstrom and Saks Fifth Avenue bags up under the bed. What he didn't know was that she was one step ahead of him. She'd learned a long time ago that whenever he wanted to catch her in a lie, he'd ask her dumb irrelevant shit like that.

"I went shopping. I told you that I was gonna go yesterday

remember?"

"Yeah, but I thought that meant you was gonna actually go yesterday. Not today."

Stacy became agitated. "What's the damn difference?" she asked. Seeing her aggravation he decided to leave it alone.

"Nothin' I was just wondering, damn. Don't be so touchy."

"What the fuck is takin' em so damn long?" Ty complained. "A nigga hungry as fuck up in here."

"Calm yo' ass down nigga," Dre said. "The food ain't goin' no where."

"If the man's hungry, the man's hungry," chimed in CeCe. Stacy quickly cut her eyes to CeCe.

"Why the hell you worrying 'bout that nigga's stomach?" Dre asked.

"I ain't worried 'bout his stomach. I'm just makin' a damn comment. Stop actin' so fuckin' jealous Dre." Dre just glared at her.

"Where the fuck is Bennie?" Ty asked breaking the tension.

"I got em on a special mission tonight," Mo said. The waiter walked over smiling from ear to ear. Apparently he smelled money in the air.

"Good evening folks. Are you ready to order?"

Before anyone else could say anything, CeCe started screaming. "Did anybody call yo' muthafuckin' ass ova here? Damn when we ready we'll fuckin' call you!" The waiter walked away embarrassed and pissed off. Dre looked at CeCe like she was crazy.

"Woman what the fuck is wrong wit you tonight?"

"Straight drama queen," Gloria mumbled.

Big mistake. CeCe heard her.

"Bitch what the fuck you say? Don't act like you part of the fam bitch. You ain't been here but a hot second," CeCe said as she squinted and glared at Gloria.

"Who the fuck you think you talkin' to?" Gloria asked, refusing to be intimidated.

"Bitch, I'm talkin' to yo' ugly ass!" Gloria turned her attention to Ty.

"Ty you betta check that hoe before I…"

Before another word could escape her mouth, her face got wet as CeCe threw a glass of water in her face. Wet and furious, Gloria grabbed a grabbed a fork, stood up, and started walking around the table. Not wanting CeCe to fuck Gloria up, Mo jumped in between them. He gave both Dre and Ty a look that told them that they'd better control both their women. Dre grabbed CeCe from behind and Ty stood in front of Gloria blocking her path.

"Aye yo' y'all cut dis bullshit out!" Mo roared, slamming his fist down on the table. "All o' y'all sit the fuck down! CeCe what the hell is wrong with you?"

CeCe stared at Mo for a good five seconds before she spoke. She wasn't afraid of Mo in the least, but she did respect him as their leader.

"Nothing Mo," she said, sitting back down in her chair.

After getting Gloria calmed down, Ty finally convinced her to sit back down in her seat. In a huff, Gloria mumbled "You lucky bitch." But this time she was smart enough make sure that CeCe didn't hear her.

$$\text{♯♯♯}$$

As he cruised up Mayfield Road in his 2008 Lincoln Navigator, Bennie's stomach started growling. He hadn't eaten anything since nine-thirty in the morning. "Shit," he mumbled. "A nigga 'bout to starve to fuckin' death'." He flipped open his cell phone and dialed a number. "Hey, it's me, Bennie. There's been a change in plans. Meet me at the Wild Wings spot on Mayfield." Before the person on the other end could respond, Bennie hung up the phone. Seconds later, Bennie pulled into the restaurant's parking lot and parked.

After shutting off the engine, he reached into his console and took out a pack of black and milds. He shook one out of the pack and stuck it in his mouth. Then he dug in his pocket and fished around until he found a lighter. After setting fire to the tip and taking a few puffs, he popped in one of Tupac's greatest CD's. He fast forwarded to the track he was looking for. *I Got My Mind*

Made Up featuring the Dogg Pound, Method Man, and Red Man blasted through the twelve inch Sub-Woofers he had installed in the back. As he bobbed his head to the beat and puffed on the black and mild, he thought about how he had pounded Audrey Murphy's guts earlier. He smiled at the thought. Bennie had a thing for white women.

He knew that most white women would have a hard time taking his ten inches without screaming and he loved to hear them scream. But Audrey seemed to be different. She actually enjoyed being pounded like that. At five feet eleven inches tall with choco- late skin, Bennie attracted his share of women. He had thick eye- brows and piercing black eyes. His chiseled two hundred and twenty pounds of solid muscle more than made up for the scar over his right eye. He had a top tooth missing just to the left of the mid- dle, although he wore a gold and platinum grill most of the time so not many people knew it. Bennie was vibin' to the beat when a knock on his window startled him. He reached down hit the button automatically unlocking the door.

"Nigga yo' ass almost got shot creepin' up on me like that."

"Sorry, wouldn't want that," Gaines replied, sarcastically.

"Whateva, just watch that bullshit dawg."

"Will you please stop complaining?" Gaines said. "You sound like my wife." The two men laughed as Gaines got in the truck. He reached into the breast pocket of his stripped blue and white button down and took out a pack of Newports. Before he could even shake one out, Bennie shot him down.

"Unt uhh," Bennie said. "Ain't no smoking in my truck bro. I'm the only one allowed to that." Gaines rolled his eyes and put the pack back in his pocket.

"I believe you have something for me, young blood?" Gaines questioned.

Without saying a word, Bennie reached into the console of his truck and took out a manila envelope. He handed it to Gaines who wasted no time opening it. He pulled out and counted one hundred crispy Benjamin Franklins. He put a stack up to his nose and smelled it as if it would somehow give him new life.

"Ahight," Bennie said. "You got what you came for. Now

beat it punk."

"In a hurry I see."

"Man, I ain't ate shit since early this morning. I'm hungry as fuck."

"Oh, no wonder you wanted me to meet you at Wild Wings."

"And," Bennie continued, "The last time I was in here the cashier was all on a nigga. Im'a try to fuck ma tonight."

Gaines just shook his head and laughed.

"What?" Bennie asked.

"Let me guess. She's white isn't she?" Gaines questioned.

"Yeah, so."

"You really need to find yourself an African American woman," Gaines said. "What do you see in Caucasians anyway?"

"Cause nigga, I like to hear them white bitches scream when I drill this dick into 'em," Bennie answered. "Plus white girls like to swallow."

"In case you haven't heard, black women do that now a days too."

"Yeah, but they do it because they know we like it nasty like that. White girls do it because THEY like it nasty like that."

"Well whatever floats your boat," Gaines said. "I gotta go. Thank you," he said as he held up the envelope.

Michael Gaines hopped out of Bennie's truck and jumped back into his silver 2002 Dodge Stratus. Hitting the horn twice, he peeled out of the parking lot. After putting in a call to Big Mo to update him of the situation, Bennie quickly got out of his truck and dipped inside Wild Wings. He casually strolled up to the counter and leaned on it. The cashier was so busy taking a call-in order that she didn't even notice that he was there. Not one to be ignored, Bennie decided to make his presence known. Clearing his throat loudly to get the cashiers attention, Bennie started to wonder if the girl he was looking for was even working today.

After putting the customer who was on the phone on hold, the cashier smiled and asked Bennie, "Are you here to pick up a call-in order?"

"Actually I was wondering if Charity was at work today.

The cashier's smile faded immediately. Bennie knew what that was all about.

"Yeah, she here," the cashier said with a lot more attitude now. "Charity!" the cashier yelled. Her name tag read Peaches. "Somebody out here to see you!" Shaking her head in disgust, Peaches had totally forgotten about the customer on the phone. By the time she remembered, they had hung up. She placed the phone back on its base, folded her arms, and stared at him with a frown.

"What the fuck wrong wit' you ma?" Bennie asked.

"No wonder I can't find a man. Y'all to busy sniffin' up these white bitches asses." Bennie wanted to laugh at her simple ass but decided that it would do more harm than good. He would never put a white girl on his arm. To him they were just sex toys.

"Don't get cha weave in a bunch ma. It ain't even like that."

"Oh, really? Tell me how it is then black man."

Before he could answer her, Charity came strutting from the back with a backpack on her shoulders. Bennie took one look at her and forgot all about his growling stomach. Charity was a white girl who acted like a sista which is just one of the reasons Peaches couldn't stand her. She had the body of a sista and knew just how to flaunt it. She had on low cut Baby Phat jeans, a pink wife beater, and pink three-inch heeled Gladiator sandals. Even through her bra, Bennie could see her erect nipples protruding through her beater.

"Hey," she said obviously surprised to see him. "What are you doing here?"

"Got a little hungry and decided to come cop me some wings," Bennie said. "You 'bout to get off or what?" he asked.

"Hell yeah. I'm out this bitch."

"Ah man, I wished I woulda got here a little earlier. Then we woulda had a chance to talk a little bit."

"Hmm," she said while she was thinking. "I'll tell you what. I'll make a deal with you. You give me a ride home and I'll share these twenty four wings with you."

"Cool. Sounds like a plan to me ma."

Peaches snorted in disgust and walked away.

"Anyway," Charity said as she gave Peaches the talk to the hand gesture, "You ready to roll big daddy?"

"Wassup wit ya girl, ma?" Bennie asked.

"Fuck that bitch. She always on some hater type shit."

Charity had hazel eyes and thin lips. Her brunette hair was pulled back into a messy pony tail. She had a mesmerizing smile to go along with flawless white teeth. Charity was barely twenty-two years old but seemed to have the wisdom of someone twice her age. Bennie, who was hoping like hell he would get some ass tonight, was being the perfect gentleman as he opened the passenger's side door for her. He wondered why she needed a ride home. The last time he saw her, she was getting into an old Ford Escort. Not wanting to offend her, he decided not to ask. It was working in his favor anyway.

"Oh, you're a gentleman I see."

"Always ma, always," Bennie responded. She didn't know that Bennie was gonna try to tear her insides out if given the chance. After getting in the truck, Bennie started up the engine. He had forgotten that he had Tupac still in the CD player. The last thing he wanted was for a part to come up with the word nigga in it. He hated it when white people would recite hood lyrics when they didn't even know what the fuck they were talking about.

"Oh, shit is that Tupac?" she asked.

Bennie nodded. "Turn that shit up daddy." He quickly scrolled through the tracks until he came to the one he was looking for. *How Do You Want It* featuring Jodeci blasted through the speakers. Charity bobbed her head with the rhythm of soul train dancer. It was at that moment that Bennie realized that this girl was totally black on the inside.

"Yo, where you stay at, ma?" Bennie asked.

"In Crystal Towers on Noble Road."

Bennie whipped out of the Wild Wings parking lot and made a right on Mayfield. If everything went according to plan tonight, he would be adding another notch in his belt.

Chapter 7

After shooting Dre the bird, CeCe walked through her front door mad as fuck. She watched Dre spin out in his green Hummer with 17 inch rapture rims as if he never wanted to see her again. CeCe wasn't mad though, she wanted him to go. That's why she'd picked a fight with him in the first place. She didn't feel like being bothered with anybody, especially Dre. For the life of her she couldn't understand why Ty was all touchy feely with this bitch Gloria. The bitch was pretty but she wasn't all that. She was highly pissed at herself for not kicking Gloria's ass in the restaurant. She walked over to her black leather recliner and plopped down. She took a deep breath hoping that it would calm her nerves.

When that didn't work, she walked over to the coffee table and picked up the half-a-blunt that Dre had left there earlier in the day. She fired it up and took a couple of puffs holding it in for about five seconds before blowing the smoke into the air. She had to calm down. By all accounts she really shouldn't be giving a fuck about whoever Ty was screwing around with. She hated to admit it but Stacy was right. She was starting to catch feelings for Ty. That's usually what happens when you start sleeping with people that you have no business sleeping with. At times she did feel bad about sleeping with her man's cousin, but Dre just wasn't doing it for her in the bedroom. He wasn't romantic, had a little dick in her opinion, and always came too quick. On top of that he refused to eat her pussy, telling her that he thought it was nasty. Nonetheless, he was her man and she was gonna look out for him as long as they were together. She just didn't know how much longer that would be. The only reason she was still with him was because for some strange reason that even she couldn't explain she did still love him. He just wasn't shit when it came to sex. She knew it was cold to think that way, but it was the truth. But Ty's different. He knows how to sex a woman. His dick was at least ten inches and he knew what to do with it, and he has no qualms about eating pussy either.

As a matter of fact, he thoroughly enjoyed it. That was very important to CeCe because she'd never been able to get off the conventional way. The only way she'd ever been able to get off is by receiving oral sex or self masturbation. So, whenever she wants sexual healing, she would hit Ty up and they would rendezvous at the Marriot in downtown Cleveland and get their freak on. She had to start keeping her feelings in check though. She almost blew it tonight with her outburst. The Chedda Boys were making too much money to let personal feelings interfere with business.

She went into the bathroom and ran herself a hot bubble bath. She was too tired to wrap her hair up so she just let it hang to her shoulders. As much as she tried, she just couldn't stop her mind from drifting to Ty. She wanted him tonight but she knew that he was probably sticking dick to that Gloria bitch. Just thinking about him caused her to get hot. After getting undressed and climbing into the tub, CeCe licked her full luscious lips with the tip of her tongue. Then she let her eyes roll to the back of her head as she pinched and rubbed her silver dollar sized nipples. Her cantaloupe like breasts seemed to float in the bubbly water.

"Oh, shit," she gasped as she finger fucked herself.

Water splashed on the floor as a result of her throwing her left leg over the side of the tub. Pre-cum oozed out of her pussy as thoughts of Ty fucking her consumed her thoughts. Pulling her fingers out of her wet womb for just a second, she felt along the edges of her neatly trimmed pubic hairs, which she'd had cut in a triangle from top to bottom. She wanted to cum so bad, her pussy hurt. Not being able to stand it any longer, she started rubbing her clit faster and faster, over and over. It took less than five minutes for her to erupt. "AAHHH SHIT!" she screamed, releasing her love juice into the soapy water. Her sex tank now empty, CeCe laid her head back on the edge of the tub and reveled in supreme satisfaction.

⚡⚡⚡

After dropping Gloria off at her house around nine o'clock, Ty felt like shooting a few games of pool. He unclipped his cell phone from his hip and called Dre.

"Yo wassup," Dre answered already knowing that it was Ty.

"You in for the night cuz?" Ty asked.

"Hadn't really thought about it. I was jus' on my way to the store to get a brew. CeCe on some bullshit tonight and I don't feel like hearing that shit."

"Meet me at Jillian's then nigga. Let's shoot a few games and toss back a few."

"I'm on my way dawg," Dre said.

⚡⚡⚡

After pulling into Jillians' parking lot at the same time, Dre and Ty jumped out of their respective trucks. Dre was in his Hummer, while Ty's choice in cars for the night was his 2009 cherry red Yukon Denali. They both walked into Jillian's with pool sticks in hand while each man bragged about the whipping one was going to put on the other. Dre briefly flirted with a dark skinned older woman with nappy dreadlocks and to much red lipstick the moment he stepped into the building. .

"Man, what the fuck you talking to that old bitch for?" Ty asked. "Her lips look like a fire hydrant."

"Man, I was just tryin' to make the hoe feel good about her self." After rubbing his chin in thought for a brief second, Dre snapped his fingers.

"As a matter of fact nigga, the last time we played I believe I was the winner."

"So," Ty said, wondering where he was going with this bullshit.

"So yo' ass is payin' nigga," Dre said as he walked toward the bar.

"Punk muthafucka," Ty said as he reached into his pocket and grabbed a lump of cash. He thumbed through the wad of bills until he found a single fifty hiding in a sea of hundreds. The impatient cashier frowned as she seemingly snatched the dough out of Ty's hands. Ty looked at her and snapped.

"The fuck wrong wit you?"

"Nothing," the attitude having cashier replied.

"Then what the fuck you snatch my money out my hand like that for?"

A tall gangly looking Caucasian with wire framed glasses, a receding hairline, and a nametag that read Mike quickly appeared on the scene.

"Is there a problem sir?" he asked.

"Hell yeah it's a damn problem. Yo' rude ass worker snatched my fuckin' money out of my hand. If she don't wanna work, she oughta take her ass home. I could be spendin' this cheese somewhere else," Ty said as he flashed the hundreds in front of the man's face.

Just then Dre walked back over with two bottles of corona. "What's up dawg?" he asked sensing there was trouble.

"Man, all I did was try to pay this broad and she gets a fuckin' attitude." Ty had to put it like that because he knew that Dre probably thought he was causing trouble again. Dre shrugged his shoulders and looked at Mike who appeared to be the manager.

"Fuck it," he said as he looked at his knot and put it back in his pocket. "After we drink these beers, we'll just take our money else where."

"Amanda, go in the backroom while I talk to these two gentlemen." Amanda's attitude disappeared when the manager said this. Now, she was afraid for her job.

"Gentlemen," he started. "Isn't there something I can do to get you to stay? I'd really hate to see you leave. I know you're good customers because I've seen you here before," he lied. "I'll tell you what," he continued. "You can shoot the first hour for free and I'll throw in two dozen hot wings. No charge."

"Works for me," Dre stated. "What you think Ty?"

"Yeah ahight," he responded. He was obviously still pissed at Amanda. Mike gave Dre and Ty a tray of pool balls and told them that their wings would be up in about twenty minutes. They walked over to table number six to get the game started.

"Rack 'em chump," Ty said.

"I won last time," Dre added. "The fuck I gotta rack 'em for?"

"Cause I'm payin' muthafucka that's why."

Dre laughed. "Whateva nigga. But I still get to shoot first."

"I'll give you that," Ty replied. "It might be yo' only shot anyway."

"Yeah right."

Dre placed the cue ball about four inches from the edge of the table. He drew back and struck the cue ball with so much force that it jumped off the table.

"Damn nigga this ain't baseball," Ty said as he picked the ball up off the floor and handed it back to Dre. After reracking the balls, Ty looked at Dre. "You knock it off this go 'round, that's shot lost nigga."

Nodding his head in agreement Dre drew back and struck the balls again. Not only did the cue ball stay on the table, he knocked in three balls including the nine. This constituted an automatic win.

"What the fuck?" a shocked Ty asked. "What kinda sucka shit is that?"

"It's called a win muthafucka," Dre boasted. "Rack 'em and stack 'em punk."

"Man this some bullshit," Ty said laughing.

෫෫෫

After being chewed out by Mike, Amanda was told she could go home for the night. That was fine with her. She didn't wanna be there anyway. The only reason she even showed up for work this night was to do what she was being paid to do. She laughed at the irony. She didn't even like niggers yet here she was setting up two for another. She didn't like being involved with black people period but she needed the money. Her sister told her that the next time she didn't have her part of the rent she was going to kick her out.

Then she would be assed out. She couldn't stay with her mother. She was married to a black man. She still remembered the disgusting feeling she had when she showed up at her mother's house unannounced one day and walked in without knocking. She almost threw up when she walked through the house and looked out the back door window. There was her mother, on the patio butt naked with an extra long black dick in her mouth. To make matters worse, it wasn't even her step-fathers. Amanda was so appalled that she ran to the bathroom and threw up. She never looked at her mother the same after that.

To this day her mother still doesn't know she was seen. After smoking her second cigarette, she looked at her watch again. It had been thirty minutes since she called for her ride to come pick her up. She got up out of the chair and stretched her thick five foot six inch frame out. A frown fell across her face as she looked in the full length mirror hanging from the door. Her ex-boyfriend used to call her the white Serena Williams because of her plump juicy ass and over developed titties. Although he meant it as a compliment she didn't take it that way. In her mind, she was and always would be fat. It didn't matter that no one else thought that, she did. Amanda took the scrunchie out of her hair and let her long brunette locks fall to her shoulders. Just when she was getting frustrated enough to call him back, her cell phone rang.

"Hello," she answered.

"I'll be there in five minutes. Be outside."

"Where are you? I called you a half hour ago," she asked.

"Bitch don't question me!" he yelled into the phone. "Just bring yo' ass outside!"

She heard the dial tone as he hung up on her. She got up and walked through the front door all the while mumbling to her self. "Damn, I hate niggers."

Chapter 8

Fat Jack sat in his truck snacking on a bag of Chips Ahoy cookies with a forty ounce of Old English 800 Malt liquor between his legs. He'd been in a bad mood ever since Ty went upside his head with his pistol three days ago. Around the way people were clowning him behind his back. He couldn't even go to the corner store without hearing people snickering. Even his girl was getting in on the act. After slapping her during a heated argument she'd told him, "You didn't slap the Chedda Boys like that."

It didn't seem to matter to people around the way that Fat Jack had a gun pointed at his head and was knocked unconscious. All they know is that Dre and Ty bitched him up. Fat Jack couldn't live with that. That's why after learning that Dre and Ty liked to hang out at Jillian's, he rolled up in there one night. After searching the parking lot for their trucks he knew they weren't there that night. When Amanda came over to serve him his drink and wings he described them to her and asked her if she knew them.

"I've seen them in here before but I can't say that I know them," she replied.

"How would you like to make two hundred dollars?' he asked her.

"By doing what?" she asked cautiously.

"All you got to do is call me the next time they come in here."

"That's all? And I get two hundred dollars?"

"That's all and you get two hundred dollars." Amanda

thought for a minute. She didn't want to get mixed up in anything shady. But the rent was due and she didn't even have her half of it.

"No one's going to get hurt are they?" she questioned.

"Look," he said. "That ain't none a yo' business and what the fuck do you care? You probably don't like black people no way." He was right about that but she wasn't stupid enough to tell him that to his face. Besides, if she didn't do it he was just going to hire someone else to. Then someone else would get that two hundred.

"Ok," she finally said. "I'll do it."

A light tapping on his window brought Fat Jack back to the present. After throwing the cane that he now had to use as a result of Dre shooting him in the leg in the back seat, he unlocked the door and Amanda hopped in.

"Wuhdup shawty? They still up in that piece?" he asked.

"Yeah they're still in there," Amanda answered.

"Cool." Fat Jack opened up his cell phone started dialing. "Yo' Shank, wuhdup dawg. This Jack. Remember that problem I told you about dat I had? Well, dem two niggas up in Jillian's right now. The soona you take care a dat, the soona you get that two grand nigga." Fat Jack listened intently for a moment. "You gon' do it tonight? Cool nigga I'm wit' dat. Just call me when it's done and I'll bring yo' dough straight to you."

Fat Jack turned and faced Amanda. "You ain't hear none of this shit right?" Amanda vigorously shook her head from side to side. "Where you stay at shawty?"

"East Cleveland."

"You want a ride home or what?"

Although she didn't feel like catching the bus, Amanda was a little afraid to take him up on his offer. Getting paid to set some-one up for him was one thing. But letting him know where she stayed was something all together different. Fat Jack saw the concerned look on her face and read her mind.

"You ain't got shit dat I want. I was jus' tryin' to be nice to yo' white ass but fuck it. Walk yo' ass in the rain den."

Looking out of the passenger's side window, Amanda had-n't even noticed that it had started raining.

"I think I'll take the ride," she said. "Thank you."

"You sure you ain't scared?" he asked sarcastically.

Normally, she would've given him a smart ass comeback but she wasn't in a position to do that and she knew it. So she just smiled and said, "No, I'm fine."

Fat Jack started his truck, turned on the windshield wipers, and peeled off. No one said a word the entire ride. Amanda was quiet because she was scared shitless. She only told him she was fine because she wanted to look brave. Fat Jack was quiet for a whole different reason. He was thinking about how much more weed he was gonna be able to sell once the Chedda Boys were taken care of. Amanda stared out of the window and quietly wondered what had happened to her neighborhood.

Once a beautiful city, East Cleveland had dramatically taken a turn for the worse. Stylish apartment buildings were now replaced by abandoned, run down shell with crackheads for tenants. School parking lots, although filled with joyful sounds during the day, was a haven for drug sells, Dice games, and shoot outs at night. Pot holes as big as moon craters lined the streets as a result of inadequate funding. The only thing left worth looking at in East Cleveland was the Nela Park G.E Light Plant at Christmas time. Every year the plant decorated the front of the building and the grass with Christmas ornaments, trees, and lights.

"Pull in here," Amanda instructed. She was thrilled that she'd made it home safely.

Fat Jack whipped into the parking lot of Crystal Towers Apartments. After coming to a stop, he reached in his pocket and took out his knot. Peeling off two Benjamin Franklin's, he handed them to Amanda.

She took them and quickly stuffed them in her pocket. She then grabbed the door handle and attempted to get out only to be stopped by Jack. *Oh shit*, she thought. *I knew this was a bad idea. Now I'm probably about to be raped.*

"Hey!" he said. She slowly turned her head to face him. Seeing the terrified look on her face made him laugh. "What you lookin' all scared for shawty?" I told you I wasn't gonna do nothin' to you." Then, little by little, the smile faded from his face.

"But you didn't hear shit right?"

She quickly shook her head from side to side. "No. I didn't hear anything."

"Good," he replied. He peeled off two more hundreds and gave them to her.

Damn, she thought. *Jackpot.* She hopped out of his truck, gently closing his door behind her.

"Take it easy shawty," he said and pulled off.

As Amanda walked through he parking lot in amazement, a thought that she had never had before entered her mind. "Damn," she mumbled to her self. "I guess all niggers aren't bad."

Fat Jack drove straight down Noble Road all the way to 152ⁿᵈ Street. Changing his mind at the last minute, he decided to get on the freeway so he kept straight until he came to the BP gas station.

"Fuck!" he screamed. He needed some gas but they were still doing construction at that particular location. "They had been working on this muthafuckin' gas station for two months," he complained. He looked down at his gas gage. The needle read that he had ¼ tank of gas. "Fuck it," he said. "I'll get some tomorrow." He continued on, going up under the bridge and making a left onto the freeway.

He looked at the caller ID of his ringing cell phone. Blocked call. He normally didn't answer them but figured it might be Shank.

"Yo, who it be?"

"It's me nigga. Shank."

"What the fuck you blockin' you number fo' nigga?"

"Uuhh…this phone be actin' stupid like that sometimes."

"You take care a dat fo' me?" Jack asked.

"Its done playa," said the raspy voice on the other end. "Dem niggas livin' wit Tupac and Biggie now dawg."

"Hell muthafuckin' yeah! I knew yo' ass was gon' come through!" Jack stated.

"Told you nigga. But peep game dawg. Instead of you bringin' me my pay, let me come by yo' crib and get it."

"Why?" a suspicious Jack asked.

'Cause I ain't at home dat's why."

"Hold on a second," Jack said. Reaching in his pocket he pulled out a knot of hundreds that added up to eight thousand dollars. After giving it some thought he figured why not. He and Shank grew up together like brothers. He could trust him. The money he was gonna make with Dre and Ty dead made the five grand he was paying Shank well worth it.

"Ahight pahtna. Come on by and get this money. We can celebrate by drinkin' Remy all night."

"What about yo' girl?" Shank asked.

"Man don't worry 'bout that bitch. She still mad at me because I slapped the shit outta her ass the other night. She over her sista's house."

"Cool dawg, I'll see you here," Shank said.

"Don't you mean you'll see me there dumb ass?"

"Huh? Oh, yeah. Dat's what I mean."

Fat Jack pressed the end button and disconnected the phone. "Backwards talking ass nigga," Fat Jack said. Not even Shanks illiterate ass could spoil his mood tonight. Bobbing his head to G-Units *Stunt 101,* Fat Jack started rapping along with the song. *"Come on now, we all know gold is getting old. The ice in my teeth keeps the cristal cold."* All he could think about was how much money he was gonna be making.

"Fuck the Chedda Boys!" he yelled at the top of his lungs.

With Dre and Ty out of the way, he figured soon he'd take over the weed game. What he didn't know was that they were only part of a bigger crew. Nor did it ever cross his mind that the call he'd just received was coming from inside his own house.

Chapter 9

Two hours earlier, Shank's girl Melony had dropped him off down the street from Jillian's. She had a bad feeling that he was about to do something sneaky and underhanded. He didn't have a steady job, but he kept a thick wad of cash in his pocket. For two years, she had ignored the rumors going around the neighborhood about him being a hit man for hire. Whenever she would ask him where he got so much money from he would simply tell her that he won it shooting dice. Knowing how much he liked to gamble, she couldn't say for certain that he was lying. People around the neighborhood wondered what the hell Melony saw in Shank. With her smooth bronze colored skin, long brown hair, light brown eyes, and model shaped body she could have any man she wanted. Her sister called her Tyra "2" caused she said she looked like the second coming of Tyra Banks.

Shank was anything but a model. The brother was light-skinned with an acne infested face. He had short nappy hair with a crooked hairline and brown-stained teeth. He was skinny but had a pot belly, kinda like those Ethiopian kids that you see on television. He had a hump in the middle of his nose, a clear indication that it had been broken before. His finger nails were always dirty. But for some reason, known to no one but her, she loved him dearly.

"Sharrod Brown, I hope you're not planning on getting into any trouble tonight."

Shank face twisted up. He hated it when she called him by his government name. "Ain't nobody planning on getting' in no trouble," he spat.

"Then why you got me dropping you off down the street from Jillian's instead of in front of Jillian's?" she asked.

"Baby, I already told you. I wanna surprise some old friends who meeting up here tonight. They don't know I'm comin'."

She didn't believe him but for the sake of an argument she decided to leave it alone. She took a deep breath and wiped her face. She had a very bad feeling about this. "If you're just going to have fun with your old friends, then why do you need your gun?"

He didn't think she had noticed when he slipped the nickel-plated three-eighty semi-automatic pistol into his jacket pocket. "Don't even start Melony. You know I carry my gun every where I go. What's the use of havin' a gun for protection if you don't have it on you to protect you?"

She couldn't argue with him on that. She'd seen enough people get their brains blew out to know having a gun while living in the hood is always safer than not having one. She leaned over and kissed him on the cheek.

"Just please be careful. Ok?"

"Always baby."

He stepped out of the confines of the dry car and into the steady flow of rain. He threw his hood over his head and slammed the door shut to Melony's 2002 white Chevy Lumina. He walked down Cedar Road at a brisk pace in a hurry to get out of the rain. After reaching the front door he looked in to see how many people felt like shooting pool that night. To his surprise, the place was relatively empty. Besides Dre and Ty there were only two other couples in the place. He laughed at the realization of what he just thought.

Two other couples, as if Dre and Ty was a couple. "Dem ho' ass niggas probably is fuckin' each other," he mumbled to him self. After taking the gun out of his jacket and sticking it in the small of his back, he opened the door and walked straight to counter where he rented a table and ordered a shot of Jack Daniels.

Not wanting to be noticed, he made sure that he rented a table in an inconspicuous part of the bar where he would work on his pool game and wait for the chance to earn his money.

$$\text{✦✦✦}$$

Amanda stepped on the elevator with a new sense of respect for black people. Although she still didn't like or trust them very much, she no longer thought that all black people were bad. She was sure that the fat ass guy that gave her a ride home was going to try something. When he gave her an extra two hundred dollars, she was so happy she almost came on her self. She knew that he was buying her silence but she was so scared she wouldn't have said anything anyway. After getting off the elevator on the tenth floor, she dragged her aching feet to apartment number 1006.

Taking her keys out of her pocket she realized that she was home two hours earlier than she should've been. Her sister had called an hour ago and asked her what time she was getting off because she was entertaining company. She had no idea at the time that she was going to be sent home.

"Shit!" she said. "Fuck it, I'm home now and I'm not going anywhere else so she's just gonna have to deal with it."

She opened the door and stepped in. After taking off her coat and hanging it on the coat rack next to the door, she walked to the living room and plopped down on the couch. The apartment wasn't huge but it was big enough to hold two bedrooms. The living room consisted of wall to wall blue carpet and the walls were painted light blue. The furniture was cheap but well taken care of.

They had a beige pleather couch and matching loveseat to go along with a wooden coffee table. The book shelf in the corner was full of urban fiction books. Amanda didn't read urban fiction. She couldn't relate to it. But her sister couldn't get enough of them. The nicest thing in the whole apartment was the 32 inch Magnavox television set that sat on top of a brown four wheeled cart and the Phillips DVD player that sat on the TV. She had begun to think that her sister wasn't at home. That thought quickly disappeared when she heard her sister panting and moaning at the top of lungs in her bed room.

"Oh, shit!" Amanda whispered to her self. "My sister's back there fucking!"

She'd come home quite a few times and found her sister laying in the bed with someone, but by that time they had already finished screwing. This was the first time she'd ever actually caught her in the act. She jumped up and grabbed one of her sisters many books off of the book shelf. She didn't even know the name of the book. For some strange reason, the cover was torn off the front.

Amanda sighed and shook her head. *What the hell does my sister see in these books?* She wondered. She made a mental commitment right then to read the whole book and find out why her sister likes urban fiction so much. She figured she would just go down in the lobby and read for about thirty minutes and then call their apartment from her cell phone. Just as Amanda reached for the door knob, her sister and the bed springs squealed louder simultaneously.

"Oh, shit!!... Ooohh hell yeah baby!! Gimme that big chocolate dick!!..."

Amanda froze in place. Her blood started to boil. She knew that her sister liked to screw black men but she didn't know if she could take seeing it. With her curiosity getting the better of her, she took her hand away from the door knob. She tiptoed through the kitchen past the bathroom up to her sisters bed room door. It was slightly ajar. She hated to admit it but listening to her sister turned her on. Her curiosity started to increase. She wanted to see what this black guy was doing to her sister that had her in sexual bliss.

She slowly and carefully pushed the door open further and further until she could get her head in the door. Her mouth fell open in astonishment as she saw her sister riding the biggest dick she'd ever seen in her life. Now, she was really turned on as she started rubbing her titties with her right hand as she held the door open with her left. Her sister got up and got on all fours. She laid her head on the pillow and reached behind with both hands.

Spreading her ass cheeks apart she begged for more. "Give it to me in the ass daddy!" she screamed. Just before he entered her she spotted her sister spying on her. Being that Amanda was embarrassed at getting caught being a peeping tom, she pretended like she had just got there.

"Charity, what the fuck are you doing!" she yelled.

"What the fuck does it look like I'm doing? And why the fuck are you spying on me bitch?"

"I'm not spying on you," she lied.

"Then what the fuck you still standing there looking for?"

"Well, when I got home I heard...I mean... shit! Never the fuck mind!"

She backed out and closed the door. Before she made it back through the kitchen, she heard her sister's pleasure cries again. She picked back up the book the she had dropped on the kitchen table. Walking back through the living room, she grabbed her keys off the coffee table and headed for the door all the while secretly wishing she were her sister.

$$\maltese\maltese\maltese$$

Mike watched as Dre and Ty ordered another bottle of Jack Daniels. He honestly didn't know how they were still standing up. Two bottles of Jack and a pitcher of beer should be enough to get anybody drunk. *Must be a black thing*, he thought. He'd already taken the liberty of ordering them another batch of wings. He planned on delivering those personally. These guys were spending big money here and he wanted to do everything in his power to keep them happy. It was amazing that he had never run into them before.

By sheer coincidence he was off on the nights the Chedda Boys rolled through. Mike also noticed that the bumpy faced man in the far corner was watching Dre and Ty. He didn't know what was going on but thought that it was strange. For a brief second he thought that the man was waiting for them to leave so he could rob the place. But then figured that if that was the case, then he would simply rob them too. Then he saw it. For one brief moment, the bumpy faced man bent over to take a shot and he saw the handle of a gun in the small of his back.

Right then he figured out what was up. He was waiting on them to leave so he could either rob them or do something much worse. The decision was easy to Mike. Instead of minding his own business, he decided to make two friends for life. He grabbed a flyer off the counter, turned it over and scribbled a message on the back, then headed toward Ty and Dre's loud voices

$$$

"Ten-eight nigga!" Ty yelled. "I'm on the comeback trail."

"Nigga you crazy as fuck," Dre said. "Ain't that much comeback on cocaine."

"Shiitt, nigga watch how I run this shit out dawg," Ty bellowed.

"Man, spare me that change. Break fool," Dre said.

Ty laid his pool stick on the table. "The fuck you doin' nigga?" Dre questioned.

"Wing check fool.

"Yeah, a nigga is getting' hungry again," Dre replied.

Just as they were about to flag down a waitress, Mike strolled over to them and sat a tray of twenty-four wings on their table.

"These are on the house my man. Thanks for your business," Mike stated.

"Damn dude you ahight," Ty said.

Mike stuck out his hand to shake Dre's. Upon making contact with Dre's hand, he whispered to him, "Read this but please don't let anyone see you do it."

Dre immediately stuffed the note in his pocket and nodded to Mike.

"Yo Ty, I gotta take a leak man."

Ty stopped chomping on a wing looked directly at Dre. "Damn nigga. You gon' call me and let me know the next time you bout to jack off too? Take yo' ass on, silly ass nigga."

Dre shook his head and rushed straight to one of the stalls so he could read the note in private. Opening up the note, he started to read.

I don't want any trouble. But the guy in the back corner has been staring at you guys for over an hour and if I'm not mistaken I could have sworn that I saw a gun tucked in the small of his back. Dre instantly got mad at him self. He was always aware of his surroundings. He was having so much fun with Ty that he slipped on his ghetto vision. Quickly, he peeped from the bathroom door only to spot Shank. He thought about him being an alleged hit man for hire. And Dre also knew that he associated with Fat Jack so it didn't take long to put two and two together. Dre put the note back in his pocket, shook his head, and laughed. He couldn't believe that Fat Jack had the balls to put a hit out on him and Ty. He slowly walked out of the bathroom and headed back toward Ty who was polishing off his fourth wing.

He didn't even look shank's way. He just stood there for a moment staring at Ty. "What the hell wrong wit' you?" Ty asked.

"Gimme a hug nigga," he said to his little cousin.

"What?"

"You my cuz man. Show me some love."

"Nigga go 'head on wit that brady bunch shit."

"Come on man. We fam dawg."

"Nigga is yo' ass drunk?" an irritated Ty asked.

"Naw man, I just wanna show my fam that I love um, that's all." Ty rolled his eyes as Dre stood there with his arms open.

"Man if I give you a hug, will you leave me the fuck alone and let me finish eatin'?" Ty asked. Dre slowly nodded his head. "Shit," Ty said as he got up. As the two embraced, Dre slyly stuck the note in Ty's pocket and whispered in his ear.

"I put a note in your back pocket. Go in the bathroom and read it." Braking the embrace Dre told Ty, "You betta go take a piss before we start this next game. I don't want no excuses when I start whupping yo' muthafuckin' ass."

"Nigga please," Ty said. "I'm 'bout to take a leak 'cause I got to not cause I'm scared of yo' ass."

After reading the note, Ty crawled out of the bathroom on all fours. He slithered around the pool table until he was next to the one Shank was shooting on. Shank's plan was to wait until they walked out together, rob them, and then kill them. He would never get the chance. Ty had to wait until the cue ball stopped on the side of the table so Shank would have to turn his back. Every few seconds, Shank would look across the room at Dre or toward the bathroom for Ty.

He thought that it was taking Ty kinda long but then figured that he was probably in there taking a shit. Ty eased his head up to see Shank bending over about to attempt a shot. He was waiting on that. He looked across the room at Dre and his Cousin nodded his head in agreement. Before Shank could even attempt his shot, Ty jumped up and put his gun to the back of his head.

"Don't move bitch ass nigga."

Shank froze in place.

"Hey man! What the fuck up?" he asked.

"Shut up muthafucka!" Ty screamed in his ear. "Don't say anotha muthafuckin' word!"

Ty snatched Shanks three eighty from the small of his back and stuck it in his waist band. Dre walked over smoking a black and mild. Standing half an arm length away from Shank, Dre took a long drag off his cigar and blew smoke in shank's face. Then he drew back and punched him in the stomach. Shank fell to his knees coughing and struggling to breathe. Ty lifted up his foot and foot-mugged him in the back of the head.

"Get yo' bitch ass up nigga!" Ty yelled.

Struggling to get to his feet, Shank tried to speak. "What…the …hell is dis…" Dre held up one finger and shushed him.

"Shut up," he calmly said. "Now, I'm going to ask you one time and one time only. Did Fat Jack hire you to kill us?"

Shank knew he was stuck. There was no sense in lying to them because he knew that they knew the truth.

"Look man," he started, "I'm just tryin' ta make a livin' out here man."

Dre back-handed him. "Nigga you sound like a fuckin' fool. How the fuck you gon' stand in my face and talk about makin'a fuckin' livin' by killin' us? Lets go"

"Wh…where we goin' man?" Shank stuttered.

"We goin' fo' a lil' ride," a scowling Dre spat.

When Mike saw Ty crawling along the floor, he knew something was about to go down. It was at that moment that he decided the less he saw the better. Sharon had left about forty-five minutes ago so it was just him and two other waitresses named Terri and Monica. They were both back in the stockroom taking a smoke break so they had no idea what was going on.

Mike was so nervous and scared that he did something that he had never done before at work. Walking over to the coat rack, he reached inside his jacket pocket and took out an already rolled up joint. Clutching it in his closed fist, he told them to stay back there until he got back because he wanted to talk to them about something. The truth of the matter was that he was trying to protect them. He didn't want them to see anything that would endanger their lives.

Stepping into the men's bathroom, he nervously flicked the lighter and set fire to the end of the white paper. It took him three pulls off the joint to settle his nerves. Whatever Dre and Ty were going to do to Shank, Mike prayed to God they wouldn't do it in there. After he was sufficiently calmed by the weed, he walked out of the bathroom and started back toward the stockroom. His heart jumped when Ty appeared out of nowhere.

Ty moved his hand up and down motioning for Mike to calm down. Reaching in his right pocket, Ty pulled out a cluster of bills and peeled off four fifty's.

"Good looking out homie," Ty stated as he handed mike the cash. "Do me a favor. Keep an eye on my truck till I get back. Thanks."

Ty strolled away without even waiting for a response. Mike continued to stare as Ty and Dre forced Shank into the truck. Mike felt like shit. But unlike Shank, he would wake up tomorrow.

Chapter 10

Amanda looked at her watch. She had been down in the lobby for a good forty-five minutes. It wasn't that she was bored. The book she'd taken off the shelf was much better than she thought it would be. She would just rather be reading it in the comforts of her apartment. Fuck it, she thought. I'm going back upstairs. I'm not staying down here all night just because she wants to get fucked.

"Ain't this a bitch," she mumbled to her self. "My sister's upstairs getting dicked down and my horny ass ain't been fucked in two months." Amanda wasn't ugly. As a matter of fact, she was fairly cute. But in her mind she could stand to lose about fifteen pounds.

She had light gray eyes, thin lips, a small pouty mouth, and her breasts looked like two big watermelons. As she got on the elevator, she couldn't help but think about the size of Bennie's dick. That was the real reason she got caught watching her sister. She couldn't tear her eyes away from the black man's love organ. She'd always wondered about that myth about blacks having bigger dicks. Now, she knew it to be true. She let her mind roam as she started to imagine the sensation of having a black dick inside of her. She wondered about how it would feel sliding between her lips and traveling down her throat.

Snapped out of her sexual fantasy by the opening of the elevator doors, she stepped off the elevator and headed to her apartment. She opened the door, stepped inside, and stood there for a moment. She listened intently to make sure she wasn't interrupting anything again. She walked to the living room and sat down on the love-seat. As soon as she plopped down, her bladder reminded her to get right back up.

"Shit," she mumbled. She got up and made her way through the kitchen. Hearing the toilet flush she figured by the time she got there Charity would be done.

Slinging open the door, Amanda yelled inside. "Hurry up girl. I gotta...Oh, God! Oh, shit I'm so sorry!" she said.

Standing there shaking his dick was Bennie. Seeing it at its full length caused Amanda to stare. Her mouth fell open in amazement at the sight of the ten inch snake hanging over her commode.

"Amanda!" her sister called from the bedroom.

Snapping out of her daze Amanda closed the door and went to see what her sister wanted. As soon as she closed the door, Bennie almost busted a gut laughing. Then he had a wicked thought. *Maybe I can fuck both of 'em.*

Amanda walked into Charity's bedroom and sat on her bed. She was still kinda embarrassed that her sister had caught her spying. She didn't want Charity to get mad at her so she decided to keep the bathroom incident to her self for now. She was sure they would have a good laugh about it later. She purposely avoided eye contact with her sister. "Are you ok?" Charity asked.

In some strange way, that made her feel good that her sister cared enough to ask her that. "Yeah, I'm ok. I'm sorry if I ruined your evening."

"Girl did it look like you ruined my evening? Shiieett sis I came four times tonight. "You coulda told me you were coming home early though sis," Charity said.

"Yeah I know. I'm sorry about that. I wasn't supposed to get off until later but Mike sent me home early."

"For what?" Charity asked.

"Well some ni... some black guy told Mike that I snatched his money out of his hand."

Charity stared at her sister for a few seconds. She knew how her sister felt about blacks. "Did you?" she questioned.

"I don't know. I might have. But you know how they are sis."

Charity rubbed between her legs and said, "Whew, do I ever."

Amanda rolled her eyes and put her hands on her hips. "You know what I mean. They're just so disrespectful."

Charity just smiled and shook her head. Walking over to her dresser, Charity stuck her hand in her purse, pulled out a twenty dollar bill, and waved it in the air. "If you can tell me what that man did to disrespect you, I'll give you this twenty dollars."

Amanda was stuck. The truth of the matter was that Ty really didn't do anything to disrespect her. She was just being a bigot. After about ten seconds of silence, Charity put the money back in her purse.

"That's what I thought," she said. "You gotta let this racial crap go sis. You're condemning people you don't even know."

"Your friend's still in there," Amanda said ignoring the comment.

"I know that. We're gonna chill for a minute. You're welcome to come chill with us if you can stand the sight of him," Charity replied. She walked past Amanda and headed out the door leaving her standing there looking stupid.

Chapter 11

Ty stood in the middle of Fat Jack's living room and nodded his head in approval. *It looks way better than that piece o' shit roach motel we slapped his ass around in a few days ago*, he thought.

Shank sat on the couch scared shitless, but trying to remain calm as the two killers kept their guns on him. He was doing his best to convince Fat Jack to come home.

Dre then motioned with his gun for Shank to hurry up and get off the phone. As soon as he hung up, Dre slapped him across the face with his gun.

"OW! Shit! What the fuck was that for?"

"That's for tryin' to be slick muthafucka!" Dre told him. "You think I didn't catch that 'see you here' comment nigga?"

Shank was trying to let Fat Jack know that he was already at his house and under duress but didn't think he got the hint. Now he was scared shitlesss. During the ride to Fat Jack's house, Dre had told him that once they had Fat Jack, they were going to let him go. He seriously doubted that. He'd been around the game long enough to know that the second rule of committing a murder was to leave no witnesses.

"We was gon' let yo' stupid ass go!" Ty screamed. "Why you gotta try to be slick?"

Mustering up courage that he didn't know he had, Shank started cursing. "You know what? Fuck y'all two punk ass niggas.

Y'all wasn't gon' let me go no fuckin' way. Do what the fuck y'all gon' do."

Dre looked at Ty and shrugged his shoulders. "You heard the man," he said. "Do what you gon' do."

Ty nodded. Without even blinking he put the Three-eighty to Shank's forehead and pulled the trigger killing him with his own gun. Shank's brains splattered the wall behind the couch he was sitting on. He slumped over and fell sideways on the couch as if he were taking a nap. Ty spat in Shanks face.

"Bitch ass nigga," Ty growled.

Dre quickly ran over to the window and peered out. Even though the music probably drowned out the shot, he wanted to make sure that no one heard it. "Yo Ty, check in that table drawer and see if this silly muthafucka got any cash in there."

Ty rushed over to the drawer and pulled it out. In it was ten thousand dollars in cash. "Jackpot," a smiling Ty said.

As he stuffed the cash into his pocket, Ty squinted his eyes and looked up to the ceiling as if he were thinking about something.

"Wassup dawg?" Dre asked.

"What the hell did he mean when he said the second rule of committing a murder?"

"Leave no witnesses."

"I thought that was the first."

"Nope," Dre said. "The first is and always will be…Don't get caught. Let's get the fuck outta here dawg."

$$$

Fat Jack pulled into his parking lot not suspecting a thing. He never looked across the street at the abandoned house where Dre had parked his truck in the back of the driveway. After grabbing his cane off the backseat, Fat Jack slid his ample frame out of the driver's side door and headed for his steps.With great effort he managed to get to his porch. He'd been having trouble balancing his weight against the cane. After a brief moment, he hobbled to his front door. Taking out his keys, he smiled to himself. This will be the best five grand I ever spent, he thought to his self. He unlocked the door, opened it, and stepped into his home.

This house was nothing like the one that he used to sell dope out of. The hardwood floors shined, and the brand new furniture looked like pieces from an MTV cribs photo shoot. He had a sixty-inch floor model Panasonic plasma HD television sitting up against the wall, and a high-dollar crystal chandelier hanging in the living room where a ceiling fan used to be.

The dinning room consisted of a marble table with six French chairs surrounding it. Fat Jack had definitely done well for himself. He flicked on the light and rubbed his face at the same time. With his eyes still closed, he hobbled over to the sofa while yawning. He sat down on the sofa and instantly jumped straight up when he felt he had sat on something. Focusing his eyes in the sofa, a look of horror fell across Fat Jack's face.

"Oh, shit!!" There was his friend Shank lying sideways on his sofa with a bullet hole in his head.

"Damn Jack. You look like you just saw a dead man," Dre smirked.

Jack's head snapped to the left where he saw Dre and Ty standing with their guns pointed right at him. Ty walked over and kicked him in the stomach. Quickly, Fat Jack doubled over in pain. Falling to one knee because of his already injured leg Fat Jack started to beg.

"Please...man. Please don't kill me," he said between coughs.

Dre started laughing hysterically. "Ya hear that Ty. His fat ass wants us to let him live. He puts out a hit on us and he wants us to let him live." Ty just shook his head. "Nigga you sound stupid as fuck. Take off yo' muthafuckin' clothes," Dre said.

"Ah come on man," Ty said. "I just ate."

"Come on man," Jack pleaded. "We can work this..."

"Take off yo' muthafuckin' clothes trick ass nigga." Ty's voice became more serious. Fat Jack started to undress and cry at the same time. "Don't cry now bitch. You brought this shit on yo' self," a disgusted looking Ty said.

Dre walked over to the CD changer and started turning knobs and pushing buttons. "How the fuck you turn this piece o' shit on?"

Fat Jack drug his bad leg over to the sound system and turned it on, hoping to delay his death. Mary J Blige's old song, *Not Gon' Cry* poured through the speakers. Dre and Ty looked at each other and burst out laughing.

"Nigga you running 'round the hood actin' like you a gangsta' and shit," Ty laughed. Dre hit the disc skip and out came the sounds of Musiq Soulchild. "You sucka-fo-luv ass ho' ass nigga," Ty said. Ty was so disgusted that he shot Fat Jack in his good leg. Fat Jack crumbled to the ground screaming in pain.

Dre looked at Ty. "Do yo' thang cuz."

Wearing black gloves, Ty picked up the Mosberg pump that he'd taken out of Fat Jack's closet earlier. "Turn around and get on all fours you nasty looking bastard." Fat Jack slowly turned around. Dre walked over to him smacked him upside the head.

"Did you really think we was gon' let you get away wit putting' a hit out on us?" Ty stuck the barrel of the shotgun on the edge of Fat Jacks asshole and forcefully shoved it inside.

"AAHHH!! Oh, God please don't!!"

Dre backed up.

"Tell the devil I said hello fat boy."

Ty pulled the trigger and blew Fat Jack's stomach inside out. Dre shook his head, looked at his cousin and smiled. "You a cold ass muthafucka Ty."

Doing his best Chris Tucker imitation, Ty wiggled his head from side to side and said "And you know this...Man!" With the music blaring, no one even heard the shot. Dre and Ty had just followed another basic rule of murder. Kill 'em with their own guns and the cops can't trace it back to you.

₵₵₵

When Dre and Ty got back to Jillian's to get Ty's truck, Ty discovered that he had left the dome light on. He tried to crank his truck but his battery was dead.

"Shit!" he yelled. Dre pulled up beside him bumping T.I.'s *Dead and Gone.*

"Everthing ahight dawg?" he asked.

"Man my muthafuckin' truck won't start. You got some jumper cables in yo' truck?"

"Naw man. CeCe got my cables in her truck."

He looked around the empty parking lot. "Mike probably had some but that white boy rolled out wit the quickness when we got back."

"Man, I really don't wanna leave my damn truck out here all night," Ty said.

"Wait a minute nigga," Dre said. "Where the fuck is yo' cables at?"

Ty was hopin' Dre wouldn't ask him that question. He felt stupid about the answer. "Man I let Pooh borrow 'em about a week ago." Dre looked at him like he was crazy. Reading Dre's mind, Ty said "I know man, I know."

"Well, it looks like you ain't got no choice but to leave the muthafucka here. You can stay over my house tonight and we'll come back tomorrow morning and jump it off."

Ty really didn't want to stay over Dre's house. It was bad enough he was screwing his cousin's woman. It was going to feel very awkward to be in his guest room again.

"Uh…why can't you just bring me back up here tonight man?" he asked.

"Cause I'm fuckin' tired that's why. Nigga ain't nobody gon' fuck wit yo' truck. Bring yo' paranoid ass on."

After locking up his truck, Ty hopped into the passenger's seat and leaned back. Guilty thoughts flooded his mind as he thought back to the night he first started sleeping with CeCe. Mo had thrown Stacy a surprise birthday party. The guest list included The Chedda Boyz of course, Chief Murphy and his wife, a couple of lawyers, tons of close family and friends, and a few high class hoochies for Ty and Bennie's benefit. Everyone had gotten their drink on and was feeling pretty nice when CeCe got sick. Dre was busy shooting dice and losing money so he asked Ty to take CeCe home for him. CeCe, already pissed that Dre was losing money, got even angrier that he asked Ty to take her home instead of him doing it himself.

After cussing Dre in four different languages, she decided that if he wasn't going to pay her any attention that night then she was gonna flirt with his cousin just to teach him a lesson. Ty had drank four glasses of Remy Martin, popped two e-pills, and smoked a blunt. His dick was so hard he was going to bust if he didn't stick it in something. The hoochies that were there had gotten so wasted that they had all but passed out. After pulling up in CeCe's driveway, Ty sat there waiting for CeCe to get out. He wanted to hurry up and get back to the party, hoping Maybe one of those drunk women wanted to screw around a little.

"Aren't you gonna make sure I get inside the house ok?" she asked. "What if somebody's waitin' in there to do somethin' to me?"

"Oh, please," Ty said. "You know damn well ain't nobody without a death wish gon' fuck wit' you."

"You got that shit right. Well, at least help me get my drunk ass up the steps."

CeCe knew exactly what she was doing. Once she got him in the house, she had planned on coming on to him just to make Dre jealous. But when she threw her arm around Ty so he could help her get inside the house, she got a whiff of his Hugo Boss cologne and her hormones kicked in. As soon as she got Ty inside the house, she pulled him down to the couch.

"Uh... CeCe what the hell are yo doing?" he asked.

"Nothin."

The way she said it convinced Ty that she was up to no good. She licked her lips and smiled and Ty figured the best thing for him to do was to get the hell outta there fast.

"Come on CeCe," he pleaded. "Dre's my cousin."

"And he's my man, but what he don't know won't hurt him."

Ty had to admit that she was looking real good that night. Still. Dre was blood and some lines you just didn't cross. With liquor impairing his judgment and arousing his hormones, Ty was powerless to stop her as she grabbed his loose fitting jeans with her left hand and reached inside them and grabbed his magic stick with her right.

"Oh, shit," Ty said. Her warm soft palm made it grow in her hand.

"Damn Ty," she replied. "What the fuck you got down there?"

Then she grabbed his left hand and guided it under her thirteen hundred dollar Yves Saint Laurent skirt until he was rubbing her pubic hairs.

Her Light Blue perfume by Dolce and Gabbana broke down his defenses and rendered him helpless. He slid his middle finger inside her and she gasped in pleasure. Gently, he pulled down her Victoria Secret underwear. Then he started kissing her feet and worked his way up to her thighs.

By the time he reached the top of her inner thighs, she was panting and sweating like she had run a marathon. He reached up and placed his hands on both knees and pushed them apart. Anticipating what he was about to do, she reached down and spread her lips open and exposed her throbbing clit. He flicked his tongue back and forth until she exploded. Even though he knew what he was doing was wrong he was so into CeCe by now that he couldn't stop if he wanted to. Not wanting to leave a job half done, he quickly climbed up on top of her. His dick now pulsating in anticipation, he eagerly entered her. When he was halfway in, she came again.

"Oh, shit baby. Is it all the way in yet?" she asked.

"Not yet baby," he said with confident swagger.

"Stop being so fuckin' gentle! "Slam that dick up in there!"

That did it. Not only was he feeling bad about screwing his cousin's woman. But now it looked like she was starting to question the way he was slinging the pipe. He grabbed both of her legs and put them on his shoulders. He would then proceed to mercilessly pound CeCe's guts until she begged him to stop. Twenty minutes and two more orgasms later, CeCe was ready to submit. She'd never had anyone sling the pipe to her the way Ty did.

"Aahhh shit!! Oh...my...God!! Ty Please. Hurry up...I ...Don't know how...how much more...I can take!"

Ty was doing this on purpose. If she was going to betray his cousin like that by screwing him, then he was going to make her pay for it. But he couldn't hold back any longer. He had to bust. "Oh, shit CeCe!! I'm 'bout to cum!!" In one swift motion she pushed him off of her. After he fell back onto the couch, she jumped up and put her head between his legs and took as much of him as she could in her mouth. "Aahhh Shit!!" he screamed as she swallowed his semen.

Quickly, she got up and walked to her bedroom door, as if they were strangers.

Right before she went inside and closed the door, they stared at each other for what seemed like an eternity. After that, their relationship would never be the same.

"Hey," Dre said. "You listening muthafucka?" Dre's voice snapped Ty back to the present.

"Oh, my bad man. What you say?"

"Nigga I said if you hear some moaning tonight don't get scared. It's just me tightening my girl up." Usually, that would have gotten a smart assed comment from Ty. But he was so guilt ridden tonight that he couldn't even smile.

₵₵₵

Big Mo woke up to a ringing telephone at nine-thirty in the morning. Trying to answer it before it woke Stacy up, he caught it on the third ring.

"Collect call from Grafton Correctional Institution. Push 0 to accept the call please."

Mo sighed and pushed 0. He already knew who it was. His brother Chaz had been locked up for close to two years for felonious assault on a police officer. His lawyer tried to work out something with the prosecutor but by the judge being the police officer's brother, he rejected all plea bargains and threw the book at Chaz. It didn't matter to him that Chaz was Chief Murphy's younger brother. When the judge went to the hospital and saw his brother lying in the bed with a fractured skull, someone had to pay.

"Yo wassup bro?" Chaz asked.

"Not much pimppin'. How you holding up in there dawg?"

"Sheeeit nigga, you know how I do. I'm practically runnin' shit up in here." Mo knew his brother was full of it but it did make him feel good to know that he was holding up pretty well.

"How da landscapin' bidness goin'?" Mo knew what he was talking about. What he was really askin' him was how the weed sales was going.

"Tryin' to plant a few more trees dawg," Mo said, meaning he was buying more pounds. "You need anything up there young 'un?" he asked.

"A nigga could use a few more dollas on his books big bro."

"Ahight. I got you bro."

"Thanks. Hey look I gotta go. I'll check wit y'all next week," Chaz responded.

"Ahight bro. You take it easy in there ok?"

"No doubt. One luv big bro. I'm out…Oh, hol' up sec!"

"What's up?"

"Jus' outta curiosity, how is yo' bitch ass brother doing?"

Mo just shook his head and laughed. He was wondering when Chaz was gonna take a shot at their other brother. He decided to just answer the question instead of embellishing him.

"To tell you the truth, I really don't know man. Sometimes he cool, but sometimes that nigga act like a bitch."

"That's 'cause he is a bitch," Chaz added.

Big Mo just shook his head and laughed some more. "Well, I'm startin' ta think somethin' goin' on wit his ass. Sometimes when I be talkin' to his ass, he be looking all spaced out and shit. I'ma hav ta start keepin' a closer eye on that nigga. And oh, he yo' bother too nigga."

"Yeah, yeah whateva dawg," Chaz replied. "Look, I gotta go though dawg, fo I have ta fuck one o' these punk ass niggas up about this phone. I'm out bro, one!" With that the two brothers hung up from one another.

Mo turned over to see Stacy smiling at him.

"What?" he asked.

"Nothin'," Stacy answered. "So, how's your brother doin'?"

"He say he runnin' shit up there," laughed Mo. "He sounds like he's holdin' his own in there though." "So, whatcha doin' today baby girl?"

"I was plannin' on havin' lunch wit' CeCe today. After that I really didn't have anything else planned. Why?"

"I was just askin."

"What about you?" Stacy asked, as she snuggled next to her man.

"I gotta holla at Rio today. He called yesterday and said he needed a couple o' pounds." "Cool. I think CeCe has a sell lined up for tomorrow."

"Speaking of CeCe, what was up wit her at dinner last night?" Mo asked.

"What do you mean?" Stacy was afraid this was going to happen. She was hoping that she was the only one to notice how CeCe was acting toward Gloria. Mo looked at her and twisted up his face.

"Now, I know if I saw it you did too. You're way more observant than I am," he said. "Yeah, she did seem to be actin' a little funny. I'll ask her about it today and see what she has to say."

"Cool," Mo said. "Cause I wanna hear about this one." As he started to get out of bed, Stacy grabbed his arm.

"And just where do you think you goin'?" she asked.

"I told you I gotta meet Rio' this mornin'".

Stacy frowned up her face, folded her arms and pretended to pout like a spoiled child. After staring at Mo for a couple of seconds, she slowly let her lips curve into a devilish smile. "You said today. You didn't say right now."

"I know, but he told me to call him when I got up. Besides, the soona I go see him, the soona we make this dough." She moved her hand to his thigh and then let it slide down to his manhood.

"You don't have to go right now do you," she said seductively.

His nine and a half inch member sprung to life. He'd wanted some last night but she'd fallen asleep right after taking a shower. *This was probably her way of making it up to him,* he thought. Both of their cell phones rang at the same time. Stacy waved hers off. Mo turned his off too. After tossing his cell phone onto the nightstand, Mo got under the covers and started nibbling Stacy's clit.

"Oh, shit," she moaned softly.

Rio would just to have to wait.

Chapter 12

Ty woke up at 7:45 in the morning. His night had been a rough one. It took him two hours before he was able to fall asleep. At first it was because Dre and CeCe argued half the night. He didn't know what they were arguing about. He'd thought that maybe it was because Dre had let him spend the night but quickly dismissed that one. CeCe wouldn't mind him sleeping there until the morning. But then he realized that it was because she wouldn't have sex with him last night. "If you were worth fuckin' then I would fuck you more," he'd heard her say. Ty rubbed the top of his head and let out a long breath. Words couldn't describe how guilty he felt at that particular moment. He had been screwing his cousin's woman so much that she'd been getting stingy with the punnany when it came to Dre.

He got up and, hoping that they were still asleep, put his shoes on and walked out the front door. He wasn't worried about getting a ride back to Jillian's. He knew too many people to not be able to catch a ride with someone. He opened up his cell phone and called Big Mo. He might as well tell him about what happened with Fat Jack last night.

Getting the voice mail, he left a message. "Yo' Mo. It's me Ty. Gimmie a call man. I saw on the news that a guy I went to school with got killed last night. Peace."

After leaving the coded message for Mo, Ty dialed Gloria's number. Although she'd been turned off by CeCe's attitude during dinner, she'd told him that she was off today and to come by if he wasn't busy. Once she agreed to pick him up, Ty started walking down Warrensville Center Road. He needed to clear his head. He didn't know how or when but at some point he was going to have to come clean with Dre.

₫₫₫

Spice flipped her cell phone open and dialed Michael Gaines's number. She wanted to let him know that she was available to meet with him earlier than she had planned. She was supposed to wait on Sugar but decided that she could do this herself. Besides, she didn't need her sister's monetary contribution to do what she was going to do. She had money her sister didn't know about. She was becoming obsessed with finding her father's killer.

Gaines answered on the second ring and was pleased to hear that she wanted to meet earlier. "That's fine," he said. "I have something to do later on anyway."

After hanging up from Gaines, she called her sister to let her know that since she was already up she would go ahead and take care of him. Her sister wasn't answering so she left her a voice mail message. *It's early,* she thought to herself. *Maybe she's still sleeping.* Then she called José to ask him how many bricks of cocaine he needed.

"I'm down to my last two senorita so you better bring me cinco."

"That's gonna cost you ocho-cinco senior," she told him.

"No problemo senorita. I'll see you in about an hour."

After hanging up from José, Spice threw on a half shirt showing her firm abs, a pair of booty shorts, and a pair of white air force ones. Then she splashed a dab of Burberry perfume on her neck, making sure she smelled good since her outfit wasn't up to par. She walked to her guest room and peered inside. Her man was sound asleep. They'd had an argument the night before and he'd stormed out of their bedroom. Not wanting to wake him she blew him a kiss and gently closed the door. he'd said some terrible things to him and planned on making it up to him when she got back home. She grabbed a large duffle bag out of the hall way closet, checked to make sure that she had her keys and headed for the front door.

After backing out of her driveway in her Jeep Wrangler, she headed down South Taylor Road on her way to Euclid Avenue. She hung a right on Euclid and squinted from the glare of the sun. She reached down and grabbed her Gucci sunglasses that were lying on the passenger's side seat. While waiting at a red light, a young thug with thunderbolt tattoos on his forearms and a black T-shirt with witness wrote in white letters across the front smiled at her. He had thick brush waves and a charming smile.

CeCe pulled down her shades to get a closer look at him. The diamond and platinum cross that hung around his neck almost blinded her. She pushed her shades back up on her face and turned her head back to the road. Turning down his radio he yelled to her.

"Hey, Mami. You lookin' good over there pretty lady." She ignored him. "Come on ma. Don't be like that," he persisted.

"You talkin' to me?" she asked as she finally responded.

"Yep."

"Sorry boo," she said. "I'm in a hurry."

"Why don't you let me give you my number then?" he asked. "That way if you get bored or lonely you can give me a call."

Before she could protest, he hopped out of his gold LX09 Lexus truck, ran around the front, and dropped his card into her lap. Then just as quickly he jumped back into his vehicle and spun off. Spice sat there with her mouth open wondering what the hell had just happened. She looked down at the card and read the name. **Darnell Carter: Real Estate Entrepreneur.**

Spice laughed out loud and threw the card into her glove compartment. *He's not even on my level* she thought.

She procedded to drive up Euclid Avenue until she came to 276th Street where she pulled into Euclid self storage. She hopped out of her jeep and walked to storage unit 6. After unlocking the door and going in she walked up to a 46 inch floor model Magnavox television.

Reaching inside her Gucci purse, she pulled out a small Phillips head screwdriver. She loosened the four screws that connected the back of the television to the front. Inside the television had been gutted. All of the electrical components had been taken out and replaced with stacks of one hundred dollar bills. She opened the over-sized duffle bag and stuffed it with fifty stacks. Each stack contained ten thousand dollars. She felt it was time to stop screwing around. If this didn't get Gaines off his ass, nothing would. Then she walked over to an old discarded sofa that she'd bought from the thrift store.

Reaching down inside the cushion, she pulled out five bricks of cocaine wrapped in plastic and dropped them into the bag. She zipped the bag up, walked out of the storage, and locked the door behind her. She hopped back in her jeep, tossed the bag onto the floor of the passenger's side, and headed back down Euclid. Euclid Square Mall was all but abandoned these days. All that was left was a few discount stores. That was the reason she had agreed to meet him there. She didn't have to worry about nosey people being in her business.

When she got to the empty parking lot, José was already there waiting for her. He was riding in a 1981 Chevy Monte Carlo. It was burnt orange in color and in mint condition. It sat on gold deep dish Dayton's with matching knock offs. The limousine styled tinted windows refused to allow anyone to see inside. Pulling up beside him, she quickly unzipped the bag, took the five bricks out, and stuffed them under the driver's seat. Then she zipped the bag back up and shoved it under the passenger's seat. She took her three-eighty out of her purse and placed it under her left thigh. It's not that she was afraid of José but she was smart enough to know that in this game you can never be too careful. José stepped out of the passenger's side of the car dressed like a B-Boy. He never ever wore suits because he'd always felt that they attracted too much attention to a person in his line of business.

He rocked a vintage LeBron James jersey, and a pair of LeBron James Zoom L23 sneakers. And attached to his back was a Cleveland Cavaliers backpack. Jumping inside the passenger's side, he greeted Spice with a warm smile.

"Hola señorita. Como es usted que hace hoy?" he asked in his native language.

"I'm doing fine José."

"Ah, I see your Spanish is still top notch señorita."

"It's ok. I haven't had to use it in a while."

"How is your sister doing?"

"She's fine."

"I'm curious as to why she's not here señorita," he asked with a frown.

"There's really no reason," she said. "I was up early this morning so I figured I could take care of this without waking her."

Jose smiled. He had an uncanny sense of knowing when someone wasn't telling him the whole truth. "So what you are really saying is that you have money put away that your sister does not know about eh señorita?" All Spice could do was laugh. "Do not be embarrassed," he said. "There is nothing wrong with putting aside a few pesos for a rainy day." Even though Spice seemed happy, José could see in her eyes that something was troubling her.

"Are you ok?' he asked her.

"Yeah, I'm ok."

He regarded her curiously as he started to rub his chin and raise his eyebrows.

"Ok," she said acknowledging that something was bothering her. "Something has been on my mind a lot lately."

Locking his fingers together in front of his face, José said "Tell me. I have time."

"But what about your ride?" she asked pointing to the car Jose arrived in.

"That is my nephew. He can wait. Besides, I'm paying him well."

"Oh, ok. Well, lately I've been thinking a lot about my father. Me and my sister have been paying someone to try and find out who killed my father but so far he hasn't been able to come up with anything concrete."

"I see," he said.

"Do you think I'm startin' to be obsessed?" she asked.

"Not as long as you don't let it interfere with your way of thinking," he answered sensitivly. "Tell me señorita. Is the person that you have working for you a private investigator or are they in law enforcement?"

She hesitated.

Holding up his hand he said, "You do not have to tell if you do not want to. I was just wondering." He looked down at his rather ordinary Timex watch.

"Well," he said, "shall we get down to business?"

"Of course," she responded. Reaching under the seat, she pulled out the bricks one at a time and handed them to him. José reached into his pocket and pulled out a folded up black plastic bag. He opened it and held it open as Spice dropped the dope into the bag.

"You ain't gon' look at it?" she questioned.

He smiled. "I've been dealing with you for quite some time now Spice," he said calling her by her nick-name for the first time. "You haven't given me any reason to distrust you. I'll check it out when I get home." He leaned forward and slid the backpack off of his shoulders one arm at a time. After unzipping it, he held it open so Spice could see what was inside. The backpack was filled with stacks of hundred and fifty dollar bills. She knew that she didn't have to count it. He had never stiffed her before and she didn't believe he would start now.

"You can keep the backpack as a gift. And try not to worry too much about your father. I'm sure something will come of your search for his murderer." As strange as she thought it was, his words actually comforted her. "I have to go now. I have another appointment I have to get to." Before he got out he gave her a hug and a kiss on the cheek. "Take care of yourself," he said as he exited her truck.

"You too," she replied. He gently closed the door, looked at her, and smiled. "What is it?" she asked as she smiled back.

"You don't have to be afraid of me Spice. I like you too much to do anything to you." He looked down and nodded at her leg. Her gun had inched its way from up under her thigh.

Covering her face in embarrassment, she laughed and said "I'm sorry."

"Don't be," he said as he walked away.

Oh my God, she thought. *He notices everything.*

Chapter 13

Thirty-eight year old José Cuevas had been around a long time. He'd been in the game since he was seventeen years old. He'd learned a lot, heard a lot, and seen a lot. He was married with two children but no one outside of his neighborhood knew it. He always felt that if anyone in the drug game knew of his wife and kids that it would expose them to unnecessary danger. Jose lived in a modest ranch style single family home in Bedford Heights, Ohio and never allowed anyone other than his immediate family to come to his home.

He owned a very lucrative electrical contracting business which he used to wash his drug money. He'd been a licensed electrician for eleven years and only hired electricians who had been to school and had some type of formal training. Jose was very well liked in his community because of the work his company had done there. He was a very very smart man who, while he possessed some nice things, lived well below his means.

The two cars that he owned were a 2009 Nissan Maxima and a 2008 Honda Accord. Every time he talked with one of his neighbors he would complain about how the car and house payments were killing him but the truth of the matter was that he owned every single thing that he had except for his house. He could've paid it off a long time ago but didn't want to bring any suspicions on himself. Over the years, José had accumulated more than twenty-five million dollars in savings. He was smart enough to know that keeping that kind of money in a bank in the United States would raise too many red flags so he kept twenty million of it in an off shore account overseas.

He kept nine point five million in three different safes hidden inside the walls of his home. His wife knew about two of them. He kept the other one a secret. No one knew about it. He had two bank accounts. One with Amtrust and the other with Huntington and had two hundred and fifty thousand dollars apiece in each one. He had far more money than any of the contacts he was buying from in Ohio. He was making over two hundred thousand dollars a year from his contracting business alone so he didn't depend on selling dope to make a living. His main customers were not even in the state of Ohio. When he sold his dope, it was usually to people in Chicago or Pittsburgh in the north and Kentucky or South Carolina in the South.

And because he didn't depend on it to survive, he would simply wait for a drought and charge his customers double what it was worth. They either paid his price or went without. He'd been doing this for the last five years. They didn't like it but there was really nothing they could do about it. They couldn't set him up because in every city he did business in, he paid off the entire police force. He was also a strong believer in your right hand not letting your left hand know what it was doing.

For some time now he'd known that Spice's sister was dating one of the guys he was buying weed from and as a precaution he'd made sure to never let them know that he was copping from both of them. After watching Spice pull out of the mall parking lot, Jose instructed his nephew Pablo to take him back to his car. They rode in silence as Pablo could tell that his Uncle had something on his mind.

"Esta usted tio de la autorizacion?," he asked.

"Si." But his uncle was not ok. It didn't take a genius to figure out that Spice and her sister was paying a dirty cop to find out what happened to their father. He'd seen the sadness in Spice's eyes as she discussed her father. In the last year he'd come to love her like a sister. She needed closure and the only way that was going to happen was for her to find out what happened to her father. He knew enough about dirty cops to know that they always knew more than they were telling. He decided to speed the process along.

𝆱𝆱𝆱

Amanda woke up in a cold sweat. Breathing heavily, she looked down at her sheets and discovered that they were soaking wet. Trying to collect her self as best she could, she couldn't figure out if she had just had a hot steamy dream or a nightmare. All she knew is that before she woke up, Bennie had her bent over one of the pool tables at Jillian's banging her back out. She was screaming his name as he pounded her with stroke after thunderous stroke. Just as she was about to cum, she woke up.

Apparently that didn't stop anything because her sheets were drenched. Charity cautiously stuck her head inside the door.

"You alright in here girl," she asked. Unable to speak for the moment, Amanda nodded her head yes.

"Damn bitch," Charity said. "The way you were in here moaning I thought you had a fuckin' man in here."

With her breath returning to her Amanda said "Sis I just had this hot ass dream. A guy had me bent over one of the pool tables at work and was just pounding this shit. I gotta get me a fuckin' man."

Charity's mouth fell open in amazement.

"You mean to tell me that a dream is about to make you do something that I've been trying to get you to do for six fuckin' months? Who were you dreaming about? Anybody I know?"

"Nope."

Amanda knew she would never hear the end of it if Charity knew she was dreaming about Bennie. Not because she had fucked him. But because he was black.

"Well, from the look of those sheets, you need to hurry up and find you a man. As a matter of fact, you don't even have to get into a relationship. All you have to do is find someone to lay the pipe to you and then you'll be straight."

"That's how you catch diseases," Amanda said with a disgusted look.

"That's what rubbers are for sis," Charity replied.

"Uhh…I don't know about that Charity."

"Fine then," Charity laughed. "Continue to not get any." She headed out the door and went to work.

$$$

Mo, Bennie, Ty, and Dre sat in a booth at Wild Wings laughing and drinking. This was the first time they had been together without any women around for a week. Dre and Ty had already told Mo about the situation with Fat Jack and Shank. Mo told them that they had made the right move. They ran C-Town and anybody trying to get in the way would be dealt with. Now, Bennie was busy telling them about what happened between him, Charity, and her sister

.　　"Let me get this shit straight man," Ty said. "That bitch was riding you and her sister walked in the room?"

"Naw man, she didn't walk in the room. Her nosey ass stood at the door and watched," Bennie said. "The tripped out part about it though is that I had already saw her ass. Man, I'm telling you she stood there for about five minutes before her sister even knew she was there."

"Ah hell naw," Dre replied as he burst out laughing.

"Hold up nigga I got some mo' shit to tell you," bellowed Bennie. "After a nigga finish ripping them guts up, I had to go piss right? Guess who walked in the bathroom on a nigga?"

Mo laughed. "Nigga quit lyin.'"

"Nigga, I swear to God that's what happened," Bennie said.

"Nigga what you shoulda did," Ty said, "is pulled that hoe in the bathroom and slung dick to that bitch."

"Damn nigga ain't you tired of fuckin' white hoes?" Mo asked.

They all stopped laughing abruptly as the waitress slammed their two dozen wings on the table. Bennie looked up to see Peaches glaring at him.

"What the fuck is yo' problem?" Ty questioned. She ignored him and continued to stare a hole through Bennie.

"Will you gentlemen be needing anything else," she asked.

"Yeah, bring us two more pitchers of beer," Mo said.

Rolling her eyes at Bennie, she turned and walked away.

"The fuck wrong wit' that skeeza?" Ty said.

Bennie waved his hand. "Man, that's the bitch that was in here trippin' when I came in here and picked Charity up. All on her Malcolm X kick actin' all mad 'cause I left wit' snowflake?"

No one said a word.

"What the fuck up wit' y'all?" Bennie asked.

"Nigga if you want the truth, you could use a few more sistas in yo' stable dawg," Ty replied.

Beenie shook his head. "Damn man. Y'all nigga's actin' like I ain't neva boned a sista in my life."

Ty laughed. "Yo' stepmother don't count nigga."

"Muthafucka I was seventeen and besides that bitch came into my bedroom that night."

"Did you ever tell yo' dad about that?" Mo inquired.

"I didn't have to tell 'em, he caught us in the act. But that's another story," Bennie said as he got up to go to the bathroom. For a full five seconds you could hear a pin drop as Mo, Ty, and Dre all stared at each other. Then in unison they all said "Ah hell naw," and burst out laughing.

"What's up Dre?" Mo asked. You kinda quiet today dawg. You feelin' ahight?"

"Yeah, I'm cool man. I just got somethin' on my mind," Dre responded.

"Spill it then nigga. We all boys here," Mo said.

Dre took a deep breath and let it out. "Man I think CeCe cheatin' on a nigga man."

"What?" Ty asked trying to act surprised.

"Man she ain't gave a nigga none in two weeks," Dre admitted.

"Ah man," Mo replied waving him off. "That ain't shit. Sometimes women just get like that dawg. Don't let that bullshit bother you. Just get you some pussy from somewhere else until she gets in the mood again."

Ty got quiet.

"Nigga don't tell me that's the only broad you fuckin'," Mo inquired.

He looked at Ty and Ty hunched up his shoulders as if to say, "Hey man I tried to tell this silly ass nigga."

"Nigga listen," Mo spoke. "I know you love yo' woman. Hell, I love mine too. But a man's gotta do what a man's gotta do. When my dick get hard nigga it needs some attention. And if Stacy don't wanna take care of it, I get somebody that will. Nigga that's the playas code."

"Hell yeah," Ty said as he gave Mo some dap. "Man what the fuck takin' Bennie so long?"

Chapter 14

Bennie walked to the bathroom smiling. He had been waiting for the right time to drop that bomb on his crew. He hadn't told anyone about that but he wanted his boys to be the first to know. As he was standing in front of the urinal draining the main vein, his thoughts shifted to Charity. Her pussy was much better than he thought it would be. He thought it would be dry but it was juicy. He thought it would be loose but it was surprisingly tight. In a way it reminded him of Audrey's womb. He laughed.

If he got the chance, he was going to try and bone her sister too. Maybe he would hook her up with Ty so he could see what he was missing. By his own admission, Ty had never been with a white girl before. After washing and drying his hands, Bennie headed back toward the table. Peaches walked toward the ladies bathroom on the opposite side. He tried to hurry past her in an attempt to avoid a confrontation, but she stepped across the aisle and stopped right in front of him. He tried to side-step her, but she moved with him.

"What is your problem?" Bennie asked.

"I just have one question for you," she said.

"Look, I ain't got time for these games."

"This ain't no fuckin' game," she snapped.

Bennie let out a sigh. "What is it?"

"What you got against black women?"

"Nothin'."

"Oh, really," she said as she put her hands on her hips. "You act like you scared of black pussy."

Bennie snapped before he knew it. "Bitch you crazy as fuck!" he said. "I ain't scared of no kinda pussy."

"Prove it then nigga."

She pushed him back into the mens bathroom, turned around and lifted her skirt. Bennie could hardly contain his self when she bent over and revealed her plump ass. He couldn't be sure but from the back her coochie looked like it was shaved clean. His dick grew so hard it almost pushed through his zipper. Assuming the position like a suspect, she looked back at Bennie with lust in her eyes. Unable to contain himself any longer, Bennie unbuckled his pants and dropped them to the floor. Spreading her ass cheeks with one hand, he forcefully jammed his thick cock into her love nest.

"Uuhhh!! Oh, shit!!" she screamed.

Bennie was gong to enjoy this. This broad had been getting on his nerves for the past couple of days. He didn't know what her motivation was for wanting to fuck but he was going to try to tear her pussy to pieces. The longer he stroked it, the juicier it got. So, instead of trying to punish her, he actually found himself enjoying it.

"Oh, shit baby! This pussy good as fuck!"

"Ooohh hell yeah baby!" she said. "Tell me you like this black pussy!"

"Shit baby I love this black pussy!"

"I suck dick much better than I fuck," she continued. Bennie found that hard to believe. This woman was rocking his world. It had been so long since he'd had sex with a black woman, he'd forgotten how good they were in bed. "Take it out and I'll show you."

Her pussy made a loud popping noise when he withdrew his penis. It was dripping with her pussy juices. She turned around and got on her knees. She circled the head with her tongue and slowly slid it into her mouth. Bennie was amazed as she put the whole ten inches in her mouth.

"Oh, shit!!" he screamed.

A satisfied smile curled up in both corners of her mouth. She knew Bennie was impressed with her deep throat abilities.

She didn't even gag as she took it to the back of her throat. Then she slowly took it out of her mouth and looked up at Bennie. "Can that white bitch Amanda do this?" she asked.

She put his dick back in her mouth and let it slide down her throat. But instead of stopping when she got to his balls, she put those in her mouth too. It felt so good to him that he couldn't hold back any longer.

"Oh, shit baby! I'm 'bout to cum!" he yelled as he squirted what seemed like gallons of cum down her throat.

She made long gulping sounds as she swallowed every drop. Bennie was so spent that after he took his love tool out of her mouth, he had to lean back against the sink to catch his breath. Peaches looked at him and jut shook her head.

"That's a damn shame," she said. "You been so busy fuckin' these white girls, I guess you can't handle a real woman no more." Bennie gave her the finger.

"Yeah, yeah whateva," she responded. "Sensitive dick ass nigga." Peaches walked out of the bathroom with a large smirk on her face. After catching his breath, Bennie walked out behind her on wobbly legs. She had definitly put it on him. When he got back to the booth, he needed a drink.

"Nigga where the fuck you been?" Ty questioned.

"I had to take a shit nigga, why?" Bennie asked defensively.

"For twenty muthafuckin' minutes?" Mo asked. Just then Peaches walked to the table carrying another pitcher of beer. "We didn't order this," Mo said.

"It's on the house," Peaches replied. She shot a wicked smile at Bennie. After she walked away, Bennie poured himself a glass of beer. He was trying to avoid eye contact with the rest of the crew. Mo, Ty, and Dre all smiled at each other.

"Nigga you must think we stupid," Dre said.

"No wonder it took yo' ass so long," Ty chimed in.

"Hold up...you fucked that hoe man?" Mo asked.

"Hell yeah. Why you so surprised?" Bennie questioned.

"Cause she ain't white," Mo replied. Dre was laughing so hard he almost threw up. "I propose a toast," Mo continued. Holding up his glass, Mo looked all of them right in the eyes. "Chedda Boyz for life."

All of them clicked glasses and repeated the last two words. "For life."

Or so they thought.

✗✗✗

Charity hopped off the number nine bus right in front of wild wings. She was getting tired of catching the bus to work. She was going to have to find some kind of way to get the three hundred dollars to get her car out of the shop. Charity walked across the half empty parking lot and smiled. She knew that some of those cars didn't belong to wild wing customers. She didn't feel like doing shit. She was still sore from the pounding Bennie had put on her. As she walked up the steps getting ready to begin her shift, Peaches walked through the door with hers just ending. The two women exchanged evil stares from one another. Peaches looked down at her watch and then back at Charity.

"You late bitch," she said.

"Don't worry about it hoe," Charity shot back.

Peaches stopped in her tracks. She turned around, stormed back up the steps and pushed the door closed just as Charity was trying to open it. "Let me tell you somethin' hoe". The only reason I ain't put my foot in yo' ass yet is because I don't want to lose my job. But if you keep disrespectin' me I'ma fuck yo' white ass up." She pointed her finger in Charity's face. "Don't make me hurt yo' ass."

Charity laughed at her. She wasn't intimidated by Peaches in the least. "You ain't gon' fuck up a muthafuckin' thing," Charity said. And you can't do shit to hurt me."

Peaches leaned forward and whispered in her ear. "That's what you think," she said. She backed up, turned on her heels, and started walking to her car. Just before she closed her car door, she blew Charity a kiss. Charity turned around and patted her ass. Then she slung open the door and walked inside wondering what the hell Peaches was talking about.

Chapter 15

Spice sat in Borders book store at a table facing the front of the store looking out the window. Checking her watch she noticed that Gaines was twenty minutes late. After finishing her café mocha, she took out her cell phone. Just as she started to dial his number, he walked in the door. It took him all of two seconds to find her. He could spot her beautiful looks anywhere. Secretly he wanted to screw her, but didn't have the nerve to pursue it. He walked over to where she was seated and plopped down on one of the chairs.

"Hello, Ms. Spice?" he asked.

She looked down at her watch and then back to him. He looked at his watch and shrugged his shoulders. She laughed at the irony.

"So, have you found out anything else yet?" she inquired.

Looking at her cautiously he asked her "You aren't going to curse me out like you did last time are you?"

She stared at him for a minute. "Look," she started. "I'm sorry about that. But this is getting very frustrating to us."

"Speaking of us, where is your sister?"

"Don't worry 'bout that. I'm handling this today."

"Ok. Sorry about that."

"No problem. Now, shall we get down to business?"

"By all means."

"Ok then. What's the progress?"

Gaines took a deep breath. He knew he was about to say something that Spice was not going to be happy to hear. "I have to tell you Ms. Spice. It seems like the closer I get to cracking this case the more people stop talking. Don't get me wrong. I am making some progress but it's not going as fast as I thought it would."

Spice sat there and listened to what she felt were excuses. Then she laid it on the line. "Look, if you can't get the job done then maybe we should just find someone else. I mean, damn Mr. Policeman. It don't seem to be hard for y'all to get the streets to talk when it's in y'all favor. Now, all of a sudden y'all can't get nobody to talk? Nigga that's bullshit."

As he opened his mouth to protest, she held up a hand to stop him. She picked up the duffle bag that she had stuffed with money earlier and dropped it on the table. After unzipping the bag, she held it open so he could see the contents. Gaines's eyes got as big as frisbees. He'd never seen that much money before in his entire life. At least none that he might actually have access to.

"This is five hundred-thousand dollars. Find our fathers killer and it's all yours." She zipped the bag back up, stood, and walked out the door.

$$$

Big Mo sat in his gold SL 500 vibin' to some old school Snoop Doggy Dog. *Gin and Juice* was his track of choice. It wasn't his favorite song on the cd but because he was drinking Seagram's Gin and Juice at the time, and loved old school music he felt it was the right song to play. He checked his watch and saw that it was almost time to meet his contact. As soon as he turned the ignition, his cell phone vibrated.

"I should'a known," he mumbled to himself. "Every time I get ready to take care of some fuckin' business, somebody botherin' the fuck outta me." He looked at his cell phone and rolled his eyes when he saw who it was.

"Yeah," he answered.

"We need to talk," Gaines said.

"About?"

"About our little arrangement."

"What about it?"

"It's time to renegotiate."

"Renegotiate! What the fuck you talking about? I'm already payin' yo' ass a grip." "I'm sorry but that really isn't much of a deal compared to what *they* want to offer me."

Big Mo was silent for a minute.

"What kinda money you talkin' about man?" he asked.

"Well, giving me more than they are will definitely change my mind," Gaines said.

Change his mind, Mo thought. *This muthafucka done decided to switch sides already talkin' like that.*

"Are you still there?" Gaines said, reacting to Mo's silence.

"Ahight man. I got you. Meet me in the parking lot of John W Raper Elementary School in an hour."

"John W Raper? May I ask why we have to meet there?" Gaines asked suspiciously.

"Cause, muthafucka, I don't want nobody to see this bag of money I'ma give yo' ass nigga."

"Oh. Ok. See you in an hour."

Mo hung up. "Fuck!" he screamed. "Where the fuck these hoes get that kinda money?"

Mo took the half smoked blunt from the ashtray and lit it. Smoking weed always helped him think better. After inhaling and exhaling the marijuana fumes a couple of times, he knew what had to be done. He finished the rest of the blunt and got out of his truck. Taking his time carefully to think over what he was about to do, he slowly walked up to his bedroom and opened the closet door. Shoving aside the mountain of clothes hanging up in the closet, he knelt down on the floor. He grabbed the edge of the rug and pulled it back revealing a secret compartment that nobody but him knew about. It was three feet deep. Opening the duffle bag that he had taken from the top shelf of the closet, he started to fill the bag with money. The more he put in the angrier he became. When he reached a hundred grand, he stopped.

"This betta be good e fuckin' 'nough," he mumbled. He

closed the secret compartment and covered it back up with the rug. Reaching back up on the top shelf, he grabbed his black 45 Smith and Wesson pistol with the silencer on it.

"I don't trust this muthafucka at all," he said to no one in particular. "His ass just might try to pop me, take my money, and then tell dem hoes that I know something about their old man getting popped."

He put his gun in the small of his back and closed the closet door. He jogged back down the stairs and out the door. Jumping back in his truck, Big Mo peeled out of his driveway and headed for the freeway. He wanted to hurry up and get this over with.

"This betta not be a fuckin' set-up," Big Mo snarled, thinking out loud. 'Cause if it is, I'm shootin' my way up outta that bitch!"

Chapter 16

Audrey Murphy stormed out of her house mad as fuck. Here she was ready to get her afternoon freak on and her husband wanted to go play golf. *He could've at least given me a quickie before he left* she thought to herself. "Golf." She spat the word out of her mouth as if it left a bad taste in it. "His fat ass needs to be at Bally's." She had tried to call Bennie for an afternoon delight but for some reason he wasn't answering his phone. She gave up on trying to get some for the time being and decided to go over to her daughter's apartment.

She knew her daughters would be at work. She told herself that she just wanted to get out of the house but in truth she just wanted to be nosey. Whenever she knew that her daughters weren't going to be at home for a while, she would go over there and snoop around. Audrey was such a sexual pervert that she got off on reading her daughter's diary. Whenever she came to the explicit details of her daughter's sexcapades, she would masturbate.

She didn't like being that way. She just couldn't help it. Sex was the ultimate drug to her and the more bizarre and kinky it was, the more she became addicted to it. She had been this way ever since she came home early from work one day and caught her sixteen year old daughter giving her black, thirty three year old neighbor a blowjob. When she walked inside the house, she heard moans coming from upstairs but assumed that it was her husband. They led a swinger's lifestyle so she was eager to go upstairs and join in.

But once she got upstairs, she started to get a little upset. She didn't mind her husband getting some pussy on the side because that's the way they lived, but she didn't want to go that far and start having ménage a trois' in the girls' bedroom. Slowly pushing open the door to her oldest daughter's bedroom, she gasped at what she saw. There was her daughter, on her hands and knees, with a huge black dick in her mouth. It had to be at least ten inches. Strangely enough though, she didn't get mad. Instead of being pissed off, it turned her sick ass on. She got so turned on, in fact, that she started playing with herself right then and there. Any normal parent would have called the police and had this pervert arrested. But not Audrey. She just stood there rubbing her clit. Listening to her daughter slob on the next door neighbor's dick caused her to explode in her pants. After she came, she eased back down the stairs and out the door. She didn't want to embarrass her daughter so she left without saying a word.

She never mentioned it to her daughter. What she didn't know however is that her daughter had seen her in the mirror. For a brief second, she got scared and almost panicked. But when she saw the pure pleasure on her mother's face she knew she was safe. She wasn't stupid. No matter how much they tried to keep it from her and her sister, she knew they were living a kinky lifestyle. From that moment on her relationship with her mother changed forever.

It turned her on to see her mother standing there jacking off while watching her. *It must be in the blood*, she thought. When she was sure her mother was gone, she decided to do something she had never done before. She started sucking as hard as she could. But instead of letting him pull out and bust in her face, she wrapped her arms around his ass and kept it in her mouth. Discovering that she actually like the taste of it, she tried to suck out every last drop of cum he had in him.

Audrey thought about that day every time she went to visit her daughters. Parking her canary yellow ford mustang convertible in the parking lot, she let the top up and got out. If she couldn't get in touch with Bennie, then she would either read her daughter's diary again or use the twelve inch black dildo she brought with her in her purse. One way or another she was going to get off.

$$fff$$

Peaches pulled into the driveway of the two-family home she was currently residing in. Deciding that she might want to leave back out later, she backed out of the driveway and parked on the street. The last thing she wanted to do was get blocked in by the dude upstairs. From what she knew of him from talking to him was that he worked twelve and fourteen hour shifts at Mid West Forge steel plant and once he fell asleep, it was almost impossible to wake him up. She'd gotten written up one day because he'd parked behind her and went upstairs and fell asleep. When she couldn't wake him by knocking on his door real hard, she had to catch the bus.They had to share the washing machine that was in the basement.

Most of the time she just went to the Laundromat and let him have free reign of it. One day when she thought he was asleep, she wanted to wash an outfit that she was going to wear to the Mirage nightclub in downtown Cleveland. Sliding on her slippers, she walked down to the basement in nothing but her bra and panties only to realize that he was awake and down there taking some of his clothes out of the dryer. Looking up at her as she stood there frozen, he'd told her that he was done.

He walked right past her without so much as giving her a second look. From that day on she was convinced that brotha was gay. Peaches lived on 117th and St. Clair Avenue. The two-family house she stayed in had a fence around it with thick grass separated by a cement walkway. It was yellow with blue trim. Blue columns surrounded the porch area and the porch was also painted blue. Walking up on her porch, Peaches stuck her hand in her mailbox to check her mail. Then she opened the door, walked in, and dropped down on the sofa.

She reached into her shirt pocket and took out a pack of unopened Newport's. After breaking the seal and opening up the pack, she shook one into her hand. She grabbed the lighter off of the coffee table beside her and set fire to the square. As she took a drag and exhaled, she started to think about what had gone down today. If she didn't need her job so bad, she would've stomped Charity's ass.

White bitch, she thought. In her book, Bennie wasn't much better. "All these fine ass sista's around and he gotta go get a cracka hoe," she said out loud.

Then she smiled. She knew it was wrong to do what she did, but she just couldn't stand that jungle fever shit. In her racist mind, blacks belonged with blacks and whites belonged with whites. That's how she was brought up and she would always feel that way. She walked to her kitchen and took a bottle of water out of the refrigerator.

She coughed violently as she twisted the cap off of the bottle. She walked to the bathroom and opened the medicine cabinet where she took a small vial of medication off the shelf. Tears started to sting her eyes and then rolled down her cheeks as she read the label on the bottle. She shook out a Retrovir, threw it in her mouth, and gulped it down with a swig of water. Unbeknownst to every one else on the planet except her mother, Peaches had full blown AIDS.

$$$

Big Mo yanked up in John W Raper parking lot buzzing. He'd finished off the cup of gin and juice on the freeway. He liked to live dangerously like that. He wanted to get there first because he didn't want Gaines getting in his truck. He would much rather get in his car. Big Mo stepped out of his truck trying to figure out exactly just how much money these broads offered Gaines. He was paying Gaines a pretty penny. So, for him to call with this bullshit, they must be offering around a hundred G's. He was in such deep thought he almost didn't see Gaines pulling into the parking lot.

When Gaines came to a stop, Mo reached into the driver's side back seat window of his truck and took out the duffle bag. After opening the passenger's side door and jumping in the seat, he got right down to business.

"Ahight," he said. "What the fuck is going on?"

"What is going on is that the younger sister, I think her name is Spice, has offered me quite a bit of money to find out who killed her father."

"Look man," Mo started out saying. "I got quite a bit of money here myself. I don't know what that bitch is offering but it's a hundred thousand dollars in this bag."

Before Gaines could even laugh at the miniscule amount Moose was offering, his cell phone went off. "Excuse me for a minute," Gaines said. Getting out of the car he said to Mo "Make yourself comfortable." When he was sure he was out of Mo's ear range, he answered he call.

"Hello?"

"Hola mi amigo. It is nice to hear your voice once again."

Gaines didn't even have to ask who it was. He knew by the heavy accent and friendly tone that it was Enrique. He wanted to tell him he was busy but Enrique was paying him well to keep him apprised of what was going on in the city. Every week he reported to Enrique what was going on with the crime scene. Enrique's reasoning was simple. The more you knew, the more power you had. He didn't tell Enrique about his deals with Moose or Sugar. He felt it was none of his business.

"Enrique my friend. How are you?"

"Alas Miguel, I have a problemo."

"I'm listening," Gaines said, with a frown spread across his face.

"I have this lady friend of mine. For a long time she has been searching for her father's killer. Word has it that he was killed right there on the streets of Cleveland."

"And that has what to do with me?" Gaines asked. He knew what Enrique was getting at. He just wanted to hear him say it.

"Come now amigo. I'm fairly confident that there is nothing that goes on in the city of Cleveland that you do not know about," Enrique said clearly trying to stroke Gaines's ego.

"You know," Gaines started, "That's a lot of detective work."

"I hear you mi amigo and I understand completely. That's

why I am prepared to pay you the sum of one hundred and fifty thousand dollars to find this person. Gaines was speechless. Not only did he have Spice willing to pay him half a million dollars to find who killed her father, now Enrique was about to hire him to find one of his girlfriends father's killer.

"I see you are at a loss for words mi amigo. But before we go on, let me explain something to you. This is not my girlfriend nor is it a relative. It is simply a friend that I care a great deal about."

"Whateva you say mi amigo." Who the hell did Enrique think he was bullshitting, Gaines thought. Nobody did shit like this for a friend. "What is this friend's name?" he asked.

"I prefer not to reveal her real name but her street name is Spice."

Gaines almost dropped his cell phone. His luck couldn't possibly be this good. Making sure to keep his back to the car so Mo couldn't try to read his lips, he smiled at the irony. He had just made six hundred and fifty thousand dollars in less than two hours and all he had to do was rat out a drug dealer.

"Mi amigo, you've got yourself a deal."

"Muy beuno. Contact me when you have the information," Enrique said.

$$$

After hanging up the phone, Enrique aka Rio aka Juan aka José Cuevas smiled as he sat on his back deck sipping cognac. His real name was Julio although his associates would never know that. It made him feel good to help out a friend. Spice was a good person and one hundred and fifty thousand dollars were mere peanuts to him. He decided not to tell her of his involvement in the matter. He didn't want to make her feel indebted in any way. If for some ungodly reason Inspector Gaines were to change his mind and turn down the offer, then he would just have to go over his head.

Someone on the police force knew something and he was prepared to go to Chief Murphy if need be. And if that didn't

---

---

work, he would go to the mayor. All three of them were on his payroll anyway. He was a very secretive man when it came to conducting his business. That's why everyone that he dealt with was given a different name. None of them would ever know that they were dealing with the same man. And that's just the way he liked it.

₣₣₣

Mo stood behind Gaines with his gun pointed directly at the back of his head. After receiving a phone call and being tipped off that Gaines was trying to double cross him, he knew Gaines had to die. The smile that Gaines had on his face when he turned around was replaced by horror as the last thing he would ever see was Big Mo's vengeful face. He never even got a chance to beg for his life as Mo fired twice into his forehead and splattered his brains all over the playground. Then he calmly walked back to Gaines' car and retrieved the bag of money. After tossing the bag into his truck, he walked back over to where Gaines was laying, pulled out his dick, and pissed on him. After defiling the dead man, he jumped in his truck and pulled off. Meanwhile, Gaines' cell phone started to ring. It rang three times before going to his voice mail.

"Michael where in the hell are you?" the voice on the voice mail asked. "We really need to talk man! When you get this call, hit me back as soon as possible! It's very important!"

₣₣₣

Charity crossed her legs and played with her finger nails as Bennie channel surfed the cable stations. An hour into her shift, she had pretended to be sick so she could leave and kick it with Bennie. Her manager didn't quite believe her but because she had never done that before, he gave her the benefit of the doubt. She was mad because she had asked Bennie to help her get her car out the shop and he didn't say yes. He didn't say no either but that was beside the point. He merely told her that he would think about it. What the fuck is it to think about? She wondered. It only cost three hundred dollars and she knew Bennie had it. Contrary to popular belief, Charity wasn't free. Meanwhile, Bennie sat next to her trying not to laugh. He was going to give her the money but he didn't want her to think he was some kind of trick ass nigga.

"Fix me anotha drink bitch," he told her without looking her way.

He was testing her now just to see what he could get away with. He was waiting on her to tell him to get it himself in which case he wasn't going to give her shit. She rolled her eyes and got up. She went into the kitchen and poured him two shots of mango flavored vodka mixed with Welch's mango juice. When she came back, three hundred dollars was sitting on the coffee table. Her face lit up as she jumped into Bennies lap and hugged his neck.

"Thank you baby," she said as she started kissing his neck. "I really do appreciate this."

"Yeah, yeah whateva," he shot back. "You just lucky yo' pussy is so muthafuickin' good."

"Naw muthafucka, you just lucky yo' dick is so muthafuckin' big," she answered back.

"Oh, is that right?"

"That's right," she said. She felt her pussy getting moist as Bennie rubbed her thigh.

"Oooh shit that feels good," she cooed. She motioned for him to stand up. After he stood up, she immediately got down on her knees. Lust filled her eyes as she unbuckled his belt and let his Roc-A-Wear Jean shorts fall to the floor. "Um, um, um," she said shaking her head at the amazement of his size. "Damn baby. I hope you don't punish me like you did last night." She slid his boxers down to his ankles and kissed the head of his rod.

"So, what you sayin'? You want a nigga to take it easy on that pussy?" He couldn't believe that he'd said nigga in front her. Either she didn't notice or didn't care. Looking up at him with a devilish grin, she reached up under her skirt and stuck her hand inside her panties.

"Hell naw baby. I want you to tear this pussy up. But first," she said as she licked his shaft, "I wanna suck this big muthafucka."

He moaned as she put half of it in her mouth. He thought back to how Peaches had stuffed all of him in her mouth and got even harder. Feeling him growing in her mouth, Charity gagged a little.

"Shit baby! Don't choke me!" Grabbing the back of her head, he pushed his dick back into her mouth.

"Stop talking bitch and suck my dick bitch," he grunted.

"Mmm hmm," she moaned. She didn't mind at all being called names during sex. As a matter of fact, it turned her on.

"Deep throat it hoe."

She pushed her head down on it until she couldn't go any further. Tears filled her eyes as she started to gag again. Not being able to go any further, she took it out of her mouth and started coughing.

"Shit! Baby, I can't get any more in." Bennie was loving this. He loved making these honkey's submit to his will.

"Don't worry about it," Bennie said. "Just keep suckin' it 'till I bust."

"On one condition," she replied. "I want you to talk nasty to me while I'm suckin' it."

"Shiiit girl, that ain't no problem at all," he said. He wasn't surprised. Most women loved to talk nasty during sex even though they would never admit it. Grabbing the back of his ass with both hands, she took him back in her mouth.

"Oohhh shit! Suck this muthafucka bitch! Make me cum in yo' mouth!" "Uuhmm hhmm," she moaned. They were enjoying themselves tremendously. So much so that they never heard the front door open and close.

Chapter 17

Chief Murphy sat behind his desk smiling. The day had been good to him so far. He'd planned to go golfing with some of his buddies but they cancelled on him at the last minute. With nothing else to do, he decided to go to the office and monitor some of his less than honest officers. He and the Mayor were jointly working together in an effort to clean up the corrupt Cleveland Police Department. Neither of them knew that one was just as crooked as the other.

They gave all Detectives and Inspectors new cell phones that were installed with a tracking device just in case they ever got into a life threatening situation. They reasoned that the time they saved with the new phones could save one of their lives one day. The part that they didn't tell them was that all of the phones were equipped with monitoring devices that allowed them to eavesdrop on their conversations. Since he wasn't above taking a bribe or two himself, he had just made an extra ten thousand dollars by informing Mo of Gaines' sinister plot. He didn't have anything personal against Gaines, but Mo was his brother so he would much rather see Gaines screwed over than Mo.

He buzzed the secretary to bring him some coffee. Leaning back in his chair he reached to loosen his tie, thought for a minute, and then snapped his fingers. He'd forgotten that he was wearing his golfing gear. Then he thought about his wife. He knew that she was mad at him this morning for not wanting to make love to her.

Oh well he thought. He'd just have to make it up to her later on. Taking a stroll down memory lane, he reminisced on when he first met his wife. It was at one of those police functions that they make the department have twice a year.

He was just a sergeant back then. She looked stunning with her long blond hair, shapely figure, and piercing green eyes. he was but a lowly file clerk invited there by her policewoman friend Cassandra. Rumor had it that both of them went both ways but no one could ever prove that. It was also common knowledge that she liked black men. She had, however, had a few kinky episodes with some guys on the force. Brad Murphy was as kinky as they came so it was no coincidence that he pushed up on Audrey the way he did. Within a year the two were married. But for some strange reason the sex was rather ordinary. At least by today's standards. Before long they were getting bored with each other. He'd confided in his brother Mo, who told him that he knew a brother who loved white women. Brad and Audrey had discussed having a threesome a few months back but so far nothing had come of it.

Then one Saturday night, he decided to push the situation along. He'd gotten his wife hot by drinking tequila with her while watching a porno movie. He'd convinced her to pop a couple of ecstasy pills telling her that it would make her even hotter. Then he had his brother make a bogus phone call to him. He pretended that it was a police emergency and that he had to leave. He'd told her not to wait up for him because he would probably be gone at least two hours. Needless to say she was highly pissed off.

She didn't know it but her night was about to get much better. Brad had paid Mo's friend to go to their house and pretend like he was stranded and needed to use the phone. He told him to wear a wife beater to show off his muscles. Brad sat at the corner and waited for him to con his way inside the house. She knew where every gun in the house was so she wasn't afraid. After he got inside the house, Brad went to the nearest bar and had a drink. He figured he'd give him enough time to charm his way into her pants. After leaving the bar, he stopped at Rite Aid and bought a tape for his camcorder which he had already stashed inside of his car.

He wanted to get this on film. When he got back to his

house, he parked on the street so his wife wouldn't hear his car. He eased his way inside the house and tiptoed up the stairs. Hitting the power button on the camcorder, he raised it up with one hand and pushed open the door with his other. When he got it focused just right, he hit the record button. Through the lens he could see his wife's legs resting high on the shoulders of another man. When she saw him, she yelled for the man to stop. "Don't stop baby," he'd told her. "I set this up." She was shocked but still pleasantly surprised. Their sex life hadn't been the same since. A knock at the door brought Chief Murphy back to the present.

"Come in."

Walking in with a pot of coffee in one hand and large coffee mug in the other was an olive skinned Hispanic woman with large hips and long reddish brown hair. She was wearing a sun dress with a flowery design on it and a white blouse that showed off her flat stomach and accentuated her perky breasts. She had a mole on the left side of her face just below her cheekbone.

"You requested coffee senior Murphy?" she asked in her high pitched alto voice.

"Yes. Pour me a cup would you please Angela?"

"Right away sir." She filled the mug three quarters of the way full and sat the pot down on an oversized coaster that sat on Murphy's desk. Then she picked up two packs of non-diary creamer that the chief always kept in his office. Tearing open both packs at the same time, she quickly poured them into the mug. She smiled as she stirred the coffee with the spoon that was already in the cup. Chief Murphy liked Angela. She kept to herself and didn't make trouble. He respected her so much he wouldn't even hit on her.

"Would that be all sir?" she asked.

"Yes that will be all Mrs. Cuevas. Thank you."

She quickly walked back out leaving Chief Murphy to his thoughts.

†††

Audrey walked into her daughter's apartment needing a

stiff drink. She knew it was kind of early to be drinking but she needed one. It would be her luck though that they didn't have any alcohol available. As she started to walk toward the living room, she started to hear oohh's and aahh's. At first she thought that it may have been the television but when she peered into the living room, reality smacked her square in the face. A sense of déjà vu came over her as Audrey had, once again, crept up on her daughter giving a black man a blowjob. But this wasn't just any man. This was Bennie. Her Bennie. The same Bennie that she was screwing regularly. The same Bennie that her husband had set her up with years ago. The same Bennie that she had been calling all damn day. Backing back toward the front door, she got light headed. She didn't know whether to be hurt, angry, or jealous. She tried to reason with herself. She knew there was no reason at all for her to be hurt.

After all, Bennie wasn't her man. He was just a black man with a huge dick who she just happened to screw from time to time. She couldn't get mad at either one of them. The first part of her reasoning justified the second. He wasn't her man and it was highly doubtful that her daughter knew anything about the two of them. She did feel a twinge of jealousy though. It was different when her daughter was sixteen. She was just a child playing grown-up games. She was no threat at all. But now she was a grown woman with a body that put any penthouse pinup to shame.

Wow, she thought. *I can't believe that I'm getting jealous of my daughters sexual prowess.*

"Are you just gonna stand there mom?" Charity asked. "Or are you gonna join us?"

Audrey was so deep in her thoughts that she didn't hear or see them creep up on her. "Oh, my God," she said covering her face. After shaking her head in embarrassment a few times, she removed her hand, opened her eyes, and stared at the two naked bodies.

Charity had her right hand on her hip and her left hand was busy stroking Bennie's manhood. Charity looked down at Bennie's crotch and shook her head. Reaching down with her other hand, charity wrapped both hands around his pole and still had some sticking out.

"Look at this mom," she said lustfully. "There's more than enough for the both of us." Audrey was taken aback by her daughter's nonchalance attitude. "Charity honey, I think there is something I should tell you."

Right in front of her mother Charity bent over and kissed the head of Bennies dick. The lewd act made Bennie's soldier stand at full attention. Trying desperately not to look at it, Audrey tried to close her eyes but couldn't. It was almost as if her eyes had a mind of their own when it came to Bennie's Johnson. Bennie hadn't said a word during this time. In fact he was kinda turned on by the whole thing. Now he knew why Charity's pussy reminded him so much of Audrey's.

"Tell me later mom. I got work to do here," she said as she started pulling Bennie back into the living room. "Oh, and just so you know mom. When I was sixteen, I saw you."

Audrey's mouth fell open. She had no idea that she had been seen. She peeped inside the living room again and saw that Bennie had her daughter bent over touching her toes. "Uuhh!...Uuhh...!" she moaned as Bennie hit it from the back. Lifting her left hand off the floor, she gave her mother the come here signal. Audrey closed her eyes and single tears rolled down each cheek. It was one thing to be turned on while watching her daughter, but to join her in a threesome was something she had never thought about. She realized at that moment that all of this was probably her fault.

In the back of her mind she knew that her and her former husband hadn't tried hard enough to keep their lifestyle away from their two daughters. Now, she wished that she had never came here. She wanted to just turn and walk away but she knew she couldn't. Her sexual addiction was much too strong.

"I've been a terrible mother," she mumbled to herself. As the tears began to flow more frequent, she walked toward her daughter. By the time she reached her, she was completely naked. She sat down on the couch and let Charity spread her legs. She closed her eyes and pretended that it was someone else.

Chapter 18

Ty walked into Jillian's half drunk from all the beer he drank at Wild Wings. Thinking about his boy Bennie, he just shook his head. For the life of him, he couldn't figure out why he wanted to keep screwing around with white girls when there were so many fine sisters in C-Town. One day he was going to have to find out what all the buzz was about. Strolling up to the table he asked for a rack of balls and a pitcher of beer.

A voice from behind him asked him "What's going on my man? Did everything work out all right for you the other night?"

"Hey what's up Mike? Yeah man. Every thing was butter." Mike stood there with a confused look on his face for a minute.

"Butter?" he finally asked.

"Smooth, Mike, Smooth."

"Oh, ok then. If you need anything, just let me know." He gave Ty the thumbs up and walked away.

"Goofy ass white boy," Ty said. He walked down the stairs and went straight to table seven.

"Hey man! I was 'bout to get that table!" a voice said, coming from three feet behind him.

Ty turned around and stared directly into the eyes of a light skinned-brother with a bright shinning cross hanging around his neck. Ty looked down at the empty table and then back up at light-skinned.

"Kick rocks cuz," Ty said. "I was here first."

"Nah nigga I was here first. I just had to go take a leak," light-skinned replied.

"Well leak yo' ass to anotha table 'cause I ain't goin' no muthafuckin' where!"

Mike quickly made his way over to table seven. By then, the few customers nearby were starting to stare. "What's the problem here?" Mike asked trying to deepen his voice.

The two ignored Mike and continued to stare at each other. Light-skinned backed down first. "Ain't no problem," he said smiling. He didn't want Mike to call the police so he played it off. "I was just askin' this gentleman if he wanted to shoot a game of pool with me and my lady friend."

Catching the hint, Ty decided to downplay it as well. He didn't need Mike or anyone else to come to his rescue. He could handle his own. "Yeah Mike, chill out man. We was just talking about pool, that's all. Not today cuz. Maybe next time."

"Yeah," light skinned said in a sinister tone of voice. "Next time."

He turned and walked to the other side of the room, passing Amanda in the process. Amanda hurried into the ladies room to wash her face. After seeing Ty talking to Mike, her stomach dropped. Fat Jack had obviously failed in his attempt to get rid of Ty and Dre. She took a cigarette out of her uniform pocket and lit it. She knew she wasn't supposed to be smoking in the bathroom but she couldn't help it. Her nerves were fried. She had probably gotten a man killed. During everything that had gone on with her catching her sister screwing and all, this was really the first chance she had to think about it.

Ty's presence snapped her back to reality. All of a sudden a thought came to her. All she had to do was remain calm. The only other person that knew what she had done was probably dead and even though she felt bad about that, she'd be a fool to tell anyone of her involvement in it. Her crotch got moist as her mind flashed back to thoughts of Charity getting her boots knocked. She just couldn't seem to get her sister's moans of pleasure out of her mind. She pushed the thought of her sister to the back of her mind and went back to work.

"Bitch ass nigga," Ty mumbled under his breath, still thinking about light-skinned.

"Did you want to order something to eat?" Mike asked.

"Nah dawg, I'm straight on that. Just hurry up with that pitcher though. A brotha thirsty as hell in here."

"Coming right up. And just to let you know sir, I did reprimand that waitress for being rude to you the other night."

"Huh?" Ty questioned. He had almost forgotten about her. "Oh, ok. Thanks cuz."

"No problem," Mike responded.

Mike walked away feeling like he had made a new homie. Ty thought he was just another corny ass white boy. Ty racked the balls and proceeded to get in a few practice shots before his beer arrived. He turned his head just in time to see Amanda sit the ice cold pitcher on the table. The two stared at each other for a few seconds before Ty broke the gaze and started back shooting pool. Before he could attempt another shot, she started to speak. "Excuse me sir." Ty sat his pool stick down and turned his head toward her. "What?" he asked.

"Well," she said as she cleared her throat, "I just wanted to apologize for being so rude to you the other night. I was in a crappy mood about my boyfriend cheating on me and I guess I just took it out on you," she lied.

He continued to stare at her. She braced herself for the cussing out that she knew was coming. Instead, he just turned back around resumed his game. That was twice in the span in the span of a couple of days a black person had surprised her. She started to feel ashamed of herself.

All her life she had hated black people because of some of the horror stories she had heard. Now, she was starting to wonder if those stories were true. She made her mind up right then and there. From now on she was going to treat each individual like a person instead of a color.

"Can I buy you a drink," she asked.

Ty looked both ways before answering her. "You talkin' to me?" he asked.

"Yeah. Let me buy you one to make up for the other day."

Ty thought about it for a minute. Her apology did seem genuine to him and he didn't think she was stupid enough to try and poison him in a sports bar.

"I'm not gonna do anything bad to it. You can come watch me make it if you want."

Smiling at her for the first time, Ty said, "You know what? Go 'head and hook a brotha up girl. I trust you on that."

"What kind of drink do you want?"

"Let me get a double Remy Martin."

Amanda strolled away and for the first time Ty noticed how pretty she was. Most people probably thought she should lose some weight but Ty thought she carried it well. Looking back at him while she was pouring his drink, she all of a sudden started feeling attracted to him. At six foot one, he was a couple of inches taller than her sister's friend Bennie. And his bronze colored skin shinned like new copper.

Ty wore his hair in tightly, freshly done corn-rowed braids. He didn't have an ounce of fat on him and his arms were cut like a bodybuilder's.On his physical, he rocked a Cleveland Cavaliers yellow throwback jersey with red numbers. His Sean John jean shorts hung just above the middle of his ass and his sparkling white Air Force Ones looked like they had just come off the line. He had a tattoo of the zodiac sign Leo stamped on his left shoulder. Amanda walked over carrying a tray of wings in her right hand and Ty's drink in her left.

"I ain't order no wings," he said, looking at the tray.

"I know, but I figured you might get hungry waiting on your shot while I kick your ass in pool."

Ty burst out laughing. He had never heard anything so funny in all his life.

"What's so funny," she asked, acting like she was offended.

"That silly ass comment you just made."

"Silly huh? I'll tell you what," she said. "We'll play the best three out of five. If you win, then the next time you come in here all the wings and drinks you want are on me."

He stared her in disbelief. "Are you serious," he asked.

She nodded her head slowly.

"Wait a minute," he said thinking. "Ain't you still on the clock?"

"Nope. Mike told me that since we're slow, I can take off for the day."

"Ok then. You got a bet."

"Uh...Don't you want to know what I want when, I mean, if I win?"

"Ok little lady. What do you want if I happen to pass out and you win by forfeit?"

She had thought about letting him win a game or two just so he would have to stay longer but because of that crack she decided to just shut him out.

"If I win you have to give me a ride home and treat me to Boston Market."

Just then Mike walked over. "Everything going ok over here sir?"

"Man you gon' have to eighty-six that sir shit," Ty said. "I ain't no old man."

"Everything's alright Mike," Amanda said. "I'm just trying to win a ride home."

Mike looked at the table and then at Ty. "You're playing her?" he asked curiously.

"Yeah, so," Ty added. Mike was silent for a minute.

"What does she get if she wins?" Mike asked.

"I gotta give her a ride home and treat her to Boston Market."

Mike looked at Amanda and twisted up his mouth.

"Hey, he accepted the challenge," she said shrugging her shoulders. Mike just shook his head and walked away. Ty looked at her through curious eyes. She gave him an innocent look.

"Ladies first?" she asked.

"Why not?" he responded.

He thought that it was strange that Mike didn't asked what he would get if he won. He was about to find out why.

Chapter 19

Stacy sat at the Honey Doo bar sipping on a cosmopolitan waiting for CeCe. She got there early because she wanted some time to herself. Big Mo had put it on her so good this morning that she had to get some more sleep. She smiled at the thought of her man. She prayed that they would go to the Bahamas soon. After all, he did promise to take her to the Bahamas. The Bahamas. Just like that her smile faded as she reminisced about the last time that she had ever spoken to her mother. For most women, the promise, of being whisked off to the Bahamas was a dream come true. For Stacy, it was bittersweet. She remembered all too well the final conversation with her mother before her death. Sitting on the couch with her mother, Janice, a young Stacy beamed with joy as her mother told her that one day her, CeCe, her husband Clarence, and her two step sisters, Sugar and Spice who she couldn't stand, would go vacationing there.

She didn't know if her mother was selling her a dream so that her mother and step father could go out. They'd told her to look after her siblings for just a while in exchange for the ultimate vacation. It sounded good so ten minutes after the promise. Janice walked out the door with her husband. Neither one of them were ever seen or heard from again. Absentmindedly, Stacy picked up her glass and discovered that it was empty. She had gotten so engrossed in her thoughts that she had finished her drink without even knowing it.

"Can I get another Cosmopolitan please?" Stacy asked.

The tall Hispanic barmaid rolled her eyes as she hurriedly poured Stacy another drink. After setting the drink down a little too hard on the table, she snatched the money off the counter and ran to the cash register. Stacy looked on with attitude in her face, as she sat Stacy's change down on the counter and went to the other end of the bar where she sat back down and continued watching All My Children.

"The fuck wrong wit this bitch," Stacy mumbled. "She betta loose that attitude before CeCe gets in here because I don't feel like talkin' her out of fuckin' a bitch up."

Apparently the woman heard her because she snorted and rolled her eyes. *This bitch must don't know how the Chedda Boyz roll* Stacy thought. Stacy was relaxed in a pair of True Religion hip hugger jeans, a yellow blouse, and a pair of T- strap sandals. After taking a sip of her drink, she leaned back and rested both arms on the bar stools on each side of her. She purposely stopped in the bar at this time of the day hoping there wouldn't be any one else in here. She was right. It was just her and the barmaid. Usually barmaids welcomed the company when the place was empty. Not this one.

She didn't seem to want to be bothered not even to get up and do her job. The bar's door creaked and in walked CeCe wearing powder blue Capri pants with matching top and white sandals. She carried a small Gucci purse that was slung around her shoulder. She strutted over to where Stacy was seated and sat next to her.

"Wazzup sis?" she asked her older sibling.

"Nothin' too much. I thought you wanted me to go with you to get rid of them thangs?" Stacy asked.

"Yeah, I did but it was early and since I was already up, I called dude and set it up for earlier."

"How much did you get off?"

"Four."

"Shit girl," a surprised Stacy said. "That's four thousand four hundred dollars."

"Nah, it's only four. I had to give dude a deal."

"I guess you did lil sis. Do the damn thang girl."

"Where the barmaid at? I need me a stiff one."

Stacy pointed to the bar maid who was still engrossed in her soap opera.

"Excuse me miss. Can I get a screwdriver please?"

The woman slowly got up and made CeCe's drink. Because she was digging in her purse for money, CeCe didn't see the woman glaring at her. After fixing CeCe's drink, the woman slowly pushed it to her. As she gave CeCe back her change the woman smiled and said "Espero que ahogar ella perra."

CeCe looked at Stacy and then back to the barmaid. "I'm sorry," CeCe said smiling. "I didn't understand you."

"Oh, I'm sorry senorita. I simply said, Bottom's up," she lied.

"Oh, thanks," CeCe said. Turning her attention back to Stacy, she asked, "Where's Mo?"

"He had to get rid of some of them thangs today too."

"Oh, cool." "CeCe can I ask you a question?"

"Sure," CeCe replied.

"Do you ever think about…"

"Stop. I don't feel like talking about the woman that abandoned us."

Holding up her hands, Stacy said, "Fine."

She knew that was a sensitive subject with CeCe. For a long time CeCe blamed herself for her mother leaving. But once she became a full fledged adult, she realized that no matter what your kids do as children, you don't run off and abandon them. She'd called her mother's cell phone number every day for a month after her disappearance. Only when it was disconnected did she stop calling.

"There is something I want to talk about though."

"I'm listening," Stacy said.

"This stays between me and you ok?" Stacy looked at her like she was offended. "I know that." CeCe took a deep breath exhaled.

"I been cheatin' on Dre."

"I kinda of figured that," Stacy responded. "I could tell by the way you had started actin' around him."

"What chu mean by that?" CeCe questioned.

"It didn't take a genius to figure it out. That's your man and you act like you don't even want him to touch you most of the time." An awkward silence fell upon the two sisters. Stacy broke it with a question that CeCe knew was coming. "So, who is this nigga?"

CeCe had prepared herself for this question but now that it was in her face, she wasn't ready to answer it. "I'd rather not discuss it right now."

"Well, whoever it is I hope their life insurance is paid up. You know as well as I do that Ty and Dre will kill him if they found out."

"I seriously doubt that," CeCe said.

Stacy started to get a knot in her stomach. She had a feeling that she knew who CeCe was screwing around with. She prayed to God that she was wrong. "So, tell me sis. What made you start sleepin' around on him?"

"To be honest with you sis, That nigga can't fuck."

"Whaaatt?" Stacy said as her mouth fell to the floor.

"Can I be straight up wit cha sis?"

"Please do." Stacy was all ears now.

CeCe grabbed her drink and downed it in one gulp. She needed some Vodka to help her spit this out, even to her sister.

"The truth of the matter, sis, is that Dre is weak in bed girl. He acts like I'm gon' break if he squeezes me even a little bit. For all that gangsta shit he do in the streets, he ain't nothin' like that in the bedroom girl."

Stacy was stunned.

"Have you talked to him about it sis?"

"Hell no!" she screamed. "Why should I have to tell him how to hit it? He likes to make love, which is ok. But sometimes I just want to get fucked! I want him to pound it!"

"Girl keep yo' damn voice down," Stacy said, looking around like there were a hundred people in the place.

"Oh, my bad sis." "But like I was sayin'. The minute I start moanin' loud, he eases up, like he gon' hurt me or somethin'."

Stacy took a deep breath.

"Let me ask you somethin' Ce. Do you still love Dre?"

CeCe looked her sister straight in the eye.

"Yes, but that doesn't mean I'm happy Stacy."

"Look Ce. Fuck what ya heard. All men are different. Some know what to do and some need to be told what to do. Sometimes you gotta…"

CeCe held up her hand. "Wait," she said. "There's more. He won't go down on me." Stacy's eyes got big and her mouth dropped open.

"You bullshitin'."

"Nope." Stacy was speechless.

"You know what sis?" CeCe said. "I'm gon' go home and tell this nigga exactly what I expect, and either he's gon' get wit the program or get to stepping'."

Both sisters shared a laugh at that one.

"I'm 'bout to jet sis," said Stacy. "I'm getting' tired." She finished the rest of her drink and got up to leave.

"I'm right behind you sis. As soon as I empty the bladder."

"Ahight then," Stacy said. "Peace out." She walked out the creaking door and dissed it on the way out. "Raggedy ass door," she mumbled. The barmaid heard that too as she flipped her the bird. Once again CeCe didn't see her. Walking into the bathroom a little tipsy, CeCe almost walked into the wall. After a few minutes, CeCe stuck her head out of the bathroom door and yelled for the barmaid.

"Excuse me miss. I can't get the water to stop runnin' in here."

The barmaid, looking as annoyed as ever, got up from doing a lot of nothing and walked into the bathroom. Walking over to the sink with a frown on her face, she turned the knob. After seeing the water pressure decrease, she rolled her eyes and shook her head. She looked in the mirror and saw CeCe lurking behind her, glaring at her. She turned around about to make a smart remark but never got the chance as CeCe punched her in the stomach.

"Ummph," she cried out as the gut shot caused her to double over in pain. A right uppercut bloodied her nose and straightened her back up. Dazed and disoriented, she began to stumble. CeCe reached inside her purse and took out her pistol. Then she grabbed the barmaid by her red and blond weave and forced her to look in the mirror.

"Aaarrgg!" the barmaid screamed as CeCe smashed her forehead into the mirror.

After spitting in her face, CeCe hit her upside her head with the butt of her pistol and let her drop her to the floor. "Choke on that bitch!" she said while walking to the door. After reaching the doorway, she turned and looked down on her fallen prey.

"The next time you cuss somebody out in Spanish, make sure they don't speak the language bitch."

CeCe, who wasn't quite tipsy as she pretended to be, walked out the bar, hopped in her ride, and drove home.

Chapter 20

After calling his brother and telling him he was on his way to see him, Big Mo had to light himself another blunt. He still couldn't believe this crooked ass cop tried to play him like that. When his brother informed him that Gaines was playing him, he probably didn't mean for him to kill the detective. *Fuck that shit,* Mo thought. Ain't no crooked ass cop gon' extort me. Pulling into the sixth district police department, Mo turned down his music. He reached into the glove compartment and pulled out a stack of cash. He had to laugh a little.

If Stacy knew that he kept this much cash in an unlocked glove compartment, she would loose it. *Oh, well,* he thought. *What she don't know won't hurt her.* He got out of his truck and walked through the twin set of double doors. Nodding and waving at the various officers in the department, he made his way to the elevator. Big Mo smiled. *These dumb asses don't suspect a thing.* All they knew was that ninety percent of the time that Big Mo came to see Chief Murphy; a drug bust came soon after that. The flat foots never knew that they were being played. Brad and Mo had set it up like that to make it look like Big Mo was a snitch.

That couldn't be further from the truth. In fact Big Mo was a more honorable man than his brother was. Big Mo knew that his brother had probably seriously thought about selling him out on a couple of occasions; especially for the murders of Clarence and Janice Johnson.

As Mo walked he thought back to that unthinkable night on July 17th 1999 that now tainted his soul. Although he had millions socked away and his future seemed as shiny as the twenty thousand dollar a pop Giovanni rims on his truck, the Chedda Boyz general had one issue that wore on his spirit. Every time he looked at Stacy, guilt washed over him like Niagara Falls. Big Mo remembered all too well that fateful night some ten years ago when he and Bennie were carving their niche in the dope game.

"Stupid muthafucka," Mo mumbled to himself recalling how Clarence, Stacy's step-father had tried to steal from him.

He could still hear Clarence's skull crack from the impact of the Louisville slugger baseball bat that Mo used to bash his head in. A Mo continued to walk it was almost as if he could still vividly see the look of horror that was still on Janice's face when Bennie dragged her inside the house and slit her throat from ear to ear. It actually hurt him to know that he had personally disposed of the two bodies by dumping them in the lake, and now has to face the women he loves. Sadly, Mo didn't find out that the couple he and Bennie had killed were Stacy's and CeCe's mother and Step father until he and Stacy had been dating for almost three months. Coming back to the present, Mo shook his head as if that would shake away the guilt.

He tried to shake the thoughts from his head still knowing that his brother was an extremely greedy man. The only thing that stopped him from turning on Mo was that he knew if he took any kind of payoff to screw Big Mo, it could end up costing him his life. If he ever decided to take a payoff in exchange for his brother's freedom, it would have to be enough that he'd be able to get away and stay hid.

Big Mo strolled into Chief Murphy's office and plopped down in the leather chair in front of the desk.

"So," Chief Murphy started. "How'd he take it when you told him that you were on to him and that you wasn't gon' deal wit him no more?"

"I didn't get a chance to ask him," Mo responded.

"What's that supposed to mean?" a suspicious Chief Murphy asked.

After a brief silence, Big Mo asked, "What does the life insurance policy pay around here?"

Chief Murphy placed his head in his hands and leaned down on his desk with both elbows.

"Jesus Mo I didn't mean for you to kill a fuckin' cop. When you said you were gonna take care of it, I thought you were gonna just stop doing business with him." Big Mo leaned over the desk and looked directly into his brother's eyes.

"Look man. I don't know who this Spice bitch is but I done heard a lotta shit about her. Now, normally I wouldn't give a fuck about her knowing that I was the one that iced her old man, but this is a problem, I don't need right now. I hear the bitch is heavy into dealing cocaine and the mere fact that not even you knows what she looks like tells me that she ain't nothin' to be fucked with. Very few people have ever seen her and I hear that she got a sister that no one has ever seen. Apparently she's handlin' some major paper 'cause I offered that asshole Gaines a hundred G's and it wasn't enough and I damn sure wasn't gon' let a crooked ass cop blow my cover. Hell, I knew the bitch probably had a few dollars but I didn't know she had paper like that. Now, after I get back from my vacation, then I'm just gon' have to dispose of this bitch, but for right now, I got other shit on my mind."

Chief Murphy stared at him through empty eyes. He still couldn't believe Mo had just killed a cop and walked into the precinct like he hadn't done a thing. He quickly shook it off. He didn't know why he was so surprised. Big Mo and his crew were capable of almost anything.

"You didn't leave fingerprints did you?" he questioned.

"The fuck I look like to you, a fuckin' amateur? Hell naw I didn't leave no prints." Just then a pencil thin woman with graying hair and a pointed nose walked through the door.

"Alice what the hell is wrong with you?" Murphy barked. "Don't you know how to knock?"

"I'm sorry sir, but Officers Rose and Peterson just called in. They say they found Inspector Gaines dead in the parking lot of John W Raper elementary school."

"What?" Murphy screamed feigning surprise. "What the

hell happened to him?"

"No one knows sir. Whoever did this to him didn't leave any clues to speak of."

Looking at Mo, Chief Murphy said "I think you'd better leave. I'm going to have my hands full on this one." Staring at Mo for a few seconds he asked "Are you sure no one's gonna find out about the surprise party?"

Big Mo caught the coded question immediately. "I'm positive. No one has a clue."

Walking through the precinct, Big Mo smiled as there was utter chaos among the department. Police officers were scrambling around like chickens with their heads cut off. They couldn't believe that one of their own had been brutally murdered and no one knew anything. One officer sat at her desk crying hysterically wondering aloud how someone was going to break the news to his wife. Calmly walking past the grieving cops at a snails pace, Big Mo, hopped into his vehicle, lit another blunt, and quickly drove off.

Chapter 21

Audrey Murphy parked her car, jumped out, and ran into her house. Once inside she went to her bedroom and fell face down on the bed where she burst into tears. She couldn't believe what had just happened. Of all the perverted and sexually deviated things she had done, this one beat them all. The worst part of it all was that her daughter actually enjoyed it. Five seconds after she creamed in Charity's mouth, Charity came all over Bennie's dick.

It's my fault that Charity is the way she is, she thought. If I had been a better mother to her, this never would have happened. Charity told her mother not to worry about it and made Bennie promise not to tell anyone. All she needed was for Amanda to find out about it. She hadn't been on good terms with her youngest daughter since she decided to marry a black man and this would just push her daughter farther away from her.

She replayed over and over in her head how her oldest daughter spread her legs apart and started to lick her inner thighs. Having a change of heart at the last minute, Audrey tried to push herself up and pull away from Charity but Charity clamped down on her thighs and wouldn't allow her to move. Sensing that her mother was about to abandon ship, Charity quickly stuck her tongue inside Audrey's vagina. Unable to break her daughter's grip on her thighs, Audrey had no choice but to stop struggling.

Once it was over, Audrey left without saying a word. From the moment she'd gotten to her car, she started crying and hadn't stopped since. After balling her eyes out in her pillow for ten continuous minutes, Audrey got down on her knees and asked God to forgive her. She prayed that he would. There was no way that she would ever be able to forgive herself.

₮₮₮

Ty sat back holding his pool stick in his hands in utter shock. Not only was he losing but he was losing badly. He was down two games to none and it wasn't even close. To make matters worse, she was constantly taunting him. Every time she made a shot she would blow him a kiss. Where in the fuck did she learn to shoot like this he wondered? Although it took him a while to realize it, it finally dawned on him that he was being hustled.

"Eight ball in the corner pocket baby boy," she said preparing to send him to defeat. Suddenly he had an idea. Just as she pulled the stick back and flung it forward to complete her shot, Ty slapped her on the ass completely throwing her shot off. "Hey!" she yelled. "What the fuck was that about?"

"All's fair in love and war baby girl. This is war."

"Oh, ok," she said. "So, that's the way you want to play it."

Ty laughed as he stood up to take his shot. His face quickly dissipated into the form of a frown when he saw how many balls he had on the table.

"Looks like you got skittles on the table baby boy," she said.

Waving his hand at the table he said, "That ain't shit. The way I'm set up, it's gon' be two to one in no time. And by the way, I don't appreciate the way you hustled my ass either."

"What?" she asked giving him her best innocent look.

"Don't play that innocent ass role wit me. You know exactly what the fuck I'm talkin' 'bout."

"Whatever man," she replied. "Are you gonna shoot or cry a damn river?"

With his competitive drive kicking in, Ty sank the next four balls and was lined up for the eight. "Like I said. It's 'bout to be two to one."

Little did he know she had a surprise for him. Now, it was his turn to be distracted. As soon as she started his forward motion with his pool stick, she reached around his waist and grabbed his dick.

"Hey, what the fuck?" he screamed.

"Oops, my bad," she said. "I guess it's my shot."

Before he could plan a revenge, she quickly ran around the table and shot the eight ball in for a clean sweep. All Ty could do was shake his head.

"Ain't that a bitch?" he said. "I need a drink. Hook me up with a double shot of Hennessey. And get that punk ass smile off yo' face." Sensing her concern that he may have gotten angry, he smiled at her to let her know that that wasn't the case.

As she went to get his drink, Ty noticed that the light-skinned dude with the cross and the broad that was with him were leaving. He did a double take as he noticed that the woman looked very familiar to him. Stepping around the table to take a closer look, he shook his head. "Naw, that couldn't be her," he said. "She ain't that damn bold." When Amanda returned with his drink, he was surprised to see that she had gotten her self one too.

"What you drinkin' on slim?"

"A cosmopolitan," she said beaming. The slim comment made her feel extremely good about her self. She always thought that she looked like a tall version of porky pig. "You know what…I'm not hungry. After we finish with these drinks, you can just take me home."

"You sure?" he asked. "I'm not one to welch on a bet."

"Yeah I'm sure. I could probably stand to skip a few meals anyway."

"Who the fuck told you that?"

"Well, I'm not slim and trim like my sister."

This was just the break Ty was looking for. Now was the time for him to pour it on thick. He figured now was as good a time as any to get his first piece of white girl pussy. "Girl you fine as hell," Ty said. "Stop payin' attention to what the fuck them bustas be talkin' 'bout." Thinking if he played his cards right, he'd be up in her in about an hour Ty kept the compliments coming. After downing the last of her liquor, Amanda was extremely buzzed.

Staring down at his crotch for about twenty seconds, she announced that she was ready to go. When they got inside Ty's truck, she decided to up the ante. Before strapping on her seat belt, she leaned over and whispered in his ear.

"When you get me home, I want you to stick every inch of that big black dick inside me and fuck the shit out of me."

Upon hearing this Ty's dick got so hard it almost ripped through his shorts. Before he knew what was going on, Amanda had unzipped his shorts and pulled his dick out.

"Damn!" she said as she finally got a real look at the size. *His is bigger than Bennie's* she thought to her self.

Being that she hadn't been screwed in a while, Amanda couldn't wait to get home. After wrapping both of her hands around it, she started to lick the head. Then she put as much of it as she could get in her mouth before she started gagging.

"Shit baby I can't wait to get home to feel this thing up in me," she said. Not wanting to waste any more time, Ty pulled off. He didn't even bother to put his penis back into his shorts.

₵₵₵

Dre sat on the couch with a bottle of Absolute in his hand. He was watching a movie about a woman cheating on her husband with her thuggish ex-boyfriend. As if he really wanted to see this shit. He didn't have any concrete proof that CeCe was cheating on him but she sure as hell wasn't giving it to him. The more he watched the movie the more he questioned his gentle manor with her. For some odd reason that he still didn't understand, women seemed to like it when a man screwed their brains out. Then one of the characters said something that stuck in his mind. Trying to school his younger brother, who wondered why his ex was still fooling around with his no good ass brother, the main character told him.

"You can't make love to your woman all the damn time. You do that bullshit every now and then. Most of the time you fuck

the shit outta her ass. And don't think that you gon' hurt her pussy. Women have fuckin' babies. You think that little bit of pounding that we put on them be hurtin' them? Nigga please. You betta drill that pussy every chance you get."

Dre sat back and thought about this. Is this the reason CeCe won't give me any? Is that the way she wants me to give it to her? He was also having second thoughts about not going down on CeCe. When he was younger, his so called girlfriend pissed in his mouth while he was going down on her. Ever since that day, he swore that he would never go down on another woman again. But now that he was a grown man, he started figuring that maybe it was time to rethink that. He had been with her for a couple of years now so maybe it was time to pleasure her that way. He was having major problems with his girlfriend and was desperate to fix them.

After all he did love CeCe. She could be a little hot tempered at times and she was dangerous as hell but that didn't change the way he felt about her.

"Fuck it," he said to himself. "Life is too short fo' a nigga not to be happy. Besides, I was only seventeen then."

He reached down and grabbed the 40oz bottle of Miller Genuine Draft beer he had sitting on the coffee table and took a long swig. Then he reached into his pocket and took out one of the e-pills that he'd copped from one of the local e dealers. Talking to no one in particular he said, "When she get's home tonight, I'm gon' fuck the shit outta her." Just then he heard her pull in the driveway. "Yeah come on in here bitch. You want it rough huh? Well I got somethin' fo' that ass today," he said rubbing his increasingly hardening dick.

He had already taken one e-pill and it was starting to take effect. He'd made his mind up. He was going to wear her ass out this time. Little did he know, that's just what she wanted.

Chapter 22

Charity looked over at Bennie who was trying to suppress a smile. They were on their way back to Wild Wings to get Charity's pay check. In her rush to get out of there and go screw Bennie, she'd forgotten it. Now she had to play the sick roll again. There's no way her boss would've believed that she had gotten better that fast.

"What are you smiling about," Charity asked.

"Nothin," he lied.

Bennie was still tripping off the fact that he had just had a threesome with Charity and her mother. During the whole time, he could tell that it was bothering Audrey but he figured that was her problem. If she didn't want to be down with it, then she should have walked out the damn door. He still couldn't believe how kinky Charity was turning out to be. She went down on Audrey like she was a full fledged dyke. He decided that it was probably better that Charity not know that he'd already been screwing her mother. He didn't think that she would give a fuck but you never know about women. Just thinking about that shit got his dick hard all over again.

"Stop lyin", she said, playfully punching him in the arm.

"Girl you wild as fuck. I can't believe you ate yo' mama's pussy like that. That was some tripped out shit to see."

"What can I say?" she asked. "I was hungry."

"Ah hell nawl!" Bennie replied letting out a loud laugh.

"Ok, time for me to get my sick face on," she said as they pulled into Wild Wings.

Getting out of the car, Charity grabbed her stomach like it was killing her. She slowly walked over to the door and pretended that she had to struggle to pull the door open. She walked to the break room in the back and noticed that all of her co-workers were sitting with their heads down. A few of the women were wiping their eyes like they had been crying. Her boss walked up to her and handed her an envelope with her pay check enclosed in it. She grabbed his arm as he turned to walk away.

"Hey, what's goin' on around here? Why is everyone looking so down?"

"Peaches is dead," he told her.

"What? Dead? What happened?"

"Her mother went to her house to visit her and found her lying in a puddle of blood. The police are still investigating but her mother thinks that the guy upstairs may have something to do with it."

Charity was shocked. There was no love lost between her and Peaches but she didn't wish anyone dead. "Oh, my God," she said as she sat down. She couldn't believe this. She had just argued with her hours earlier. When she was able to speak again, she asked, "Why does her mother think that the guy upstairs had something to do with it? Was he stalking her or something?"

"She doesn't know," Mike said.

"According to her, she'd only met him twice but he acted real strange both times. She said that she just got a bad vibe from him."

Hearing a car horn blowing reminded her that Bennie was waiting on her. "I gotta go guys. My ride is waiting on me. But keep me posted about what's going on with the investigation." They agreed and she walked out of the sports bar. Surprisingly, she was almost in tears.

As soon as she hopped in the car, her emotions flowed. "Oh, my God Bennie, one of my co-workers, Peaches is dead."

"Word."

"Yes, the shit is so weird. It's like I just saw her."

Bennie pulled away from the curb, thinking at least he'd gotten some ass.

Charity continued to ramble, "I mean the fact that she had full blown AIDS is crazy!"

Instantly, a lump formed in Bennie's throat, and a petrified feeling filled his gut. "AIDS?" he asked with fear.

"Yep. AIDS," she responded shaking her head.

$$\text{↯↯↯}$$

Ty and Amanda stumbled into the elevator. They were both tipsy from the drinks they'd had at Jillian's. Since he had been drinking before he'd even went to Jillian's, Ty was three quarters of the way to being drunk. Amanda was horny as hell. She'd had her eyes on Ty's crotch ever since they'd left the sports bar. As soon as the doors closed, she reached down and grabbed it.

"Damn girl," Ty said. "You don't waste no time do you?"

Shaking her head, Amanda palmed his ass and grabbed the back of his head. Before he could say a word, she pulled his head down and jammed her tongue in his mouth. She was beginning to see why her sister and mother liked black men.

When the elevator stopped, she snatched him out of it so fast he almost caught whiplash. *Shit*, Ty thought. *This bitch must ain't had no dick in a long ass time.*

Once they got inside the apartment, Amanda couldn't get out of her clothes fast enough. By the time they got to the bedroom, she was already down to her bra and panties. She was tired of hearing about how big black men's dick's were and how good they fucked. She wanted to find out for her self. After unbuckling Ty's jean shorts and letting them fall to the floor, she pulled down his boxers.

"Damn!" she said once again marveling at his size.

After licking her lips, she wasted no time putting it into her wetness. She didn't know if she could get all of it inside her mouth but she was sure willing to try. This was the first time she'd ever had something this big in her mouth. She wondered why it took her so long.

"Oh, shit!" Ty moaned. She cupped his nuts with her right hand and grabbed the back of his ass with her left. She relaxed her throat muscles and controlled her gag reflex just enough to get all ten inches down her throat.

"Fuck!" Ty screamed.

He'd never had a woman take all ten inches before. Not wanting him to cum yet, she took it out of her mouth and started licking his balls. She reached behind her back and unclasped the hooks on her bra. Her titties were huge. They looked like two giant casaba melons. Ty crawled back on the bed with Amanda climbing on top of him. Ty was a titty man. He loved a woman with big breasts. That was good because Amanda was well blessed in that area. He grabbed one and started licking on Amanda's silver dollar sized nipple.

"Ooohh baby, that feels so good."

After sucking on both titties for a while, Ty flipped her over. Then he leaned over the side of the bed and reached in his pocket and pulled out a condom. After tearing it open, he pulled out the extra large magnum and slid it over his throbbing love pole. He was just getting ready to enter her when she stopped him.

"Wait...hold up a second," she told him. Reaching into her nightstand, she took out a tube of K-Y Jelly. "Ain't nobody been up in here in a while baby." She squeezed some in her hand and rubbed it all over his condom enclosed dick. After placing it back in her drawer she growled, "ok...I'm ready."

Ty eased the head in and she gasped. He went in further and she gasped a little louder.

"Uuhhh!!... Oooo Shit!!" she moaned loudly as he shoved it all the way in. When he thought she was loosened up enough, he started going at a faster pace. Then when he was sure of it, he started slamming it into her.

"Damn baby this pussy good as fuck!" he yelled. He was hitting it so hard, all she could do was moan louder.

"Aahh!...Aahhh!!...Aahhh shit!!! Baby please don't stop!! Fuck the shit outta me baby!!" She clawed the back of both of his shoulders, drawing blood as he pounded her relentlessly.

She'd never had a man go this deep up in her before. It

felt like his dick was touching her sternum. Not able to withstand her back scratching any longer, he leaned back, lifted both her legs up, and put them on his shoulders. He was going to make her pay for scratching up his back. With all the force he could muster up, he repeatedly drove into her as deep as he could.

"AAAHHH!!!...AAAHHH!!!...OOOHH MY GOD!!!," she screamed. "Shit!" he yelled as he felt the condom burst. He pulled out just in time to splash cum all over her stomach and titties. She threw her arms around him as he collapsed on top of her.

"Oooh shit baby that felt sooo good," she cooed. He had to agree. For this being his first time with a white woman, he was extremely satisfied. "Oohh hell yeah!" she said still breathing heavily.

This made it official for her. Now she knew what the saying 'once you go black you never go back' meant. After this experience, she had no intentions of ever sleeping with any other man except a black man. She turned her head to the right and her eyes got as big as the moon. Her mouth dropped open. Standing there in the doorway with her camcorder was Charity. She had filmed it all.

"Congrats, sis. You're now a porn star."

₣₣₣

Big Mo figured he needed a break. After being forced to blow Gaines' brains out, now would be the perfect time to take a vacation. He hadn't planned on leaving so soon, but after what had just happened he wanted to get out of town quickly. Unlocking his console, he reached into a black IMG Jewelers bag, took out a blue box and opened it up. In it was a seven thousand dollar three and a half carrot white gold diamond engagement ring that he planned to give to Stacy when they got to the Bahamas.

It took him three months to find what he considered the perfect ring and he couldn't wait to give it to her. He had grown to love her just that much. Ever since she'd met him at the Odyssey bar on St. Clair and cried on his shoulder about her mother walking out on her and CeCe, he knew she was the one for him. Not realizing until six months after they had become a couple that it was his fault that her mother had left her and CeCe, he decided that it would be more beneficial to keep that to himself. He put the bag back into his console, locked it, hopped out of his truck and went into the house. He wasn't worried about anyone breaking into his truck. Shit, he was big Mo. After pulling out his bank card, Mo flipped open his cell phone and dialed his travel agent to arrange the trip. He couldn't wait to tell Stacy the news.

His face grew angry as he thought back to his meeting with his brother. This Spice bitch had to go. He wasn't going to spend the rest of his life looking over his shoulder and wondering if this hoe was going to come after him for killing her old man. The only reason he hadn't disposed of her ass yet was because he felt it was more beneficial to pay off a crooked cop than to take a chance on getting knocked on a murder charge. But when Gaines started getting greedy, he had no choice but to kill him. He was crooked plus he knew too much. He always knew in the back of his mind he might have to kill Spice sooner or later but what he was really hoping was that she would give up the search. Having Gaines in his back pocket and paying him to give Spice the run around made more sense to him.

Chapter 23

Amidst all of the confusion and chaos going on at the police station, no one paid attention to one Miss Angela Cuevas as she calmly walked into Chief Murphy's office and removed the voice recorder she had taped underneath his desk. She smoothly placed it in her pocket and walked out the door.

$$\notin\notin\notin$$

Upon hearing of Inspector Gaines' demise, Julio Cuevas was greatly disturbed. He was sure that offering the Inspector a large sum of money would do the trick. And it probably would have if he hadn't gone and gotten himself killed. Someone was going through a lot of trouble to make sure that Sugar and Spice didn't find out who killed their father. Julio had a strong suspicion that he knew who it was but so far he had been unable to attain any proof.

Sitting back with a glass of cognac in his hand, he pondered his next move. Someone knew something but for some reason they weren't talking. In his experience, he had learned that there were only three things that kept people quiet when money was involved. More money, family, and fear. He just had to figure out which one he was dealing with. He took a sip of his drink and stroked his chin. His vibrating cell phone broke him out of the deep thought he was in. A broad smile broke out across his face when he saw who was on the other end of the phone.

"Hola papi," a light voice resonated from the other end.

"Hola mi querida hija. ¿Cómo están ustedes hoy?" Julio asked.

"Muy bien," she answered. "Listen papi," she said, switching back and forth between Spanish and English. "I have something in my possession that I am certain you would like to hear. I did as you asked I think your suspicions may have been warranted."

"Bien, bien," he said. "Bring it to me once you leave there."

"I'll be there in thirty-five minutes."

After hanging up from Angela, Julio nodded his head and smiled. About a month ago, he had his daughter, who coincidentally works for the police department as a secretary, tape a small voice recorder under Chief Murphy's desk. Julio had a gut feeling all along that he knew something about Sugar and Spices father's murder. His next step was to bribe him but was hoping that he would be stupid enough to talk about it to someone in his office. That way he would have no reason to bribe him.

To his delight, the Chief did prove to be just that stupid. Not knowing if that what was on the recorder, he tried to temper his enthusiasm. For all he knew it could be anything from a big drug bust on the way to someone he knew getting killed. Angela had no idea what he was looking for when he'd asked her to plant the device nor did she ask any questions. She simply did as she was told. Taking another sip of his drink, he leaned back and wondered if this was the break he was waiting for. One things for sure. He hoped Chief Murphy wasn't involved.

ϟϟϟ

Chief Murphy felt like he needed a drink. After seeing Inspector Gaines' brains scattered all over the playground and listening to the Mayor chewing him a new asshole for fifteen minutes, he definitely felt he deserved one. Straight, fuck a chaser. He pulled up in the driveway and noticed that his wife's car wasn't there. Actually, he was glad. He was in no mood to hear her mouth plus he wanted to talk to his other white bitch. Even though he knew what had happened to Gaines before anyone else in the department knew, it still sickened him to see the fist sized hole in the back of his head. He walked up the cement steps of his brick layered ranch-style home and took out his keys. With his hands shaking, he unlocked the door, walked in, closed it, and slid the deadbolt across the door. That way if Audrey came back sooner than he expected she'd have to knock on the door. He walked over to a brown chestnut table with a locked drawer. It was always locked and he had the only key. To keep Audrey from bitching about it, he'd told her that the drawer contained confidential police papers and that he kept them at home so that he didn't have to keep an eye on them at work.

After unlocking the drawer, he reached into it and took out a small saucer laced with five lines of cocaine and a razor blade. A straw was lying next to the saucer. He walked over to his couch and dropped his overweight two-hundred eighty-five pound frame down on the overworked cushion.

"Damn!" he yelled forgetting his drink.

He got back up and walked over to his bar cabinet and took out a bottle of Crown Royal. Disregarding a glass, he took the cap off and took it straight took the head. "Arrghh!" he cried out as the burning alcohol flowed down his throat burning his chest. Then he went and sat back down on the couch. Calmly lifting up the saucer with one hand and the straw with the other, he joined them together in marriage. A large vein appeared in his forehead as the cocaine traveled up through the straw rushing through his nostrils and into his bloodstream. It only took a few seconds for the white ghost to take effect on his system and for the moment he transcended to his own world.

$$\text{\textit{\$\$\$}}$$

Charity had just gotten back home when she'd heard the pleasurable screams of her sister getting her back blown out. She just couldn't resist grabbing her camcorder and recording her uptight sister getting her pussy popped by a black man.

"You sneaky little bitch. How long have you been record-ing this shit?" Amanda screamed as she tried to cover her self up.

Damn Ty thought. *Her sister finna than a muthafucka.*

"Don't get your panties in a fuckin' bunch," Charity shot back. "You act like you ain't ever done that shit before."

Ty looked at her with raised eyebrows, although he was not that surprised. He could tell she had a little freak in her by the way she attacked him on the elevator. Looking at her sister, he could tell why she would be insecure about her appearance. He still didn't think she had any reason to have low self esteem. But her sister's body was banging. She looked like a swimsuit model. Amanda shot daggers through her sister.

"You just gonna put my business out there like that huh bitch?"

"Oh, my bad," she said nonchalantly. "My man had just dropped me off when I heard you in the back with your little friend here So… how did you like your first piece of black meat?" Char-ity asked.

"Fine Charity. The shit was the fuckin' bomb all right? Is that what your 'wanna be right all the time ass' wanna hear?"

"Hey," Charity said. "Don't get mad at me because you liked it."

"Whatever," Amanda replied. "Close the door on your way out."

Amanda turned around to face Ty with a gleam in her eye. She walked over to him and threw her arms around his neck. "Damn baby," she said. "You fucked the shit out of me and I en-joyed every minute of it."

So, did Ty but he had to maintain his cool posture. "Is that right?"

"Hey," she responded. "I gotta go to the bathroom but when I come back, I want you to put it back in my mouth. I wanna taste your cum."

"Shiieet girl you ain't got to tell me twice!" a now excited Ty replied.

Bennie had told him before that white girls loved to do

nasty shit. When Amanda was far enough down the hall, Ty took out his cell phone and texted Bennie, Mo, and Dre. *Yo' man we gotta hook up later. Y'all ain't gon' believe the shit that just happened to me.* Bennie texted him back. *Nigga please. Wait to you hear the shit that happened to me today.* Then Bennie sent Ty a picture text showing Audrey Murphy being ate out by a younger woman. He didn't know who the younger woman was because all he could see was the back of her head.

"So," Ty whispered to himself. "A bitch eatin' anotha bitch. It ain't like I ain't seen that shit before." *Maybe it's more to it*, he thought. *I guess that nigga will give me the scoop later.*

Thinking about Dre caused guilty feelings to kick in. He had to stop fuckin' wit CeCe. He picked up his cell phone and dialed her number. She didn't pick up so he left a message. It proved to be a lethal mistake.

ϟϟϟ

"Damn…nigga… what the fuck got into you?" CeCe asked. She was breathing heavily and after three orgasms, was almost completely out of breath. "Whew!" she said, kissing him on the neck. "Now, that's how you fuck a bitch!"

That comment surprised Dre. He had no idea that's how she felt about sex. *Damn* he thought. *All this time I been tryin' to be gentle wit her ass when I shoulda been tearin' this pussy to pieces.* "You liked that shit baby?" he asked.

"Hell yeah baby I loved that shit. Especially wit you finally goin' down a on a sista."

She couldn't believe that was the first time Dre had ever eaten pussy before. He was just too good at it. His tongue game alone caused her to have two orgasms. Just then their house phone rang. "Answer that baby," CeCe said. "I gotta go take a shower."

"Tell it," Dre replied answering the phone.

"Yo man this Mo. Is CeCe there with you?" he asked.

"Yeah, she in the shower. Wassup?"

"I'm callin' an emergency meeting. Get here soon as you can."

"Ahight, bet." Dre hung up and went into the bathroom with CeCe. "Yo' we gotta hurry up CeCe. Mo just called an emergency meeting at his house. Scoot over."

Moving over so Dre could take a shower with her CeCe asked Dre if he knew what the meeting was about. "Nah, he didn't say."

While they were getting showered, Dre's cell phone was in his pocket vibrating. CeCe's had fell under the bed after Dre had ripped her panties off. She was so pleasantly surprised by his rough sex tactics that she didn't even notice.

Chapter 24

Ty left Amanda's apartment feeling weak in the knees. She had sucked him dry and drained almost every drop of energy he had. After receiving the call from Mo about the emergency meeting, he reached down into his ashtray and picked up a half smoked blunt.

"Oh, shit!" he said. Messing around with Amanda almost made him forget he had to meet Hector in E-Z's parking lot on 80th and superior. Making a u-turn in broad daylight on Euclid Avenue was not a smart thing to do. But he had to get to E-Z's.

Adding on what Hector already owed Ty, this was a six-thousand dollar trip. After getting caught by a red light, he reached up under the driver's seat and pulled out four-one pound bags of weed. "Hector betta have my muthafuckin' money this week," he thought out loud. "I'on wanna hear no bullshit."

Hector was a small time marijuana dealer in the Superior area. He copped from Ty and sometimes Dre. Because he had bought so much shit from him in the past, Ty fronted him an extra bag the last time he did business with him. So, with his mind on his money and his money on his mind, Ty mashed the gas.

$$
\maltese\maltese\maltese
$$

Still in shock from what had transpired earlier, Audrey Murphy drove her white Toyota Celica convertible on the I 90

Highway going west. When she reached the 72nd Street exit, she made a right and pulled in to where most people do their fishing at in Cleveland, Ohio. Trout and Bass were the last thing on her mind at the moment. Feeling like shit anyway, she reached down and grabbed the bottle of Smirnoff Vodka she'd brought with her. After opening it, she took a quick swig. What kind of mother has a threesome involving her own daughter? She'd asked herself that question a thousand times. She took another swig of Vodka and felt the vibration of her cell phone on her hip.

After unclipping it from her belt buckle Audrey looked at the picture and almost threw up. She couldn't believe that slimy bastard Bennie took a picture of that shit. There was no telling how many other people he had sent that picture to. If she wasn't so ashamed of what she had done, she would tell her husband what was going on and ask him to take care of Bennie. But that would mean that she would have to tell him what happened and she didn't want to do that. She couldn't live like this. It was eating her up inside. She knew she had to come up with a solution. She had to do something. But what?

$$$

Julio Cuevas couldn't believe what he'd just heard on the voice recorder. This was so much more damaging than even he could ever imagine. Big Mo had quiet a few skeletons in his closet. Not only had he murdered Sugar and Spice's father but their stepmother as well. Angela hadn't listened to the voice recorder since she started recording Chief Murphy's conversations a month ago so there were quite a few on there that she hadn't heard. When she called her father and told him that there was something he needed to listen to, she had only listened to the one conversation that she was referring to.

She had no idea that the dialog on this little piece of machinery was about to wreck havoc on the Chedda Boyz Crew. Julio just shook his head.

"This poor girl is going to be extremely upset," he said to himself.

Still shaking his head, he flipped open his cell phone and dialed Spice's cell number. No answer. He hung up and called a different number that only a select few had. He wondered why she didn't answer her primary cell phone but didn't harp on it. Maybe she lost it or left it somewhere. *No matter*, he thought. *As long as I can get in touch with her.* She answered on the first ring.

"Hello?"

"Hola Sra. Spice. ¿Cómo están ustedes hoy?"

"Muy bien senior," she answered. "What can I do for you today?"

"Well," he started out. "There's something that I need to discuss with you that is muy importante."

Spice wondered what could be so important. The product that she gave him was of grade A quality. "How important is it?"

"Muy, senorita, muy."

"Ok, I'm listening."

He took a deep breath. "I took the liberty doing some investigative work on your behalf my friend. By doing so I think I have found what you have been searching for."

Spice didn't have a clue as to what he was talking about. "Forgive me senior but exactly what are you talking about?" Not wanting to waste words with her, he dropped the bomb on her.

"Spice, I've found out who killed your father."

Silence.

"Hello? Hello?"

On the other end Spice was saying the same thing. "Damn," she uttered as she looked at her cell phone. "I didn't hear you," she said, not realizing at first that the call had been disconnected. "I'll just call him back later," Spice stated, once she read the dropped call message on the screen. She still didn't a have clue as to what he was talking about.

Julio tried to call her back, but it went straight to her voice mail. He decided to leave a message. "Senorita Spice. I don't know what happened with the call, but I have some important information for you. Call me back at your earliest convenience. I know who killed your father."

Spice's phone beeped once letting her know that she had a

voice mail message. Already in a hurry, she waved it off.

₵₵₵

When every member of the Chedda Boyz crew had arrived, Big Mo walked to the bar and pulled out a bottle of Don Perrion.

"Yo', what's the occasion Mo?" Ty asked. He was still buzzing from his first sexual encounter with a white girl.

"Waddup niggas and nigetts," Big Mo said. "Thanks for comin' over here in such a hurry for me. But peep game though. Me and Stacy goin' on a little vacation. We'll be gone for a week. Bennie will be in charge while I'm gone."

"Man you coulda told us that shit on the phone," Dre said.

"Nah," Mo replied. "We leavin' tonight so we wanted to see you ugly ass niggas before we left."

"Ugly?" CeCe responded. "Sheeiit. My baby fine as hell," she said, as she rubbed Dre's leg. She was still on cloud nine from their lovemaking session.

Damn Ty thought. *He musta put some serious dick on her today.*

He was cool with it though. He had hoped that his cousin would change his approach to dealing with CeCe. She was tough as hell but when it came down to it, she was still a woman who needed a strong man in and out of the bedroom. Just then Stacy came down the steps glowing like a fluorescent light. In full travel mode with J-Brand jeans and a black witness T-Shirt, she slid across the floor in her Black Prada multi flowered wedge shoes

"Damn girl, slow down," CeCe said.

"Unh uh," Stacy said, shaking her head. "I been waiting to get the fuck outta Cleveland for a minute now. I'm ready fo' this girl."

"What time does your plan leave?" Bennie asked.

Looking at his watch Mo said, "We got about three hours before takeoff. I'ma need you to take us to the airport though Bennie."

"Bet nigga, you know that ain't no problem." Although Bennie agreed, it was clear something was troubling him. Deeply.

The fact that he'd fucked Peaches and could possibly have AIDS sent chills up his spine. "I'ma go get the car cleaned up," he said, walking toward the door. In reality, he needed air. And an AIDS test.

Dre's cell phone went off as soon as Bennie left the room. After a brief conversation, he disconnected the call and said, "Yo' I gotta make a quick run. My dude wants a couple o pounds." He was disappointed that he had to leave the little get together.

"Man don't even sweat that," Mo said as he saw the expression on his friend's face.

"You betta go make that cheese." Dre walked up to Big Mo and gave him a hug and a pound.

"If I don't get back before you leave man, have a safe trip." He walked over to Stacy, hugged her, and kissed her on the cheek. "Enjoy yourself girl."

"Oh, you know I will," she sassily replied.

Grabbing CeCe around the waist, he pulled her to him and kissed her passionately on the lips. The room fell silent. He'd never shown that kind of affection to her in public before.

"See you at home baby," he said.

"Ok," she replied blushing.

With that Dre was out.

♴♴♴

Twenty minutes later, Dre rushed into his house and ran straight to his bedroom closet. He was anxious to get the sale over with. He wanted to make it back to Mo's house before they left. After grabbing two bags of weed and stuffing them in a green adidas duffle bag, he headed for the door. But before he got out of the bedroom he heard a buzzing sound. Not knowing what it was he stopped and listened carefully. He heard it again and discovered that it was coming from under the bed.

He knelt down and looked under the bed and saw CeCe's cell phone laying on the floor. Picking it up, he just shook his head. *Damn woman would lose her head if it wasn't attached to her body,* Dre thought. Looking at the display screen, he noticed that she had a voice mail message. He knew her four digit code. He'd seen her punch it in on one occasion and remembered it. Going back and forth in his mind, he decided to listen to it. It might be about some business and he didn't want them to miss any money. He punched in her 2141 code and waited for the message. What he heard next ripped his heart out.

$$$

The minute Audrey opened her cell phone and saw the picture text, she was in shock. She couldn't believe that Bennie would be such a snake as to record her performing oral sex on her daughter. She had to get him to erases it somehow. Without any regard for the law or her own safety, Audrey sped toward Bennie's house doing ninety miles an hour.

Chapter 25

After dropping Mo and Stacy off at the airport, Bennie decided to go home and chill out for the rest of the night. He was the second in command but he didn't really like it. He would much rather lay in the cut, collect his money, and do his own thing. But Mo had confided in him that he didn't trust anyone else to do the job, so, reluctantly, he agreed. Plus he had other things on his mind. Although he really wanted to figure out how to get Charity and Amanda to have a ménage trios, he needed to get to a doctor's office.

He knew Charity would be down for wild sex but her sister seemed kinda uptight to him. She would need some convincing. Bennie pulled into the driveway of his single family home off of 93rd and Superior. Walking up on his porch he noticed that his door was slightly ajar. He reached behind his back and took out his nickel plated nine millimeter. He carefully pushed the door in, cocked the hammer back, and pointed his gun inside the house. When he reached the living room, he uncocked his gun and lowered it.

"What the hell are you doing in my house?" he asked.

Audrey Murphy sat in his brown leather recliner chair puffing on a cigarette and sipping on the same bottle of vodka she had earlier.

"I made myself comfortable. I hope you don't mind," she said.

"You didn't answer my question, bitch. What the fuck are you doing in my house?"

Audrey crossed her arms and tilted her head to the side. "You have a lot of fuckin' nerve trying to get mad at me!" she yelled. "Why in the fuck would you do that to me?"

"I ain't do a muthafuckin' thing to you. Ain't nobody tell you to open yo' legs and let yo' daughter eat yo' ass out."

That comment cut her to the bone. Although she hated to admit it, he was right. If she would've just turned around and walked out the door, none of this would have ever happened.

"I know that!" she spat. "But why did you have to take pictures of that shit? I don't want anyone knowing about that."

"I ain't showed that shit to nobody," he lied. "Calm the fuck down."

Audrey dropped her head and started to cry. "Would you erase it please?"

Bennie saw an opportunity to get some quick head. "Maybe," he said as he unzipped his pants and smiled at her. Then Bennie pulled out his dick and shook it at her.

Audrey stood up and put her hands on her hips. "And just what the fuck do you want me to do with that thing?" she sassily asked. Seeing a dick changed her mood instantly.

"I want you to suck this muthafucka until I bust a nut."

"Then will you erase it?" she asked.

"Yeah I guess so," he replied.

Audrey wasn't convinced. But seeing Bennie's extra large dick made her mouth water. Getting down on her hands and knees, she crawled toward him like a jungle cat until his stiff pecker touched her forehead. She reached up and grabbed it with her right hand while balancing her self with her left. Bennie moaned as she flicked her tongue across the head. Audrey was a pro's pro.

She knew more about sucking dick than a two dollar hoe, and with the extra motivation that that picture provided, she was going to put a little extra into this blowjob.

"Oh, shit!" he screamed when she put the whole thing in her mouth.

She had always seen Bennie's dick as a challenge to her.

The first time she sucked it, it felt like someone was stabbing her tonsils with a javelin. While she was busy giving Bennie a blowjob that would make Janet Jacme envious, she smoothly slipped his gun out of his hand. He was enjoying her skills so much that he didn't even notice. Sucking faster to keep his attention, she stuck the gun in the small of her back. The white Capris she had on kept it snug.

Focusing her attention on Bennie once again, she started to slurp loudly on his baby maker. Hearing her slurp like that had always turned him on. Simultaneously she grabbed his ass cheeks and he grabbed the back of her head. His legs started shaking as he neared his climaxed. She started messaging his balls with her left hand. She could almost feel the semen swishing around in his sacks.

"AAHH FUCK!" he yelled as he sprayed cum all over her esophagus. "Oh, shit wait, baby, wait," he said as she licked his now ultra-sensitive head. Wanting to taste some more cum, she continued to jack off his still rock hard dick. "Ooohh shit," he cried out as his last squirts of cum streamlined to her chin and traveled down her neck. Drained, Bennie dropped down on the couch. Audrey got up and walked back to the recliner.

After wiping off her chin, she asked "Do we still have a deal?"

"What deal? I ain't make no promises," he said, with a sinister grin on his face.

"What!" she screamed as she jumped up from the chair. "You black son of a bitch. We had a fuckin' deal!"

Bennie started laughing hysterically. His plan was to let her do her thing and then escort her ass out the door. Reaching behind his back, he grabbed nothing but air. He looked to his left and then to his right. Nothing. Turning his head to face her with a puzzled look on his face, he found himself staring at the barrel of his own gun. He laughed some more.

"Oh, so you think this is a fuckin' joke?"

"Bitch please," he replied. "Yo' ass ain't gon' shoot no…" Pow!!

He yelled as she shot him in the stomach. When he doubled over in pain and fell to his knees, she shot him again, this time in the shoulder. As he collapsed on the floor, she walked past him, spitting on him as she went by. Snatching his cell phone off of his hip, she instinctively stuck it in her purse. As she walked out the door she looked back one last time. Although she'd shot him, deep in her heart, she really didn't mean to kill Bennie. All she wanted was for him to erase the picture text but when he started laughing at her, she snapped.

Shaking her head, she mumbled to her self, "dumb nigger."

$$$

Dre sat in his truck at Gordon Park. He was hurt, but he was also mad as fuck. How in the fuck could he not see this shit? His cousin had been fucking his woman right up under his nose. The more he thought about it the madder he got. He wanted to take his gun and blow both of their brains out but he wasn't trying to go to jail over a bitch. Taking a big swig of the Old English 800 40oz bottle, he thought of an ingenious plan to payback his backstabbing cousin. He knew that Ty was secretly selling cocaine on the side. He was also paying one of Ty's customers to keep him apprised of what Ty was doing.

"Payback is a bitch," he said as he punched numbers into his cell phone. He loved both Ty and CeCe, but he wasn't going to let them make a fool out of him.

"Hello," the voice on the other end answered.

"Yo' waddup Hector. Listen my man. How would you like to make two grand?" Dre asked.

This got Hector's attention. Pushing his cell phone tightly against his ear Hector said, "I'm listening amigo."

$$$

Spice sat in front of the house on Desoto Street in Cleveland Heights puffing on a blunt. She thought about the message that Julio had left her on her cell phone. After calling him back and confirming what had gone down about her father's death, Spice was heated. She found out much more than she anticipated. This ruthless bastard had taken away not one but two people she cared about. After taking a couple more hits from her blunt, she put it out and walked up on the porch and made her way to the door. She rang the doorbell twice and folded her arms as she waited for someone to open the door. When the door finally did open, a sly smile crept across her face. A look of shock registered on CeCe's face as she stood face to face with her step-sister.

"What the hell are you doing here?" CeCe asked.

"Nice to see you too sis," Spice said as she walked past CeCe.

"Did I say you could bring yo' ass in my house?" CeCe was irritated.

"Oh, please bitch. We both know that you were going to let me in."

CeCe sighed. "What do you want Charlotte?"

Spice looked at her and rolled her eyes. "Yeah, that's right I called you by your government name."

"Anyway," Spice said, holding up her hand as if it would somehow stop CeCe from talking. "We need to talk."

"What could you possibly need to talk to me about? There is nothing you can say that would interest me."

"Yes… there is," Spice said. "As a matter of fact," she said as she took out her cell phone, "I don't have to say anything. Just listen."

CeCe reluctantly sat down on the couch, and listened intently.

$$\text{ʄʄʄ}$$

After letting CeCe hear the evidence for herself, Spice made a call to Sugar. When she heard Spice's recording of what she had learned from her friend Julio, Sugar was livid. She didn't know if Stacy knew what was going on or not but there was no way she was going to let this shit slide. And if Stacy knew about it, then she was less than a woman in her book. However this thing was going to shake out, Stacy was going to have to pick a side.

She shook her head in an attempt to reason with her self. Stacy didn't know about this. She didn't get along with her step-sister but she never viewed her as a weak woman. She thought about Julio. This man had some major connections.

Not only was he able to find out what they hadn't been able to, he even knew that Big Mo and Stacy were going to the Bahamas and what hotel they were staying in. Sugar smiled and quickly called Cleveland's Hopkins Airport to make reservations to the Bahamas. This was the chance that she had been waiting for. Her father's killer was within her reach and she was not going to let this opportunity slip through her fingers. Thinking ahead, she also made another phone call as she sped toward the airport. Fifteen minutes later she was pulling up into the parking garage. She didn't even go home to pack. She figured that whatever she needed, she would just buy when she got there. Her cell phone rang just as she stepped out of her car.

"Hello," she greeted.

"I will have it for you when you when you get here," the voice on the other end replied.

"Thank you," she said before hanging up. Sugar flashed a wicked smile. "He's gon' pay for this shit," she mumbled to her self.

Chapter 26

Hector didn't have a clue as to why Dre was trying' to set his cousin up. Nor did he give a damn. All he knew was that he was getting paid a grip to help do it. If Dre and Ty were beefing with each other, then that was none of his business. After calling Ty and telling him that one of his partners in Akron wanted to cop two bricks of cocaine for him, he met Dre down at Slymans Deli on St. Clair Avenue. When he got there Dre was sitting in his truck eating one of Slymans famous corned beef sandwiches. Hector hopped in the passenger side of Dre's ride and stuck his fist out expecting some dap from Dre. All he got was a hard stare.

"Muthafucka don't you know how to knock?" Dre questioned.

A confused looking Hector remained speechless with his palms facing upward.

Dre burst out laughing. "Man, I'm just fuckin' wit you." Hector smiled and relaxed a little. Just then Dre's cell phone went off. He'd been expecting this call for the last thirty minutes or so. "Speak on it," he said, answering the phone.

"Yo' waddup cuz," Ty said.

"Wassup man."

"Yo' man check this out. I gotta roll to Akron to handle some business in a few. You not gon' need me in the next few hours are you?"

"Nah, go 'head and handle yo' business nigga. I'll holla at

you when you get back."

He hung up without saying another word. Turning his attention back to Hector, he reached into his jeans and pulled out a knot of one hundred dollar bills. He peeled off twenty of them and handed them to Hector. Then he sat back and continued eating his corned beef sandwich.

Feeling like he was being dismissed, Hector said "gracias señor," and got out of the truck.

What Dre was about to do could get his cousin locked up. *Too bad* he thought. *He shoulda thought of that shit when his was bonin' my woman.* It didn't matter to him that in the message he'd heard said that they were going to stop screwing around. They should've never been doing it in the first place. He let his mind slowly drift to CeCe. He cracked a sinister smile. She was going to pay for betraying him like that. If it took his last breath he was going to make sure of it.

$$$

After Spice left, CeCe sat on her couch fuming. She wondered if anyone else in the crew knew what was going on. That would be the ultimate insult. Her eyes became red as she thought about these last few years and the hatred she had carried around for her mother. Now that she knew the truth, she would give anything to be able to apologize to her. The more she thought about what Mo had done, the more she wanted to blow his brains out. He had taken more from her than he'd ever know. She wanted so badly to cry on Dre's shoulder yet she also wanted to be alone. A sudden thought occurred to her. What if Dre knew about it? What would she do then? Did he have anything to do with it? Knowing that there was only one way to find out, she picked up her cell phone and dialed his number.

$$$

Dre looked at the caller ID on his cell phone and sat it back down. He didn't feel like talking to CeCe after what he had learned earlier. All he wanted to do was sit back and wait on his homeboys call. Right after he'd talked to Ty, Dre had called his childhood friend Chop. He got that name because he'd always brought pork chops to school for lunch. Since he'd moved to Akron before Dre and Ty had started hanging out together, Ty didn't know him. His father was a cop and pushed him hard to go into a career in law enforcement. Now, he was a state trooper earning his stripes. Dre told him he had overheard a conversation about someone transporting cocaine from Cleveland to Akron today and gave him a description of and the license plate number of the truck. He'd told him that he felt it was his duty as an honest citizen. Chop had no idea the type of stuff Dre was involved in but he knew his friend wouldn't give him a bogus tip. So he sat with his partner and waited on the Drug bust that was sure to come.

$ $

Ty cruised along Highway 77 going south on his way to Akron. He was going to have to give old Hector a bonus for this one. This was going to net him twenty-five G's. Hectors partner was going to meet him at Shoney's restaurant off the highway. He wasn't going to get to close to him because when he talked to him on the phone, he sounded like he was sick. Ty didn't know that he was still talking to Hector. Hector just pretended it was a three-way call and simply covered his cell phone with his hand and made his voice raspier. It wasn't until he changed CD's that he heard the sirens blasting behind him.

"Shit!" he screamed as he looked into the mirror. "Ok, calm down," he said out loud. "I ain't did shit and my license is good."

Ty was starting to feel confident that the worse thing that would come out of this would be getting a ticket. He still didn't know what the fuck he did to get pulled over. But when a cop wanted to stop you that didn't mean shit. His confidence was short lived. When he saw the dog get out of the back of the police car, he knew he was fucked.

Chapter 27

Sugar sat in the Emerald Palms hotel sipping on a mixed drink. Her large Prada sunglasses masked the infuriation in her eyes. Her extra large hat covered most of her face. Being that she had visited this hotel on many occasions, Sugar felt right at home. She'd even made a few friends that she kept in touch with from time to time. Caught up in her thoughts, she almost didn't notice the tall, wavy haired man with the milk chocolate skin and pearly white teeth walking through the lobby. She smiled as their eyes locked on to one another. ooking like a taller more muscular version of Billy Dee Williams, he returned her smile. Leaning down and grabbing her hand, he kissed her gently on the cheek.

"It's nice to see you again Patrice and before you start, let me just say that I have never called you Sugar and I'm not going to start now."

She laughed. "You musta knew what I was thinkin'."

"I just know that for some reason you hate your given name. I don't know why. I think it's a beautiful name," he said. He sat down across from her and sighed. "So, let me get this straight," he said. "The person who murdered your father is here and you wish to take care of him."

"Yes," she responded with no hesitation.

"Are you sure young lady?" he asked. "Because once you take a man's life there is no coming back from that." There was no reason to tell him that she had killed before. He had always thought that she was so sweet and innocent. She'd rather for him to continue to think that.

"I know," she said. "But this is something that I have to do."

"Your sister didn't come with you?" he asked only because he knew that Charlotte was the more vicious of the two.

"No. I don't need her to handle this," she replied taking offense.

He stared at her for a moment. "Are you sure you don't want me to handle this?" he asked. "After all, this is just as personal to me as it is you." Upon seeing her roll her eyes and shake her head, he held up his hands and conceded. He got up, walked around the table, and hugged her tightly. "Be sure to call me when it is over."

"I will," she replied.

"I love you Patrice."

"I love you too, Uncle Charles."

Leaving the black bag he was carrying with him sitting on the floor next to her feet, he calmly got up and walked away. Sugar picked up the bag and sat it on the table. Inside the bag was a Desert Eagle simi-automatic pistol with a silencer next to it. Now it was time for plan two. Sugar got up and walked to the hotel counter. Standing there staring at a computer was a petite young woman with honey colored skin and long flowing sandy brown hair.

"May I help you ma'am?" the woman at the counter asked.

"Yes you may," Sugar said. "The sign on the ladies room door says that it's out of order. Is there some place else I can go to use the bathroom?"

Looking around nervously the young woman said, "I don't know ma'am. I could get in trouble for this."

"Please," Sugar begged. "It will only take a second."

"Well, ok. Follow me please. The bathroom is back here."

She led Sugar to the employee restroom in the back. Looking around to see if anyone was watching, she turned around to face Sugar. In one swift motion, she turned around and slapped the shit out of Sugar. Momentarily stunned, Sugar briefly saw stars.

"Oooww!" the woman screamed as Sugar grabbed the back of her hair and yanked it. Then she took out the gun that her Uncle had given her and put it up against the woman's head. The woman laughed as if she wasn't afraid.

"Bitch," she said to Sugar. "Why haven't you fuckin' called me?"

"I been busy hoe," Sugar responded. Putting the gun back into the black bag, she then tongue kissed the smaller woman in the mouth. The woman responded by squeezing Sugar's right tittie.

"Damn baby, I missed yo' ass," Sugar said when they broke the liplock.

"Oh, really? I can't tell." the woman stepped back, folded her arms and leaned to the side.

"Look Trish, I told you that I had a few things that I had to take care of."

"You also told me that you were going to take me back to the United States with you," an upset Trish stated.

"I know I know, just give me a couple more days baby. You waited this long, two or three more days ain't gon' kill you ok?"

"Yeah alright." Sugar grabbed Trish by her collar and pulled her close up to her.

"I know what you want, you sweet pussy bitch."

Sugar stuck her tongue in Trish's mouth. After tongue wrestling with her for about ten seconds, she removed it from her mouth and started licking her neck. Trish started to moan when Sugar reached up under her skirt and massaged her clit.

"Ooohh Baaabyyy stooopp," she purred as she pushed Sugar's hand away. "You gon' get me in trouble. Can't we finish this later?" she asked.

"We sure can," Sugar said smiling. Reaching in her back pocket, sugar pulled out a picture of Stacy and Mo. "But first, I need to know what room these two are staying in."

"Ok, but why?" Trish asked. "Ask me no questions, I'll tell you no lies."

After that comment, Trish figured that she was better off not knowing.

"Follow me."

$$$

Stacy sat in her plush hotel room staring out the window. She and Big Mo had just made love for the third time since they had gotten to the Bahamas. When they were done he showered, threw on some shorts, and went down to the lobby gift shop.

"Be back in a minute honey," he told her. "I saw a hat down there that I just gots to have. I wanna get it before anybody else does."

With that comment he was out the door. This gave Stacy some time to her self. She was really enjoying her self. Looking out the window at the white sanded beach, she started to daydream. She thought about settling down and giving Mo some Children. She was sure he was going to marry her. She just didn't know when he was going to pop the question. She got giddy thinking about what she would be wearing when she walked down the aisle. She thought of CeCe being the maid of honor. She even thought about squashing the beef between her and her two step-sisters. Maybe they would want to be involved in the wedding. The opening and closing of the door interrupted her thoughts. Big Mo walked back in looking disappointed.

"Why you back so fast?"

"Some jackass got the hat," Mo replied.

"I'm sorry baby," Stacy said, trying to comfort him.

"Ah well," he said. "I'll find something else. And oh, by the way, tomorrow I got a surprise for you.

"What is it," she excitedly asked.

"I ain't telling you that. That's why they call it a surprise."

"Asshole," she said.

"Just for that, you gon' wait two more days."

"I was jus' playin', I was jus' playin'."

"Uh huh," he said. "Oh, I almost forgot. They havin' a party in the lobby tonight. You game?"

"Hell yeah. I came here to have fun."

"Well," Mo said. "I plan on partying all night so I'ma lay here and get me some sleep."

"Sounds like a plan to me," she responded. She climbed in the bed and curled up next to him. They both drifted off to sleep.

₣₣₣

Sugar carefully slid the key card into the slot. When the light turned green, she turned the lever and pushed the door open. It was dark inside but she could still see two bodies intertwined on top of the sheets. She wanted to shoot him right then and there but Stacy deserved to know the truth. Walking over to a desk that was sitting in the corner, she turned the chair around so she would be facing the bed. Then she took the gun out of the bag and screwed the silencer on. She placed a small digital voice recorder on desk. As she sat there thinking about what this man had taken from her life, she became angrier and angrier. Sugar tilted her head so she could get a good look at her step-sister. This was going to cause her immense pain but it had to be done. The code of the streets is an eye for an eye. It was time to collect. She banged the handle of the gun down on the desk so hard, it produced wood chips. Stacy and Mo sat straight up in the bed. Instinctively Mo reached for his gun. At home he'd always kept it on the nightstand just in case. For one brief moment he had forgotten where he was.

"Shit!" he yelled. He blinked a few times as he tried to get his eyes to focus.

"What is it?" Stacy asked as she shook her head and rubbed her eyes.

Sugar remained silent. When Mo finally focused enough to realized that a woman was in front of him, he cracked a slight smile. In his warped mind he thought that maybe Stacy was setting up a threesome. That thought quickly disappeared when he saw the forty-five in her hand.

"Bitch, who the fuck are you? And what the fuck are you doing in my room."

Sugar still remained silent. Mo started to get up but quickly sat back down when she cocked the hammer back on the pistol. Finally gaining enough focus to recognize who it was, Stacy finally spoke. "Sugar?" she said. "Is that you?"

"Hello Stacy. Long time no see."

"Wait a minute," Mo said. "You know this bitch?"

"Yeah," Stacy replied. "She's my step-sister."

Mo looked confused. "Step-sister...you never told me you had a step-sister."

"You gotta lotta muthafuckin' nerve!" Sugar screamed. "It's some shit you ain't told her either."

Mo tried to think but his brain hadn't started working yet. He was still half asleep. "Sugar what are you talkin' about?"

"Ask your man."

Turning her head to look at Mo Stacy asked through pleading eyes "Mo honey, what is she talkin' about?"

"I don't..." Mo looked down at the voice recorder and it caused him to hesitate. He locked eyes with Sugar and she smiled at him.

"Will somebody please tell me what the fuck is going on?" Stacy yelled.

Sugar stood up and pointed the gun at Mo's forehead.

"Stacy, what I want you to do is come over here by me," Sugar said calmly.

"No," she said as she grabbed Mo's left arm.

"Have it your way," Sugar said. With no hesitation, she shot Mo in his right arm.

"AAHHH SHIT!!" Mo shouted.

Stacy started to scream but Sugar shook her head and pointed the gun at Mo's chest.

"The next one's going through his heart! Get the fuck over here now!"

Stacy eased out of the bed and slipped on the outfit she had on earlier. Then she walked over to Sugar and looked her dead in her eyes. "I hate you," she said.

Smiling at her Sugar said, "No you don't. But after this is all over, you're gonna hate him." Stacy was at her breaking point.

It was bad enough that her step-sister had barged into their room, was holding them at gun point, and had shot her man. Now, she seemed to playing games.

"Sugar, what the fuck do you want?" she yelled as she clenched up her fists.

"I know you don't understand Stacy but this will explain everything."

Sugar reached down and pressed play on the voice recorder. Mo's eyes grew to twice their normal size when he heard his voice. Tiny sweat beads formed on his shiny bald head when he realized what was being discussed on the recorder. Stacy just stood there with tears in her eyes. Her mouth had dropped completely open.

By the time they were done listening, tears were flowing down her face. She felt as if someone had reached inside of her and ripped her guts out. Mo stared at Sugar with pure hatred in his eyes. He purposely avoided eye contact with Stacy.

"Does Spice know?" Stacy asked Sugar.

Sugar nodded.

"What about CeCe?"

"Yes. I sent Spice to tell her."

Mo still had a confused look on his face. What the fuck does Spice have to do with this he wondered?

Reading his mind Sugar looked at him and said, "Spice is my sister.

Mo closed his eyes and shook his head. Getting madder by the minute, Stacy looked at him through cold, dark, slits. "You bastard! You fuckin' bastard! You killed my mother? I've talked to you a hundred fuckin' times about tryin' to find her when you knew that she wasn't comin' back! How the fuck could you do that?"

Big Mo sat there stone faced. If he had known that Spice was Stacy's step-sister, he would have killed her a long time ago.

"Say something!" Stacy spat.

"Stacy, I didn't know that that was your mother at the time. When I found out I was afraid to tell you because I didn't want to lose you. I love you Stacy."

"That may or may not be true," interjected Sugar. "But the

simple fact remains that not only did you kill her mother. You killed my father as well. Ain't no way in hell I'ma let you get away with that shit." She pointed the gun at Mo's forehead but before she could pull the trigger Stacy jumped in front of the gun.

"The fuck are you doing? This muthafucka murdered yo' moms."

"I know that Sugar. Just give me a second. Please."

"Fine," Sugar said, lowering her gun. "But I'm not leaving this room."

Turning to look at Mo, Stacy had a thousand thoughts running through her head. She'd been raised by the street code *an eye for an eye.* She knew what that meant and as much as she wanted to get mad at Sugar for walking in there and upsetting her life she couldn't. This was something that she needed to know. She had no doubt that Mo was going to propose to her the next day. She'd snooped around in his suitcase and seen the engagement ring before they'd left. Now she had a decision to make. Could she get married to a man who'd killed her mother and lied about it for the past three years, or would she follow her street ethics and get revenge. Looking deep into his eyes she asked him "Do you love me?"

"Yes," he replied.

"Then why didn't you just tell me and let me make up my own mind about staying or leaving? Are you that selfish?"

Mo searched his soul for an answer but couldn't come up with one. Feeling ashamed of himself, he dropped his head. Stacy, with tears still flowing, turned around to face Sugar.
"What if I said that I wanted him to live?" Stacy asked.

"Then I would walk away," Sugar replied.

The statement was only half true. She was going to walk away but only after she blew Mo's head off. If Stacy sided with Mo, then she was going to kill her too. They weren't that close and if Stacy wanted to stick by a man who had killed her mother, then Sugar would lose the little respect that she did have for her. Stacy walked over to Mo and kissed him on top of his head.

"I love you too baby," she said. Then she turned and walked to her step-sisters side. "But you killed my mother. And

I'll never be able to forgive that." Stacy looked at Sugar and nodded her head.

Closing her eyes, she started to remember all the good times she and Mo had together. For five seconds the room was eerily silent. The unmistakable sound of a body falling to the floor broke the silence as Sugar fired two bullets into Big Mo's heart. Sugar opened her cell phone and called her Uncle.

"Hello?' he answered.

"It's me," she said."

"Is it done?" he asked.

"Yes. Send a cleanup crew to room number 22. My friend Trish will let you in." After hanging up, she looked at Stacy and said, "I'm not gonna ask you if you are all right because that would be a stupid question. But what I am gonna tell you is that we need to get out of here. Pack up as much as you can as fast as you can. I booked a flight for two back to the United States. I'ma go outside the door and talk to my friend. Be ready to go when I get back."

Stacy hurriedly gathered what she wanted to keep. It took her all of five minutes to pack the things that she felt was important to her.

"You ready?" Sugar asked as she stuck her head in the door.

"Yeah, I'm ready." When she got to the door, she turned around and looked as her fiancée lay dead on the floor. A single tear rolled down her face as she closed the door behind her.

₣₣₣

Stacy leaned back in her seat on the plane in deep thought. She went to the Bahamas expecting a marriage proposal and left behind a dead fiancée. A headache started to set in as an avalanche of thoughts attacked her mind. She still couldn't believe that the man she loved so dearly, the man who was supposed to become her husband was the same man who'd murdered her mother. Looking over at her sleeping step-sister, she was void of emotions. She truly didn't know whether to be angry or grateful. She knew in her heart that Sugar was doing what she thought was right. As hard as she tried, she just couldn't erase the scene of Big Mo's dead carcass lying on the hotel floor. She was hoping that this was a dream from which she was about to wake up any second. She needed something to calm her nerves. Since she couldn't smoke a blunt on the plane, she had to settle for a drink. When the stewardess rolled the beverage cart down the aisle, she ordered two shots of Jack Daniels.

Sugar woke up just in time to see her finishing off the first one. "You ok over there sis?"

Stacy wanted to tell her, "I ain't yo' fuckin' sister," but instead, she remained silent. Not wanting to make a bad situation worse, Sugar leaned back and tried to go back to sleep. She'd gotten what she wanted. Revenge on the person who killed her father. A sudden thought occurred to Stacy. *How was she going to explain this to the rest of the crew?*

Their leader was dead and her step-sister was the one who had pulled the trigger. Big Mo was gone. Forever. Big Mo. The love of her life. Thinking about him brought her to tears. Her sniffling caused Sugar to open her eyes and look in her direction. She got mad instantly. She leaned over to Stacy and started whispering in her ear.

"You know what? You's a weak ass bitch."

Stacy turned to her in shock.

"Yeah that's right. I said it. You up in this muthafucka sheddin' fuckin' tears for a man that killed your mother. Now I didn't wanna tell yo' ass this but yo' mama died a terrible death Stacy. Not only did he kill her, that sick son of a bitch cut her up, stuffed her body in a garbage bag, and threw her in the fuckin' lake. So, stop sheddin' tears fo' this muthafucka."

"That's easy fo' yo' ass to say," Stacy said. "You didn't even know him. You didn't know shit about him."

"I knew all I needed to fuckin' know. This asshole killed my father, cut him up, and threw him into the lake." Sugar leaned in so close to Stacy, she could see the plaque on her teeth. "And he did the same thing to your mother. Remember that."

Stacy sat back and let Sugar's words resonate through her head. Although she hated to admit it, she knew deep in her heart that Sugar was right. No matter how much she cared for this man, he did kill her mother. The more she thought about it, the more she started to hate him. He was never going to tell her what he had done. He was going to go right on letting her think that her mother was still alive when he knew that she wasn't.

"Now," Sugar said, after giving her a few minutes to collect her thoughts. "When we get back to Cleveland, I have a business proposition for you. Are you interested?" Stacy sat there in silence for a moment. Until just that moment, it hadn't occurred to her that Big Mo was the one that brought in the dough. She had some money stacked but that wouldn't last forever. "Well?" Sugar asked.

"Yes, I'm interested," Stacy replied.

Because no mater what happened to Big Mo, Stacy had to live. Chedda still had to be made. She just wished that she knew what happened in the past that brought her to this present.

Chapter 28

Back in Ohio, Stacy hopped off the plane and headed straight for the nearest bar. She needed a drink in the worst way. Sugar was right on her heels.

"Damn sis, slow the fuck down."

"How many times do I have to tell yo ass that we ain't sisters?"

"Ah sis, don't be like that," Sugar teased.

Stacy stopped dead in her tracks and wheeled around to face Sugar. Sugar, caught off guard, took a step back. "Look Sugar, Syrup, Sweet-N-Low, or whatever the fuck you wanna be called now a days. Get this through yo' thick ass head. We're not sisters and technically speaking, we ain't even step sisters no more. Furthermore, I just watched you blow my fiancées brains out and that ain't something I can easily forget."

Stacy walked into the Max and Erma's and took a seat in the booth. "Now, you said you had a business proposition for me so lets hear the shit."

Sugar glared at her as she sat directly across from her. "First of all, don't you ever fuckin' talk to me like that again. I ain't no muthafuckin' child and more importantly, I ain't YOUR muthafuckin' child. And you can lose that high and mighty attitude 'cause if I remember correctly, Ms. Thing, it was you who gave me the go ahead to clip his punk ass. You need to start reminding yourself that it was him that robbed you of a life with your mother."

The waitress appeared out of nowhere and quickly took their orders. Neither woman wanted any food, but both of them were dying for some sort of alcohol. Stacy ordered two long island iced teas. After the day she had, she felt like she deserved it. Sugar, a stone gut in her own right, ordered a double martini. The waitress left and the ladies continued their conversation.

"So, do we at least have a civil understanding?" Sugar asked.

"Yes, Patrice, I guess so." Sugar's smile faded. She hated being called by her government name and Stacy knew it. "Oh, my bad 'Sugar'," Stacy said like she didn't know that she had just hit a nerve.

The two women sat in silence for a moment as each one gathered their thoughts. Sugar stared Stacy up and down. It had been a long time since she had seen her step sister and was pleasantly surprised at how well her body had filled out. She didn't even realize that she was staring until Stacy said something.

"Bitch, what the fuck are you staring at me like that for? You some kinda dyke or somethin'? Cause if you are, I don't play that *bush on bush* shit. I'm strictly dickly baby."

"Don't knock it till you've tried it baby girl," Sugar smirked.

"What? I was just fuckin' with you! You a dyke for real?" Just then the waitress made her way over to the table with their drinks. She sat the drinks down and smiled a very seductive smile at Sugar letting her know that if she ever wanted to go a few rounds in the sack with her, she was ready, willing, and able. The unspoken communication wasn't lost on Stacy.

"Damn, that bitch act like she a dyke, too."

Sugar shrugged her shoulders.

"You betta get wit the program honey. We're everywhere. Now, let's get down to business. How long was y'all suppose to stay in the Bahamas?"

"For three more days, why?"

"Cause I think it would be best if you stayed at a hotel, at least until we come up with a story for the rest o' your crew." That did present a problem Stacy thought to herself. She had no idea what she was gonna tell the rest of the crew. "I'll do that," she said quickly. "Now what's the proposition?

⚡⚡⚡

Audrey walked into her house in a daze. She couldn't believe that she'd just killed a man over a cell phone photo. She stood at the door for a few moments trying to assess the situation. She was racking her brain trying to figure out if she should tell her husband or not. Maybe he could make this go away. After all he was the Chief of Police. Upon walking into her living room she looked down and saw her husband stretched out on the couch. After staring at him for a few seconds, she reached down to wake him but quickly pulled her hand back. Nervous and fidgety, she took a deep breath and rushed upstairs. She'd just have to talk to him about it later.

At about eleven thirty the next morning, Brad woke up from his trip to a higher ground. The way he was feeling told him that he had scored some potent cocaine this time. He didn't feel this good the first time he'd done it. He staggered up from the couch and went to his desk drawer. Reaching into it, he took out his second helping of the white lady. His cop's ear thought it heard his wife talking to someone upstairs but he quickly dismissed it to get back to his woman on the side. He went and sat back down on the couch and for the second time in less than twenty-four hours beamed up Scotty.

After hearing her husband moving around downstairs, Audrey quickly ends her conversation and heads downstairs to tell him what happened, but when she gets downstairs, he's already started getting high. She shakes her head and walks back up the stairs.

⚡⚡⚡

With his ears being pierced by the constant beeping sound, Bennie tried to open his eyes. The blinding sunlight crashing through the window caused him to close them back up. After willing his eyes to stay open, he tried to sit up but the severe pain in his right side convinced him to remain in the horizontal position. A little disoriented and still groggy from the medication being administered to him, he slowly let his eyes sweep from side to side. It didn't take him long to figure out that he was in a hospital. He had so many tubes attached to his body, he thought he was a science project.

Every time he tried to move, the pain reminded him who was in charge. Just then the door swung open and Charity walked in blowing the steam off the top of a cup of hot chocolate. The redness and puffiness in her eyes was a clear sign that tears had recently lived there. She stopped dead in her tracks when she saw Bennie open his eyes. A smile quickly took hold of her face when she realized he had awakened.

"Hey sleepy head. About time you woke up," she said.

"Was…sup," he replied weakly.

As a result of the shooting, Bennie had suffered a tremendous loss of blood. Charity walked over and sat down next to him. Tears formed in her eyes once again as she thought about how close she had come to losing her new lover. Luckily for Bennie, after picking up her car from the shop she had, unaware by him, followed him home just to find out where he lived. This particular day, she was gonna surprise him by showing up at his house wearing nothing but a coat and a smile.

While undressing in her car, she saw her mother walking toward Bennie's house. At first she was gonna follow her to the door but decided to wait just in case they were screwing. That way she could bust in and join the party. Just thinking about what had gone down between the three of them got her juices flowing. She couldn't wait to taste her mother's moist clit again. Reaching into her purse, she pulled out an already rolled blunt. After taking a couple of puffs of the herb, her mind started to twist and bend. The seat underneath her was drenched due to her dripping wet womb. She touched her now ultra sensitive clit and almost came right then. She started fingering her self and heard a popping sound. Naturally she thought it was her coochie making the noise.

She couldn't take it anymore.

She had to have some dick, pussy or both. Just as she started to jump out and head towards Bennie's house, his door opened up. Her mother shot out of there like a bullet and walked extra fast to her car. Charity ducked down low enough so that her mother couldn't see her but not so far that she couldn't see her mother. The look on her face and the way she was looking around told Charity that something was wrong. As soon as she pulled off, Charity hopped out of the car and ran toward the house. She knocked on the door a couple of times and got no answer.

"Bennie, you in there?" she remembered calling through the door.

After not receiving an answer, she tried the doorknob. To her surprise, the door opened up. Bennie didn't strike her as the type of man who would just leave his door unlocked even if he was there. She poked her head inside the door and called his name again. When he didn't answer for the second time, she carefully walked in and closed the door behind her. Then she tiptoed into the living room and found Bennie lying in a pool of blood.

Her heart sank as she tried to remain calm. Reaching into her coat pocket, she quickly pulled out her cell phone and dialed 911. When the dispatcher asked her where she was calling from she had run outside and checked the address on the house. She didn't know what was going on or why her mother had put a bullet into Bennie's stomach but was determined to find out, especially if he didn't make it. The warm feel of Bennie's hand touching hers brought her back to the here and now.

"What is it baby? You ok? You need the nurse?"

Shaking his head no, Bennie simply asked, "What... happened?"

"You don't remember baby?" she asked.

He shook his head no.

"You got shot baby. You've been in and out since the surgery. Do you remember anything at all? Do you remember who shot you?"

When Bennie shook his head no, Charity felt a huge sigh of relief. The last thing she wanted was for Bennie to seek revenge on her mother. She hadn't known him for very long but he didn't seem like the type of man to let someone shooting him slide. She hoped and prayed that he would never remember.

Chapter 29

Trish stood at the baggage claim waiting for her suit cases to come off the line. Her girl Sugar had finally made good on her promise to bring her back to the states. Although she wanted to come back with Sugar instead of having to catch a later flight, she really didn't have much choice in the matter. Sugar had informed her to answer all questions presented to her by the authorities and wait for further instructions. Having accumulated a considerable amount of vacation time allowed her to leave the island without much suspicion.

She simply told her boss that with the stress and shock of what had happened in the hotel room, she needed to get away for a while. It also didn't help the Bahamian police's case that the surveillance tapes had mysteriously disappeared. The hotel manager suspected that Trish was involved somehow but since he couldn't prove his theories, it was better that he kept his mouth shut. The thing that made him suspicious was that, since he was screwing Trish from time to time, she was the only one other than himself who knew where the tapes were being recorded from so deductive reasoning told him that if he didn't remove them, then she must have.

As Trish stood waiting patiently for her luggage, she could feel the stares of men as well as women upon her. She had on skin tight guess jeans and a black button down blouse. Her sandy brown hair was now pulled back into a tight ponytail. Her Gucci sunglasses hung just above the bridge of her nose to give her that cool seductive look. At a glance, she kinda looked like Vanessa

Williams from soul food.

When her bags finally did come around, the airport flunkies were tripping all over themselves trying to be of assistance. The lucky winner was an overweight buffoon with flaky dry skin, bad breath, and less than a snowballs chance in hell at ever being with a woman that looked like Trish. He sported a short nappy afro and a raggedy, unkempt beard. His teeth were white as snow but there was only one problem with that. He was missing about six of them. After he escorted her to a cab, she gave him a twenty dollar tip and prayed to God that he used ever dime of it on some lotion and mouth wash. The cab took her to downtown Cleveland where Sugar had already booked her a room at the Marriott. After the long flight from the Bahamas to Miami to Cleveland, all she could think about was taking a long hot bubble bath. Her plans to kick back and relax were nothing more than a pipe dream. As soon as she entered her room, Sugar and Spice were all over her.

"Hey, what the…?

Her words disintegrated into thin air as Sugar roughly pushed her tongue into Trish's mouth. Trish didn't fight it as she wrapped her arms around Sugar's neck and returned her kisses. Spice fell on her knees behind her and had reached around Trish's waist and was unbuckling her jeans. When she finally got the tight fitting pants pulled down, she proceeded to bite Trish on her ass cheeks. From there, she dragged her tongue all the way down to her calf muscle. Trish started to shake.

It had been a long time since she had felt Spice's silky smooth tongue on her flesh. While Spice was busy tasting Trish's sweet flesh, Sugar was relieving her of her shirt and bra. All three women slowly glided over to the king sized water bed and crawled onto it. It took them less than thirty seconds to get completely naked and start devouring each other. Spice's mouth started to water as Trish spread her legs and revealed a low cut diamond shaped bush. While Sugar and Trish were busy tongue wrestling, Spice dove headfirst into Trish's deep ocean.

"Oooohhh Yeeesss," Trish moaned as Spice sent her to an-other world.

Sugar reconfigured her body so that her lips were just

above Trish's breasts. The heat from Sugar's breath caused Trish's body temperature to rise ten degrees. Each woman came at least twice that night and all three drifted off to sleep drowning in total satisfaction.

✦✦✦

Audrey's body snapped up in the bed like a mousetrap. Her face was covered in sweat and her mouth was as dry as the Sahara desert. For the second time during the night, the nightmare of Bennie and his crew gang raping her, then blowing her brains out caused her to lose sleep. Each time she calmed her nerves down by telling her self that Bennie was dead and her husband was the Chief of Police so she had nothing to worry about. She looked to the other side of the bed and discovered that her husband still hadn't joined her.

From the moment she walked in the house and saw him passed out on the couch, she knew that he was stoned to death. She didn't even try to wake him up. She just shook her head and went upstairs. In a way it was good that he was asleep. She still hadn't decided if she was going to tell him about Bennie or not. She still couldn't believe that she had shot a man over some pictures but in no way did she ever want to be reminded of what she did with her daughter. Reluctantly dragging herself out of bed, Audrey needed a cup of coffee in the worse way.

She passed through the living room and noticed that Brad was still on the couch asleep. She waved her hand at him in a dismissive gesture and continued into the kitchen. Before she could even start brewing the coffee, the telephone rang.

"Hello," she said still halfway asleep.

"Hi mom, it's me Charity."

"Oh…uh… hi honey. What's going on?"

This was the first time the two had spoken since the incident and the uncomfortable tone used by Audrey wasn't lost on her daughter.

"Nothing much. Uh…Mom are you busy today?"

"Not really, why?"

"Because I think we need to talk about something."

This was the moment Audrey was dreading. She didn't want to talk about that day to anyone. She was determined to push it to the far corners of her mind. "Charity, I really don't want to talk about what happened the other day. I feel ashamed enough as it is."

"This ain't about the other day. This is much more serious. Meet me at Bob Evans in Mayfield Heights for lunch and I'll fill you in."

"Lunch? What happened to breakfast?"

"Uh, mom. It's 11:30."

Audrey looked at the clock hanging over the stove and was surprised that it indeed was 11:30. "Uhh...ok. What time?"

"In about an hour."

"An hour?"

"Yeah. Is that gonna be a problem?" Charity asked.

"Uh...no honey, I can make it."

"Ok. See you there."

After hanging up Audrey started to speed up. First thing first though. She had to have that cup of coffee. She hurriedly set the coffee pot to brew and ran upstairs to take a shower and get dressed. Last night she was too dazed to do anything but go to bed but before she went out in public again, she had to wash the stench of murder off her body. After hopping out of the shower and getting dressed, Audrey quickly zipped downstairs and into the kitchen. She clumsily poured herself a cup of coffee, spilling nearly half of it on the floor.

"Shit," she uttered to herself as she knelt down with a paper towel to get it up. She speedily drank the half cup and walked back through the living room. On her way to the coat rack, she called to her husband.

"Brad! Brad! I'm about to go... Ah fuck it, I'll call his ass later." She figured he'd just decided to take the day off, since he had been talking about it for the past two months anyway. She grabbed a light jacket and ran out the door. Her curiosity was killing her. She had no idea what Charity wanted to talk to her about but she was anxious to find out.

Chapter 30

Stacy sat on the soft hotel bed in Beachwood, Ohio reflecting on the last two days of her life. She couldn't help but feel sad about the way things had gone south for her. Sugar showing up at their hotel room in the Bahamas was a surprise but when she revealed that it was Stacy's own fiancée that was responsible for her mother's death was a total shock. The mixed feelings she had were battling each other. On one hand she was down in the dumps over losing the love of her life.

Big Mo had been her friend, lover, and confidant for the past three years and in a short time, he was going to be her husband as well. She was now feeling a great sense of loss. But on the other hand, the man she loved and was set to marry was solely responsible for her mother's death. The fact that he didn't bother to tell her about it when he found that it was her mother that he murdered made it even more sickening. She understood why he didn't tell her but that didn't make it right. Just the thought of it made her nauseous.

She was pissed beyond belief but she would have to move on with her life, especially now that she had taken Sugar up on her offer of joining forces. She'd already told CeCe through a coded message over the phone that the Big Mo situation had been taken care of. Now, all she had to do was tell CeCe that the Chedda Boyz was about to join forces with Sugar and Spice. Not an easy task considering CeCe's dislike of her step sisters. A light knock on the door interrupted her thoughts.

"Come in," she said.

CeCe slowly walked in wearing a red Nike sweat suit and a pair of air max sneakers. The two sister's eyes connected and held each other's for what seemed like an eternity. Seeing the tears in her sisters eyes caused CeCe to rush over to her and embrace her in a tight sisterly hug.

"You ok big sis," CeCe asked after the two sisters broke the embrace.

"Not really sis. This shit fuckin' wit a bitch, ya know?"

"Yeah, this whole situation is fucked up," CeCe said. She opened her mouth to say something else but Stacy held up a hand and stopped her.

"CeCe, I know just what you're about to say. He killed our mother and he deserved what he got. But I can't turn my emotions on and off like that. We were together for three years."

"And he's been lying to you the whole fuckin' time."

"I know that CeCe, but like I said, my feelings don't run hot and cold."

"I know sis and I'm sorry if it sounded like I was suggesting that. I just hate seeing you like this." Stacy took a deep breath and shrugged her shoulders.

"I'll be alright sis. It's just gon' take a lil time for me to get it out of my system, that's all. Have you heard anything from the rest of the crew?"

"Nah, I ain't heard shit from neither one of them niggas. I ain't seen or heard from Bennie or Ty since we met up at your place and Dre's punk ass ain't answering the phone. I don't even know if he came home last night to tell you the truth. I tried to wait up for his ass to give him a treat but I guess he had better things to do."

"That's strange," Stacy said.

"I know, especially since he ain't answering his cell phone either. Every time I call, it goes straight to his voice mail." CeCe walked over to the bed and plopped down.

"So, now what?" she asked her older sibling. "What are we

gonna tell the rest of these clowns. Even though Mo getting disposed of was justified, the rest of the crew might not see it that way, especially Bennie's ass. You know how close they are…were. Stacy winced at her sister's choice of words. 'Disposed of' sounded so cold to her.

"Yeah I know. But I think I've come up with a plan that will take care of that, at least for the time being."

CeCe listened intently as Stacy broke down her plan to keep Big Mo's demise a secret. She also told her of Sugar's offer to collaborate and become one functioning unit. This earned a cold stare from her sister.

"Stacy, you know we couldn't stand them hoes when we was growing up. You really wanna go into business wit these bitches?"

"I just think it's time that we expanded our horizons, baby sister. Them hoes got the yayo hookup fo' real. They caked the fuck up and this is our chance to get our hands into some of that flour."

CeCe thought about it for a minute. They were making plenty of money, but if they could make more then why not go for it? "What they talkin' 'bout sis?" a cautious sounding CeCe asked.

For the first time that day, Stacy smiled.

"Well, for starters they talkin' 'bout frontin' us two birds a piece. All they want back is the cost of the dope and ten percent. Even with that we should still make a good eight to ten grand off of it. Like I said sis, these bitches caked up like a muthafucka."

Just as CeCe was getting very, very interested her cell phone went off. She listened for a minute. "What!" she said in a loud voice. "Fo' what?" she continued. "I'll be there in about thirty minutes." After hanging up, she looked at Stacy and shook her head. "Un-fuckin'-believable."

"What's wrong?" Stacy questioned.

"Ty's ass is in jail."

"Jail? For what?"

"He says it's an old warrant but I don't believe that shit for a second. Ain't no tellin' what the fuck Ty done got himself into. He said he tried to call Dre but I guess he can't get in touch with him either. I don't know why the fuck he ain't answering the phone but he better start pickin' up soon. I'm starting to think his ass is with another woman."

Stacy gave her an incredulous look. "I kow, I know," she said. "I gotta boogie though sis, and get this knucklehead outta the pokey.

"Alight, just remember though. In a few days, we start to put this plan into effect."

CeCe nodded and walked out the door.

₰₰₰

Dre extended his right arm to the coffee table and reached for the bottle of Belvedere. He'd been drinking non-stop since he'd found out that his backstabbing ass cousin was fuckin' his woman. For a split second he actually thought about getting Ty out of jail but then came to his senses. If he did get out, somebody else would be footin' the bill. He still hadn't figured out how he was going to exact his revenge on CeCe yet. But whatever he did, he was going to have to be extremely careful. CeCe was dangerous. She would kill a muthafucka just to watch him die. Whether it was a man or a woman. He knew CeCe didn't give a fuck.

₰₰₰

Amanda frantically dialed her sister's cell phone number. For some unknown reason, her mother wasn't answering hers. Trailing the EMS truck to the hospital was the last thing that she expected to be doing today. She had gone by her mother's house to show off the car she had bought, but when she got there her mother wasn't there and her step father was lying on the couch foaming at the mouth. Although she didn't particularly care for the man, she didn't wish death on him. The paramedics told her that he was still alive but that was going to have to get him to the hospital ASAP. She'd tried to call her mother twice but to no avail so she figured that she'd try her sister.

"Shit!" she yelled after the phone went to voice mail.

Hopping out of the Silver 2003 Toyota Celica that she'd purchased just that morning, she made a beeline to the receptionist in the emergency room. The car was over six years old but to her it might as well been brand new. After having to ride the bus or catch a ride with someone as she much as she had in the past year she was grateful for anything she could get. She quickly walked up to the desk where a rotund Hispanic woman appeared to be in a daze while filing what was left of her nails.

"Excuse me Miss," Amanda stated. "I came here with a Mr. Bradley Murphy and was wondering if you could give me some information on him please."

The woman looked at Amanda and, with a surprisingly pleasant attitude, proceeded to answer her question. Yes, I'm sorry but we really don't know anything right now. As you know, they just brought him in so when the find out anything we'll be sure to let you know. Are you a relative of his?"

"I'm his step daughter."

The woman gave Amanda a look that said 'ok step daughter where the hell is his wife.'

"Ok, we'll let you know something as soon as the doctor finds out what's going on."

Amanda tried to sit down and relax but couldn't. The magazines on the table weren't worth looking at so she ran to her car and grabbed the novel that she'd just bought from the passenger's seat. Ever since reading her sisters book, she'd been hooked on street lit novels. Reading that book made her rush out to Borders and look around. After reading the synopsis to *Marked, by Capone*, she purchased it and read it in one sitting. She just couldn't put it down. Her most recent choice was *Millionaire Mistress, by Tiphani*. Amanda sat down and thought for a minute. She knew that if she opened that book, she wasn't going to be able to put it down so she decided to try to call her mother one last time.

Chapter 31

Ashim Goldberg walked into Grafton Correctional Institution with his brief case in his hand and a smile on his face. For the past eight months he had been working to get his client's conviction reversed as a result of improper procedure by the Cleveland Police Department. The police Department thought they had his client dead to rights until new evidence showed that the officer failed to identify himself as a Police Officer when he physically detained the young man.

So, instead of it being assault on a Police Officer, it turned into just plain assault, a misdemeanor that carried a far less sentence than the one his client was convicted of. From the beginning the police knew it was just a matter of time before Goldberg would have the conviction overturned so in true pig fashion, tied the case up in so much red tape that it took it nearly a year to unwind. He smiled as he sat across from his client in what has become a painful ritual for Chaz Mays to absorb.

Having gone through this process a number of times, Chaz subconsciously expected something to go wrong. His mind temporarily wondered as he thought about all the money he would make and all the bitches he would be able to kick it with hanging out with Mo and Bennie, if he could just get the fuck out of prison. He looked his lawyer in the face and smirked.

"What's the fuckin' problem this time," he snapped at his lawyer. It seemed to him that every time his lawyer came to see him, it was more bad news.

"Actually, I have some good news for you this time Mr. Mays. Apparently a tape has surfaced that shows you and the officer exchanging words before you two came to blows."

"Yeah so," Chaz said.

"So, by him not revealing that he was a police officer, and by you having no way of knowing that he was, means that the assault on a police officer conviction will probably be thrown out." Chaz' eyes grew big as a big smile broke out on his face.

"You mean to tell me I could be getting the fuck outta here?"

"It looks that way Mr. Mays." Chaz's smile faded temporarily as a sudden thought came to him.

"Wait a minute nigga. You done said some bullshit like this before and I'm still sittin' up in this muthafucka."

"But this time it's coming straight from the judge."

"That's what up!" Chaz yelled as he could barely contain himself.

"Well," Goldberg stated.

"Well what man?" Chaz asked as the scowl returned to his face.

"Nothing really. It's just gonna take time for the paper work to get done, that's all."

"That's all? How long Goldberg?"

"About a week, maybe two."

"What?" Chaz yelled again. He started to get mad but then he thought about it. He'd been in the joint for over a year so what the fuck was another one or two weeks? "Ahight man. Do the damn thing. I'm more than ready to get the fuck up outta this place." Chaz dropped the phone and got up and walked away without even saying goodbye.

"Ungrateful nigger," Goldberg mumbled.

Chaz stopped dead in his tracks and turned around. "You say something Goldberg?"

"No, I didn't say anything."

"Oh, ok."

Chaz had heard him quite clearly. He just wanted to see if

the thin bearded man would have the guts to repeat it so he could hear it. He figured that he wouldn't. There wasn't much he could do about it anyway as the thick glass that separated them offered Goldberg the comfort of protection. But he would definitely address the racial slur that was just hurled his way when he got out. For right now he still needed him. He would just go back to his cell and make sure that he didn't do anything to get any time added to his sentence.

$$\oint\oint\oint$$

Bennie sat up in the bed and stared intently at the television. It was three o'clock in the morning and he was highly pissed. Instead of being at Charity's apartment laying the pipe to her fine ass, he was laid up in a hospital bed. He thought back to the precise second before the bullet pierced his abdomen. Make no mistake about it, Bennie remembered every little detail about who shot him. There was no way he was going to tell the police anything. He was a soldier of the streets and the number one rule of the streets was no snitching. He would handle the situation himself but didn't want Charity to know that he knew it was her mother who had shot him. He wanted to keep fuckin' her a little while longer before she had to bury her mother. He looked at the clock above the TV and rolled his eyes. He knew that the nurse would be in soon.

Ever since he'd gotten out of surgery, nurses were bringing him medication every three hours. He wouldn't mind if the nurses were good looking. But these dogs needed to be in a kennel! Right on que, Nurse Payne entered the room with a needle on a tray.

"Sorry Mr. Bennie," she uttered. "We need more blood."

"For what?" he asked holding his arm out.

"Well the doctors see an acute infection in your blood stream," she said sadly. "Not sure what's going on, but they wanna take a closer look."

"I know they told you something."

"Your plasma viremic levels are high. That's all I know."

"What the fuck does that me?"

Nurse Payne looked at Bennie with a pitiful stare as she filled the vile with blood. "I'm just a nurse Mr. Bennie. That's all the information I can give you."

"Damn, Nurse Payne. That shit hurt."

Her name fit her perfectly, Bennie thought. Every time he looked at her face it made his stomach hurt more than the needle. She was a rail thin woman with a perm that desperately needed a touch-up. Her jaws were sucked in and dark spooky eyes that were sunk into her head. If Bennie would have seen her on the street, he would have sworn that she was a crackhead. After giving blood, then taking his meds, Bennie drifted off to sleep. Tomorrow he would call his comrades and inform them of what happened, and what needed to be done

Chapter 32

Charity sat in a corner booth eating a plate of sausage, biscuits and gravy and washing it down with a glass of apple juice. She turned the heads of quite a few old geezers when she sauntered in wearing a white mini skirt and a blue and white stripped blouse. Checking her watch, she saw that it was just about time for her mother to arrive so she tried to hurry up and finish her meal. Not even ten seconds after she was done, Audrey slid into the booth across from her.

"Hey first born," she said. "What's up?"

Audrey tried to keep the mode light although she was embarrassed about what had happened with her, Charity, and Bennie.

"Not much mom. I was just wondering if me, you, and Bennie could sit down and talk about what happened the other day. You seemed very uncomfortable about it and we just wanted to put your mind at ease."

"Oh, ah... there's no need for that honey. I'm a big girl. I'll be alright."

"I know, but Bennie wanted to apologize to you in person. He really feels bad about it." Charity wanted to see if her mother was gonna come clean. "Mom? Did you hear me?"

"Uh...yeah honey. I don't think that would be a good idea."

"Why not?"

"Charity, I'd just rather put the whole thing behind me." A look of fear suddenly came across Audrey's face.

"What's wrong?" Charity asked.

"Honey you didn't tell your sister about this did you?"

"No, I didn't tell her mom."

"Oh thank goodness." Charity got up to leave. "Where are you going sweetheart?" her mother asked. "I thought that we were going to hang out for a while."

"I can't mom. I promised Bennie that I would stop by today. Plus I want to tell him that you said everything was ok. He was really concerned about you. I tried to call him right before you got here but he's not answering his phone."

As soon as Audrey heard the word concern and Bennie in the same sentence, she knew something was wrong. She knew Bennie well enough to know that giving a damn about anyone's feelings had never been a strong suit of his. An awkward silence filled the air as the two women just stared at each other for a minute. Audrey gave her daughter a half smile and shook her head. She knew that her daughter knew something.

"Sit back down honey," she said. After looking around to make sure know one was going to hear her, she leaned in close to Charity. "You know don't you?"

Charity responded by slowly nodding her head.

"Jesus Christ," Audrey said as she put her hands in her head. "I swear to God Charity, I didn't go there to kill that man. I only wanted to talk to him to and try to convince him to erase those pictures that he took.

"What pictures mom? What are you talking about?"

Audrey's head snapped back up. "You didn't know that that nigger took a picture of us on his cell phone?"

"No, I didn't know that."

"Well, he did. And stop looking at me like that. Just because I'm married to one doesn't mean that I don't know a nigger when I see one."

"Just tell me what happened."

"Like I said Charity, I went over there to try and get him to delete that picture. I even did him a sexual favor hoping it would soften him up."

Charity felt her blood start to boil. Although she had gotten a little kinky with her mother and Bennie, She didn't appreciate her mother sucking Bennie's dick behind her back. "But it didn't."

"No, it didn't. He laughed in my fuckin' face and I lost it."

A thought suddenly occurred to Charity. Her mom said that she didn't mean to kill Bennie which meant that she didn't know that he was still alive. She thought about telling her, but decided against it for the time being.

"Good God mom, does Brad know?"

"No. When I got home last night, he was asleep on the couch and when I left this morning he was still there. Which reminds me."She took her cell phone out of her purse. "I'd better turn this thing back on just in case someone is trying to call me."

No sooner had she turned it back on, it vibrated in her hand.

"See what I mean. Oh, it's your sister." Hello…What! Amanda…Amanda, slow down! What happened! Oh, my God. I'm on my way!" she yelled into the phone.

"What's going on," Charity asked.

"Amanda said that she stopped by the house an hour ago and found Brad lying on the couch unconscious. She called EMS and they rushed him to Cleveland Clinic Hospital. I gotta go," she said as she fumbled trying to get her keys out of her purse.

"I'll follow you," Charity said. And with that Charity dropped some money on the table and ran out the door behind her mother.

₣₣₣

"Good lookin' Ce. Thanks for snatchin' a nigga up outta there," a dingy, jailhouse smellin' Ty replied.

"Good lookin' my ass nigga. What the fuck was you doing in jail and don't give me that weak ass warrant excuse either homeboy. I just spent a grip to bail yo' ass out so spill the beans, my nigga."

"CeCe, I wouldn't na even called yo' ass if yo' man woulda answered his muthafuckin' phone. The fuck that nigga at anyway?"

CeCe looked at Ty like he had lost his marbles. Not only was he obviously avoiding the question, but now he was trying to check her on the where a bouts of her man. "First of all nigga, you can lose that muthafuckin' attitude wit me. I just did yo' ass a favor so don't jump fly wit me. Second of all I don't know where the fuck Dre ass at. He ain't answering my calls either. Why the fuck you ain't just call Bennie?"

"Shit, I couldn't even remember that nigga's number Ce," he lied. CeCe saw right through it. It was as plain as day that he didn't call Bennie because he didn't want Mo to find out. She didn't know why. It wasn't like it was the first time Ty had been in jail before. "Which brings me back to my original question muthafucka. What the fuck was you in jail for?"

Ty tried to think of a lie, but couldn't come up with something that she would believe so he tried a novel approach. The truth. "Ahight, look CeCe. I'ma tell you but you can't say nothin to nobody, cool?"

"Nigga, spare me that change. It ain't like we ain't keepin' secrets from the rest of 'em anyway so drop the juice nigga."

Ty ignored her last comment. He'd address that later. "Yo' it's like this Ce. I was on my up to Akron to get rid of some yayo and got knocked. Real spit."

"Yayo? Nigga when you start slingin' powder?"

"Yo, I been at this shit for a minute now and don't get me wrong. We making nice money fuckin wit Big Mo, but I'm trying to make a real come up. Know what I mean?"

CeCe smiled to herself. *That's one soldier down,* she thought. And if Ty was down, she would definitely get him to help her convince Dre to be down. She thought it would be hard to convince the rest of the crew to join forces with Sugar and Spice, but by the hungry look in Ty's eyes, this was gonna be easier than she thought.

"Yo Ce, you hear me girl?"

"Huh, oh yeah don't tell Mo, I hear yo ass nigga." Ty had no idea at the time, but Big Mo being pissed at him was not going to be a problem at all. Not in this lifetime.

$$$

Melony sat in a bar on Cleveland's East Side sipping on a

cosmopolitan. She had just received some bad news about her man, Shank, a couple of nights before. He'd been found shot to death along with a childhood friend of his named John "Fat Jack" Wilson. Although Shank wasn't the best man and did some unsavory things at times, even to her, she still loved him. The last time she talked to him, she remembered getting the feeling that he was about to get into something dangerous.

He'd told her not to worry, kissed her on the forehead, and walked out of her life forever. Red, the bartender handed her a napkin but it wasn't for her drink. She was so engrossed in her memories of her loved one that she hadn't even realized that she was crying. She downed the potent drink and quickly asked for another. Seeing that she was gonna be here a while, Red decided to water the rest of her drinks down. The last thing he wanted or needed was some strange woman leaving his place of establishment lit up like the fourth of July and running into a light pole.

Looking at Melony's face and figure, he concluded that that would be an awful waste. In his opinion, this woman had stunningly good looks. She kinda reminded him of Tyra Banks, but just a tad thicker. If she was in here just chillin' instead of weeping over some guy who probably wasn't any good anyway, the bartender would be tempted to get his Mack on. Red was five feet five and light skinned almost to the point of being Caucasian.

"Another time, another place" he mumbled.

The bar was surprisingly empty for this time of day. It was now happy hour and people usually flooded the bar around that time. Red thought it was just gonna be him and the grieving Tyra banks look-a-like until a tall white man walked in looking like someone had stolen his dog. He sat three stools down from Melony and stared blankly at the counter.

"What you need playboy?" Red questioned.

"Let me have a double shot of crown royal."

Red was surprised by this. The clean cut preppy white guy didn't look like the crown royal type to him. Nevertheless, a buck was a buck. *This muthafucka must be blind* Red thought. *He's sitting a few stools down from this fine ass woman and ain't even looked her way. Muthafucka must be a fag.* He sat the man's drink down and quickly pulled his hand away. He had a phobia about gay people.

His brother was gay and died of AIDS before his twenty second birthday. He knew that you couldn't get it by casual physical contact, but he just couldn't help not wanting to come in contact with people that had the disease. His two patrons sat there quietly and sipped their drinks. His services were not needed at the moment so he went back to watching Sports Center. For a period of two seconds, Melony and the preppy dude exchanged glances and nods. Melony sized him up. Although she was sad about Shank the liquor she was drinking had her feeling a little horny not to mention the fact that she had been secretly wanting to sample some white meat for some time now. Sliding down the bar a couple of stools, Melony made her move.

"Buy a bitch a drink?"

The man continued to stare into his drink. It was obvious that he had something on his mind.

"What's your name," Melony asked, refusing to give up.

"Mike," he grunted through clinched teeth.

"You married?" she continued, as if she cared.

Mike turned his head and faced her with irritation in his eyes. "No, I'm not married! I'm twenty-eight years old and I'm a manager at Jillian's! That's the news, you want the weather?"

Melony's face twisted up in a mask of anger. "Who the fuck you think you talkin' to like that white boy? I just asked yo' bitch ass a question! You know what... fuck you," Melony shouted as she got up and walked to the bathroom.

"Wait, Ms. I'm sorry," Mike said as he reached for her arm.

"Get the fuck offa me!" she yelled, snatching her arm away.

Mike felt like an ass. He'd just pissed off a woman who had nothing to do with his situation. He thought that by coming to the bar and drowning his sorrows in alcohol that he would feel better but in reality it made him feel worse. He got up, paid his bill and left an extra twenty bucks on the counter, instructing the bartender to give the woman twenty dollars worth of drinks on him. As soon as Mike got out the door, Red folded up the money and put it in his pocket.

Chapter 33

After Dropping Ty off, CeCe figured she'd try to find her man once and for all. She didn't know what the fuck was going on with him but it was starting to put her in a bad mood. After the screwing that he'd laid on her a couple of nights ago, she thought things were finally starting to get better. She still thought his meat was a little suspect on the length side but he worked the fuck out of his five and a half inches the other night. She doubted if another woman was involved but if there was, two funerals would be held.

The one thing she wasn't gonna tolerate was disrespect. Out of the rear view mirror, she noticed a car following a little too closely behind her. Instantly, CeCe smelled trouble and reached in her purse for the nickel plated three eighty she always carried. She drove slowly down the street until she came to a deserted looking apartment building. Her gut feeling told her trouble was brewing and if she had to lay someone down, she didn't want any witnesses. The less killing she had to do, the better. She wheeled around to back of the building with her hazard lights on to make it appear as if she were having car trouble. Once she got to the back, the car that was following her stopped about twenty-five feet behind her.

CeCe popped the hood and got out of her car with the three eighty entrenched in her pocket. She walked around to the front of her car and pretended to be looking at something under the hood. Out of the corner of eye, she paid close attention the two female bodies talking in the car. She took the gun out of her pocket and put it on the top of the engine. She had already made her mind up that as soon as the car started moving she was gonna shoot it the fuck up. She couldn't tell who the two females were and didn't know what this was about but if some shit was gonna pop off, then she would be ready. She tensed up as the doors opened up on the gold Grand Am. As the two women started walking toward her, she noticed something vaguely familiar about the one who emerged from the driver's side. The one on the passenger's side looked and walked like Chyna, the WWE wrestler. Then all of a sudden it hit as to the identity of the other woman. It was the barmaid whose ass she had whipped in the bathroom a few days ago. As they walked closer to CeCe's car, CeCe stuck her hand in her pocket.

"Yeah bitch, wassup up now?" the barmaid screamed. "I thought that was yo' ass dropping that ugly muthafucka off! Now wassup hoe?"

"Hol' up mami, una momento! You let this skinny ass broad do that to your face? You must didn't know who you was fuckin' wit mami," the Chyna looking broad said as she stared into CeCe's eyes.

"What I do know, is that you hoes must have a death wish fuckin with me," CeCe said. "Y'all betta breeze on before y'all get squeezed on!" The two women cracked up laughing.

"Yo listen to this bitch," the bar maid said. "You sure are talkin' a gang o' shit for someone who's about to get fucked up." She reached into her back pocket and pulled out a straight razor. Simultaneously, her friend popped open a switch blade. CeCe smiled as the bar maid rubbed the scars on her face. "Yo' look what the fuck you did to my face!" she screamed.

"What?" taunted CeCe. "All I did was make you look a little better, slut!"

The two women stared at each other in disbelief. They couldn't believe that CeCe was outnumbered and talking so much shit. If they would've paid a little more attention, they would have noticed that CeCe never took her hand out of her pocket. If they were listening they would've heard the hammer click when she cocked it back.

"Let's fuck this bitch up," Chyna said. She took a step toward CeCe and got no further as CeCe pulled her gun out and shot her in the right thigh. "Ah Shit!!" she screamed. When she grabbed her leg, CeCe shot her in the other one. Calmly and without remorse CeCe walked up on her and put the gun to her temple.

"Oh, God no please don't sh..."

That's as far as she got before CeCe blew her skull in half. CeCe looked up and saw that the barmaid was trying to run. Although she probably couldn't do it again if she tried, CeCe put a perfectly placed hollow point right in between the crack of the barmaid's ass cheeks that traveled through her body and tore open the front of her stomach. Amazingly, the woman was still alive, but not for long if CeCe had anything to say about it. She walked over to the now whimpering woman, who had turned onto her back and gave her a depraved smile. The woman tried to beg for her life, which pissed CeCe off even more.

"Bitch, die with some dignity," she said as she put the pistol in between the woman's legs, pulled the trigger twice, and walked away.

✝✝✝

Dre awoke from his drunken stupor to the sounds of his Ludacris ring tone on his cell phone. His head was pounding and his stomach felt like a volcano. It took him a minute to locate the damn thing which had now started to get on his nerves. By the time he got to it, it had stopped ringing. Looking at the caller ID, he saw that it was CeCe. He knew that he couldn't avoid her forever and he really needed to make a decision on whether he was gonna leave her or not. But now wasn't the time. He felt like shit. His phone beeped to indicate that he had a message. Being that he hadn't talked to her in a minute, he thought it was best that he checked the message.

He punched in the appropriate codes and listened. *"Dre, I don't know what the hell is going on or why yo' ass is avoiding me, but I got into an altercation today and need to tell you about it."*

An altercation, Dre thought. *Who in their right mind would be dumb enough to fuck with CeCe?* He quickly dialed her number.

"Dre, where the hell have you been?"

"Hello to you too," he responded.

"And what's wrong with you? You sound fucked up."

"I feel fucked up. You gon' tell me what happened or are you gon' bitch some more?"

"What? Nigga I'ma bitch some more. You wasn't at home when I got there last night and you was gon when I got up. I don't even know if yo' ass came home last night. Where the fuck was you at? I know you wasn't somewhere fuckin' with some other bitch."

Dre pulled his cell phone away from his ear and stared at it like it was possessed.

"I know her ass didn't just accuse me of cheatin'," he said to himself.

"Dre you listening to me?"

"CeCe! What the fuck happened?" Seeing that he wasn't about to argue with her, CeCe figured that she may as well tell him what the deal was. She wasn't so much as mad at him as she was the situation.

"A few days ago, I got into it with a barmaid and had to rough her ass up. I guess the bitch saw me rolling and decided to follow me so I pulled into the back of that abandoned building on page in East Cleveland. The bitches followed…"

"Hol up Ce. Did you say bitches, as in more than one?"

"Yeah it was two o' them hoes. Anyway, I popped the hood of my ride and waited on 'em. Well, to make a long story short they asses got ghost."

"Anybody see you?"

"Naw, I'm clean."

"Ahight. You might as well come on home then."

"What, you mean you gon' spend some time with me today?" While laughing at her own sarcastic joke, she suddenly realized that Dre had hung up on her.

✚✚✚

Dr. Yuseff was of Arabic decent with dark curly hair that came down to his shoulders. He had gray eyes, a thick beard, and perfectly white teeth. He was a slender man of medium height, who could not have weighed more than one hundred and eighty pounds on a good day. His long angular face searched the room for the family of Bradley Tyrone Murphy.

"Family for Murphy," he called out.

Audrey, Charity, and Amanda rushed across the waiting room floor to meet with him. His long angular face was ashen and his eyes had the look of a man who hadn't slept very much lately. "Mrs. Murphy?" he asked, extending a boney hand toward Audrey. She nodded absently as Charity and Amanda flanked her holding an arm a piece.

"Hi, my name is Dr. Hasaan Yuseff. I'm the attending physician treating your husband. He is unconscious but alive."

"Thank God," Audrey said as she breathed a sigh of relief.

"Can you tell us what happened Dr?" Charity asked.

Dr Yuseff looked at Audrey.

"It's ok," she said "You can talk in front of them."

Amanda popped her lips as if she was offended. He ignored her. "Well, Mrs. Murphy, Your husbands heart seized up from ingesting a large quantity of a substance that looks like cocaine."

"Excuse me, what did you just say?" Audrey questioned.

"He said that Brad almost died from an overdose of cocaine, mom," Charity replied.

Audrey gave her a death stare. "I know what the hell he meant, Charity." Audrey put her hands to her temples and massaged them. She felt a migraine coming on.

"Luckily, he made it here in time. Another ten to fifteen minutes and this conversation would be going a lot differently."

"Can we see him?" she asked.

"Yes, but only for a moment."

The Doctor led them to back to the intensive care unit to see Brad. They all checked their cell phones to make sure that they were off. Amanda smiled as she saw that she had received message from Ty.

$$$

Ty sat on the toilet smoking a blunt. He knew that this shit was far from over. He still had to go to court on some very serious charges. Drug trafficking over state lines carried some heavy time. As he replayed the incident over and over again in his mind, he still couldn't understand how he got caught. It almost seemed like the state trooper was just sitting there waiting on him. He'd been sitting on the toilet for the better part of thirty minutes. His bowels were backed up because he simply refused to use the jailhouse commode.

He had already called Amanda and left her a message telling her that he wanted to pick her up later but gave her his address just in case she could get a ride from her sister. He told her that he was purposely leaving his door unlocked and for her to just come in when she got there. Ty lived in a red brick apartment on Lakeshore blvd. He'd moved in a couple of years ago hoping to escape the hood. He would always have the hood in him, but he didn't want to live in it. That was two years ago and now Lakeshore was starting to resemble what he was running from to begin with. After finishing up the blunt and wiping his ass, Ty jumped in the shower. Since Amanda hadn't called back, he figured that she was either busy or at work. After washing the stench of the jail cell off of him, he walked into his bedroom and was pleasantly surprised when he saw Amanda lying there on his bed in her birthday suit.

Ty's dick jumped to attention as he eyed Amada's thick frame and enormous breasts. Seeing his love soldier standing at attention caused Amanda to lick her lips. "Come and get it big daddy," she said as she spread her legs open.

Ty didn't need anymore convincing as he dove in head first and started eating Amanda out.

"Oooo yes baby, eat it."

Ty flicked his tongue back and forth across the clit until

Amanda was on the verge of coming.

"Oh, God baby wait, please, I don't wanna come yet," she cooed.

Ty wasn't trying top hear it. If he had his way, Amanda was going to come three or four times.

"Uhhh…Ahhh shit!" she screamed as she squirted cum juice all over his dick.

Ty then mounted her and entered her slowly. "Oh, shit," he moaned.

Amanda's pussy wrapped around Ty's dick like a hot glove. It felt so good to him that he wanted to scream, but in true g fashion, he bit his tongue. He tried to hold out for as long as he could, but when she curled her legs around his back and grabbed his ass, it was a wrap. Ty exploded inside of her and the two lovers passed out together.

$$\text{\bf ≠≠≠}$$

After calling her husband's job and explaining the situation, Audrey walked over to her bar and poured herself a scotch and soda. Charity offered to come and stay with her if it would make her feel better, but Audrey refused. She appreciated the gesture but right now she preferred being alone. She didn't know why Amanda left so abruptly but after being in the ICU a total of five minutes, she left. She knew that Amanda didn't particularly care for Brad because he was black. She must've figured she had done her good deed for the day when she called 911. Audrey couldn't help but think that this was her fault. If she would have paid closer attention before she left, her husband might be conscious right now. She wasn't surprised that he was doing drugs. She'd smoked weed with him on occasion herself. But she had no idea that he was this far gone. After taking a few guzzles of her drink, she laid her head back and closed her eyes as tears invaded her pupils. When the telephone sitting next to her rang, she didn't even bother to look at who it was.

Chapter 34

Melony's apartment was cheap but clean. The wall to wall carpet was grass green and the beige colored walls were void of any scratches or blemishes. Her sofa and love seat were dark brown and the plain coffee and end tables were of a tan color. Strangely, she had a small fish tank with two goldfish in it sitting in the corner.

After grabbing the remote, she clicked on the nineteen inch color television that was sitting on a milk crate and walked to her kitchen.When she opened her refrigerator to take out the Old English forty ounce bottle, reality started to set in. She had always depended on Shank to get her over the hump while she was working part time and going to school. He'd always helped her with her rent and groceries but what was she going to do now. Melony didn't have a dime saved up and although she was going to miss her lover the thought of going without scared her more than she ever thought it would. She sat down on the couch, tilted her head back, and took a long swig. Just as she got comfortable, someone knocking at the door snatched her out of her zone. She didn't feel like it but she got up and walked to the door.

"Who is it?" she yelled through the door.

When Melony didn't receive an answer, she walked to her purse and took out her pistol. She then walked back to the door, put the chain on it, and with gun in hand slowly opened the door. A broad smile broke across her face when she saw who was standing on the other side.

"You really need to tell the landlord to put a peephole in this fuckin' door. It's dangerous opening the door like this. You never know who's gonna be on the other side."

In the blink of an eye, Melony closed the door, unlatched the chain, and snatched Chaz inside. Before pleasantries were even exchanged, she had her tongue in his mouth trying to jam it down his throat. Chaz was Melony's first true love. They played the boyfriend, girlfriend game all throughout Jr. High and High school. It was Chaz who, on a cold winter night when her mother was at work, broke her cherry in and took her virginity. She had loved him from the get go and it has never went away. Unfortunately, Chaz did and she played a big part in it.

The reason Chaz got into it with the fellow who turned out to be an officer was because he disrespected Melony. Chaz didn't want her at the trial for fear of retaliation by some crooked cops. He didn't know if Brad or Mo could protect her but he wasn't willing to take that chance. Before he was shipped out, he gave Melony two things and asked her to make him a promise. He gave her his driver's license and a key. He told her that he was under no illusions that she wouldn't screw around while he was away. All he asked was that she give him a chance to win her heart back once he got out. She agreed. When she allowed him to come up for air, they gazed into each others eyes for a second before either one spoke. Finally, Melony broke the silence.

"When did you get out? The last time I talked to you, you told me that they said it's gon' be a couple o' weeks."

"That's what I thought. I guess the judge was going on vacation or something and didn't want to leave the next dude with his mess, so he processed me out before he went."

"That's what's up," a smiling Melony said.

She grabbed his hand and led him to her bedroom. The bed wasn't even made up but Chaz didn't give a fuck about that. All he was thinking about was getting into some pussy. He pushed her back on the bed started tearing off his clothes. She was amazed at how thick and well defined his body had gotten since he was away. Just looking at his washboard abs made her mouth water. She had a brief moment of sadness thinking about Shank, but that all went away when he dropped his pants and revealed his cement hard eight and a half inch dick.

"Baby you gon' get undressed or what?" he asked.

"Nope," she said staring at his groin area.

"Nope? The fuck you mean nope?"

"Cause, nigga, I want you to undress me."

"Shit you ain't got to tell me twice baby." Chaz attacked her like she was the last woman on earth. He popped every button on her blouse trying to get it open.

"Damn, brute ass nigga take it easy!"

"Fuck that shit! You know how long it's been since a nigga had some pussy?"

"Betta be the last time I gave you some," she said as she slid out of her skirt. The way he tore her top off, she wasn't going to give him a chance to tear up her skirt. He roughly kissed her neck and groped her body with his right hand while tugging her panties down with his left. As soon as he got them off, he grabbed both of her ankles and spread her legs in a giant V.

"Baby wait. Did you bring a con...Oh, shit!" she screamed as he plunged deep inside her womb.

Chaz took two years of pinned up frustration out on Melony's love hole. He pounded her from one side of the bed to the other, doggie style and missionary, with her lying on her back and bent over. Just when she was ready to submit and tell him that she couldn't take any more, he shot his seed deep inside her.

"Oh, shit! Oh, my God!" she screamed as she felt the flow of semen travel through her canal. "Shit! I hope you don't plan on fuckin' me like that all the time. I don't know if my pussy hole can take it."

Chaz didn't say a word. He just laid there with a pressure relieved smile on his face.

Bennie picked up the phone and dialed Dre's cell phone

number. He figured it was time to let his crew know what happened. He was feeling much better this morning. The doctors were even talking about releasing him because he was healing so quickly. He hoped like hell they did. He was getting tired of eating the nasty ass Hospital food they were giving out. After getting the voice mail, he figured he'd call CeCe. Bennie knew that Mo and Stacy wasn't getting back in town until tomorrow and he didn't want to call Ty's erratic ass. CeCe picked up on the second ring, answering the call from the hospital cautiously. She didn't know of anybody that was in the hospital. After explaining most of what happened to her, CeCe was livid.

But the difference between her and Ty is that she wouldn't go off without thinking. Ty woulda wanted to shoot every enemy in sight. CeCe was a killer, but she wasn't gung ho with it. She was an efficient assassin. Bennie didn't want to tell anyone of Audrey's involvement just yet. To assassinate her would take some careful planning with her being the Chief of Police's wife. But there was no way he was gonna let her get away with shooting him. He didn't care who she was, she had to die. And if Charity and Amanda got in the way, then they would get it too.

Chapter 35

Stacy and CeCe sat in Applebee's restaurant waiting on Sugar and Spice. After hearing about what had happened to Bennie, they decided to push the meeting back an hour.

"Let me get this straight," Stacy said. "This nigga got shot, in his own apartment, and he don't know who the fuck shot him?"

"That's what he said," CeCe responded.

"Do you believe him?"

"I don't know. Bennie ain't never been the type to lie to the crew, but then again he might be embarrassed."

"Why would you say that?"

"You know how Bennie is. For one he wants to be macho. Plus, it coulda been one of those white hoes he be fuckin' with."

"Is everything straight with Ty?"

"Yeah he straight. He's gonna be easy to convince. He already thinks he should be making more money." Stacy glanced at the door and saw her step sisters walk in. They took a seat directly across from Stacy and CeCe.

"What's good?" Spice asked.

"Shit, we was hoping you could tell us," CeCe replied.

"Well, we got our partner going shopping for us in a about a week. If all goes well, and I don't anticipate it going any way other than that, then we should be in business," Spice said.

"Have you had a chance to talk to your crew about what we talked about," Sugar asked.

"No, but we have a meeting scheduled in a couple of days. I don't anticipate any problems from my people either, she answered.

The four women sat silently and stared at each other for a full minute. Finally CeCe broke the ice.

"What the fuck? Are we gonna sit here and stare at each other or are we gonna get reacquainted?" With that statement, the tension was lifted as all four women burst out laughing.

"Look," Stacy said. "If we are gonna be working together, then we need to start gettin' the fuck along."

The waitress walked over with a tray of wings and four glasses of wine. Stacy grabbed her glass and held it in the air. "To starting new partnerships and letting old grudges go." The other three women clicked glass with her and a seal was formed.

"Stacy, I hate to bring this up," Sugar stated," "but are you gonna be able to do this?"

"Don't worry about me," she replied. "I'm straight."

Sugar nodded her head approvingly and tossed back her drink.

ꟍꟍꟍ

Audrey was so tired of hearing the telephone ring that she wanted to take it off the hook. Being at the hospital for that long had her exhausted. She had hoped to see her husband's eyes open so she could try to comfort him. But she never did. She really needed another drink but didn't feel like getting up. After willing herself to the kitchen and pouring herself another stiff one, the phone rang again. Since she was already up, she figured she might as well answer it. She was pleasantly surprised when she saw that it was the hospital. Her spirits picked up and her energy returned as she picked up the phone and gave whoever was on the other end a cheery hello.

"Mrs. Murphy?"

"Yes, this is me."

"Hi Mrs. Murphy, this is nurse Lang. I was calling to let you know that the doctor would like for you to come back to the hospital immediately. He needs to talk to you."

"Oh, ok. How is my husband doing? Has he regained consciousness yet?"

Heavy silence filled the air.

"Hello?"

"Yes Mrs. Murphy, I'm here."

"Did you hear me?"

"Mrs. Murphy, hold on for one minute ok?"

Before Audrey could even respond, the nurse had put her on hold. A few seconds later a different nurse came on the line.

"Mrs. Murphy?"

"Yes."

"I'm Nurse Jackson. I was here when you left a few hours ago. We've been trying to reach you for the last few hours."

"Is everything alright?"

"I'm afraid not ma'am. About ten minutes after you left, your husband fell into a coma. I'm sorry to tell you this, but your husband passed away about two hours ago."

Chapter 36

Chaz woke up to the smell of slightly burned bacon. He smiled at the reality of not waking up in a jail cell but to the comfort of a soft, warm bed. He wondered if Melony had a man. If she did, she hadn't said anything about the him, so he wasn't gonna worry about it. He sat up in the bed as Melony walked through the door carrying a food tray with a plate on it filled with bacon, eggs, grits, and toast.

"Good morning baby," she said, greeting him with a warm smile.

"Why the fuck you walkin' like that?"

"Why the fuck you think nigga? My pussy sore."

"Oh, my bad ma. A nigga was backed the fuck up fo' real."

"Yeah right," she said. "Yo' ass ain't sorry. It's a good thing a bitch on birth control pills or I'd be good and pregnant with all that nut you bust up in a bitch."

"Birth control pills huh?" Chaz replied. This was the first sign that he had received that she was screwing around with someone. Melony dropped her head.

"Yeah. I had a man."

"Had? What you break up wit that nigga or somethin'?"

"No. He got killed the other day."

"Oh, I'm sorry to hear that Mel, I really am."

Tears started to leak from her eyes and onto the floor. Chaz got up and wrapped his arms around her. He really didn't give a fuck bout her man getting sent to hell but figured that this was a way to gain brownie points.

"It's ok ma. I'm here now. I'ma take care of everything from now on."

She squeezed him tight as he kissed her on her forehead. For as sad as she was about Shank being gone, Chaz was the man who had her heart. She'd always loved him.

"Eat your breakfast baby. I'ma see if the newspaper came yet."

Chaz watched her walk out of the room wondering if she was still wifey material. At one point, before he got locked up, he even considered proposing to her. But first things first. When she got back, he was gonna ask her for his driver's license and the safety deposit key he'd left with her. He had moves to make. The second he stepped out of prison, he made his mind up to either ball or fall. She came back with the paper and sat down next to him. Before he was locked up, he was never a big reader but figured since she had taken the trouble of getting it for him, he might as well look at it. The first page headline slapped him in the face like a ton of bricks. *Chief of Police Brad Murphy dies from mysterious illness.'*

"What's wrong baby," Melony asked.

"Huh? Oh, nothin'. Just checkin' out some of' the bullshit in the world today."

Since Brad and Chaz had different last names, not many people knew that they were brothers. Chaz preferred it that way. He was cool with Mo, but he hated his other half brother with a passion. They had the same mother but different fathers. Brad always looked down on Chaz. He didn't like him because he was a product of an affair. t has been said that he could have done more to keep Chaz out of jail. Money wasn't the problem as Big Mo held him down on that tip. A satisfied grin graced his face. *Mysterious illness my ass,* he thought. He'd seen Brad snort cocaine before he even became Chief of police. Truth be told, He'd dreamt about blowing his half brother's brains out many a night while in prison.

He then turned to the next page and shook his head as he

read the next headline. *Witnesses left stunned as local sports bar manager jumps to his death.* With a slight smirk on his face, he read on. *Police identified the body of Michael Green after 911 calls flooded the lines about a man who jumped off the east 72nd Street pier to his death. Witnesses there told the police that the man was acting very strange and talking to himself just before running full speed and diving into the river. By the time authorities arrived on the scene to help, it was too late.*

"Weak ass muthafucka," Chaz mumbled. "Went out like a straight bitch."

"What you say baby?"

"I was just reading about this lame ass cracker that killed his dumb ass self," he told her, holding the paper up where she could see it.

As soon as Melony saw the picture, he mouth fell open.

"What, you know that muthafucka or something?"

"I don't really know him. I just saw his ass in a bar yesterday. I had to cuss his ass out for gettin' fly and shit."

"Well, his ass won't be getting' fly wit nobody else," Chaz said. "Hey, you still got that for me?"

"Hell yeah. You know I kept my word to you baby." She got up and walked over to her dresser and pulled it out. Grabbing a screwdriver that lay on the floor next to the dresser, she removed a plate that covered a hole in the wall and took out his license and a key.

"That's what's up!" Chaz replied as she handed them to him. Chaz had big plans. His brother may have had the weed trade in Cleveland locked down, but he wanted to be larger than weed. Mo told him he was gonna put him on when he got out but the only thing he wanted to do with weed was smoke it. He had bigger dreams.

"What's the key to baby?" Melony asked.

"You know what? You ask too many questions," Chaz said as he pulled her down on the bed. For the second time in less than twelve hours Chaz commenced to blowing out Melony's pussy.

Chapter 37

(One week later)

Stacy sat at the head of table in her basement explaining the false version of what went down in the Bahamas. CeCe didn't feel the need to say anything so she just sat there quietly. She was still trying to figure out why Dre was acting so strange. When the rest of the Chedda Boyz questioned her about the whereabouts of their leader, she responded by telling them that Big Mo stayed in the Bahamas trying to get them hooked up to another business opportunity. She'd also told them that he'd accidentally left his cell phone on the plane and he would get another one when he got back to the states.

They also wanted to know who the two women were that were allowed to sit in on their private meeting. Bennie especially wanted to know, since he was second in command and know one had bothered to inform him of strangers infiltrating the Chedda Boys camp. It was bad enough that he was fresh out of the hospital, after leaving without being released. He still didn't feel too well, but listened on as Stacy continued to talk. After explaining that good changes were in store and that they were all on the verge of being able to make some serious money, Stacy felt that the time was right to introduce her step sisters.

"That's where these two ladies come in."

Sugar and Spice stood up met the uncertain gazes of the rest of the crew. While Dre and Ty had their eyes glued on Stacy and CeCe's voluptuous step-sisters, Bennie was staring disapprovingly at Stacy, making it known how he felt about being left out of the decision making loop. She ignored him as she waited to see if anyone had anything to say. When no one spoke up, she proceeded.

"These two women are Sugar and Spice, our step sisters. By hooking up with them and using their connections, we stand to make quite a bit of money."

"How much money we talkin' 'bout," Dre asked, rubbing his hands together at the thought of making more money.

"Let's just say that if you stick with us, each one of you niggas stand to make as much as a half a million dollars in only a couple of months."

"Now that's what the fuck I'm talkin' bout!" Ty yelled. "Man y'all know what kinda bitches I can get to suck my dick making that type o' dough?"

Dre cut his eyes at Ty. He wanted to shoot him in the face right then and there.

"Hold up a second dawg," Bennie said as he looked at Ty. "This shit don't sound right. You mean to fuckin' tell me that we can make this kinda cheese and Mo aint here to oversee it? And why do we need this connect if Mo is talking to one in the Bahamas?"

"I didn't know about this connect until I got back Bennie, damn," Stacy said. She was getting increasingly irritated by Bennie's questions. "And why does Mo have to be here to oversee this shit? Nigga didn't he leave yo ass in charge?"

"Yo' I'm just sayin' I think he should be here if we gon' make a big ass decision like this."

"Ok, Bennie," Stacy replied. "Let's say we wait and they find somebody else to plug in. Then we miss out on millions."

"Find somebody else? Damn, she yo' step sister, she can't wait?"

"Hell naw we can't wait," Spice said, speaking for the first time. "Look Bernie or Bennie or whatever the fuck your name is. We tryin' to put y'all on to make some major paper. Now, if y'all niggas got kool aid pumpin' through ya veins, then me and my sister can just roll the fuck out."

"Bennie, dawg I'm loyal to Mo too man," Dre said, "but we

gotta chance to make some heavyweight paper here dawg. I think we should take it."

Bennie looked at Stacy, who held up her hands and shrugged.

"It's yo call Bennie," she said.

"Fine," he said holding up his hands. "Let's do it."

"That's what's up," Ty stated. Although he agreed to the deal, Bennie still couldn't shake the feeling that Stacy was hiding something.

$$\text{\textcurrency}\text{\textcurrency}\text{\textcurrency}$$

Enrique sat in a quiet corner booth in Borders sipping the foam off the top of his latte. With his nose pressed firmly against the inside of a Wall Street Journal newspaper, the smiled as he noticed that one of his investments in the stock market was doing quite well. He looked at his diamond Rolex and frowned. He didn't like it when his business associates were late for meetings. He returned to reading his paper and looked up just in time to see a starry eyed young woman approaching him. He then looked over to the booth next to the window and motioned for his two body guards, who were trying to look inconspicuous, to be ready in case some bullshit jumped off. Trish wiggled her frame into the booth seat directly across from Enrique smiling from ear to ear.

"May I help you young lady?" he asked.

"Uh…Sugar sent me," she said, suddenly appearing very nervous.

Enrique immediately got upset. He didn't like to do business with runners. In his experience, those were the ones that got you knocked. He stared at her for a few seconds and got up, motioning for his bodyguards to follow him out the door.

"I'm am sorry senorita, but I do not know this Sugar that you speak of."

He walked out the door leaving Trish sitting there looking lost. As soon as Enrique got to his car, he opened his cell phone and called Sugar.

"Senorita Sugar, please explain yourself," he said. "Not only do you not show up for the meeting but you send someone that I do not know. I know you don't expect me to send ten of them with a total stranger.

"Oh, shit!" Sugar screamed on the other end. "I'm very sorry my friend. I was in another meeting and the time got away from me. I meant to call you and let you know that I would be sending someone in my place. I'm working on a very big deal that could be profitable to all of us, especially you."

Hearing this made Enrique perk up a little bit.

"Profitable you say?"

"Hugely!" she exclaimed. "I'll meet with you later and fill you in on the details."

Enrique snapped his cell phone shut and smiled as he sensed more cash would soon be on the horizon.

$$$

Audrey sat on her bed with her hands in her head. The constant flow of tears streaming from her eyes had all but soaked the top of her black dress. She had just got finished burying her husband an hour ago, and now her house was overrun with police and family. The police force took the liberty of picking up the tab for the catered repast. She just couldn't believe that her husband was gone. The only thing good to come out of this was the five hundred thousand dollar life insurance policy she had on him. At least she wouldn't starve.

"Mom, are you ok?" Charity questioned as she walked in without knocking.

"Not really sweetheart. It's gonna take time for me to get over this. I've been with that man a long time and I'm going to miss the hell out of him."

Charity wrapped her arms around her mother and hugged her tight.

"I know mom. I'm so sorry."

Just then Amanda walked in with a concerned look on her

face.

"Hey, how you guys doing?"

Charity nodded toward her mother and shook her head, letting Amanda know that Audrey wasn't taking it too good. "I'm about to go to the store mom. Do you need anything?"

"As a matter of fact I do. Bring me back some skins."

Both sisters looked at each other. They knew what that meant. Their mother wanted them to pick up a pack of white owls. Whenever Audrey got depressed about something, she would blaze up a joint, hoping that it would take her troubles away. She also wanted to be alone, which is why she sent both of them.

"How many more people are downstairs?" she asked.

"Only four and I think they're getting ready to leave," Amanda said.

"Good. I'm sick of them being here anyway. Bring me back a pack of white owls, but go out the back door. Maybe the rest of them will get the hint and leave."

"Are you going to the store with me, Amanda?"

"No, I have to run home right quick. I'll see you when I get back."

$$\maltese\maltese\maltese$$

Chaz walked inside National City bank feeling and looking like new money. He had just convinced Melony to give him her last two hundred and fifty dollars so he could go cop some gear. After buying a Cleveland Cavaliers jump suit, a fitted hat, and a fresh pair of kicks, he had her take him back to her place where he could shower and change. He did do a quick wash up before he left to go to the store but figured why shower when he was gonna put the same clothes back on? Melony asked him if he wanted to wear some of Shank's old clothes and got cussed out for her troubles. Chaz wouldn't be caught dead wearing another niggas shit.

She wanted to kick it with him all day, but he nixed that idea quick. He wanted to get nice and didn't feel like having a bitch beside him, all in his ear fuckin' up his groove. Besides he wanted to stop by and surprise Mo later on. He thought about calling him but figured the shock of Mo seeing him would be better. Plus, she had to go to school, and if it was one thing he learned from muthafuckas in the joint was that knowledge was power. He was going to encourage her going to school to the fullest. He walked in the lobby and took a seat. He wasn't there five minute when a white, grey haired man with freckles approached him.

"Hi sir, how may I help you?"

"Yo, I need to get into my safety deposit box dawg."

Chaz handed him his license and showed him the key.

"Just one minute sir," freckles said. After typing something on the computer, he walked back over to Chaz. "Follow me sir."

Chaz followed him, smiling all the way to the back.

Chapter 38

Bennie watched as the last car drove away from Audrey's house. Parked in a school parking lot down the street, he sat in his whip smoking a blunt. His red eyes stared holes into the house as he remembered the pain of the bullet shredding part of his insides. For the time being he was now forced to walk with a cane and hated every minute of it. He would talk to Stacy later about the arrangement that they had made with their step sisters. It struck him a little odd that Mo hadn't mentioned anything to him about it. Being that he was second in command, he felt he had a right to know about these things beforehand. A light tapping on the window broke his train of thought. He unlocked the door and let his passenger in.

Dressed in all black with a black hoodie pulled over his head and dark shades covering his eyes he handed Bennie a slip of paper. Bennie wrote down Audrey's address and handed the paper back to him, along with an envelope containing ten thousand dollars. The shadow slid out of the whip and made his way back down the street. Walking with speed, he looked at the paper one last time and then pulled a lighter from his pocket. With one flick he set fire to the paper and dropped it on the ground. When he got to the address, he looked around quickly. With no one paying attention he threw what appeared to be two bottles of beer into the house.

Bennie sat back and smiled as he watched the two cocktails blow Audrey and everyone else in the house to smithereens. Ten minutes after the explosion, he was still sitting there watching as the smoke and ashes from the blown up house rose toward the clouds. Smiling from ear to ear, he reached into his console and took out a freshly rolled blunt. After taking a few puffs from the thick get high stick and blowing the toxic fumes into the air, he jumped and instinctively reached for his gun at the sound of the passenger side door opening. Two seconds after she got in the car, Charity was sticking her tongue down Bennie's throat. Her left hand started unbuckling his belt while her right hand started unzipping hi pants.

"Damn girl, let a nigga catch his breath," Bennie said. She smiled and leaned back in the seat.

"Pull that muthafucka out baby. I'm about to celebrate by giving you the best fuckin' blowjob you ever had in your life."

She glanced down at the vibrating cell phone on her hip and unclipped it. Her cell phone had been going off for the last ten minutes. There was no need to answer since she already knew what it was about. Although she didn't mind having a threesome with her mother from time to time, there was no way in the world that she was going to let her mother come in between her and the juicy black dick that she had come to love. So, when she began to believe that her mother was making plans to take Bennie back, she figured the best way to solve the problem was to eliminate her from the equation.

Bennie was shocked when Charity first introduced her plan to murder her mother but since he planned on killing her anyway he decided to go along with Charity's plan. Charity turned off her cell phone, grabbed Bennie's dick, and proceeded to give him the blowjob of a lifetime.

$$$

Trish went into the restroom at Borders and splashed cold water on her face.

"What the fuck did I just do?" she mumbled to herself.

She knew she was gonna be a little nervous when Sugar

told her that she needed her to go make the transaction with her connect but now she was wondering if her nervousness had caused him to get up and walk out without making the deal. She was supposed to return with ten kilos of cocaine but instead she would be going back empty handed. Trish panicked when her cell phone vibrated and Sugar's number came up on the caller I'd. Having no idea how she would explain her failure, Trish nervously answered the phone.

"He...hello?"

She listened intently for a minute and then breathed a sigh of relief after Sugar told her that she had forgotten to make the call to Enrique. After having that load off her mind, Trish needed a drink. She wasn't a total stranger to Cleveland so she knew just where to go to toss back a few. Hopping in the 2008 Acura Legend Sugar provided for her, it only took her ten minutes to get to the bar. Five minutes after she sat down and ordered her drink, a young muscular dude sat down on the stool next to her.

Looking like a baller in his saggy blue jeans, Sean John shirt, and crisp Air Force ones he preceded to get his Mack on. "What's poppin ma?" Chaz asked with a smile on his face.

Trish looked around the place for a minute before pointing a finger to herself.

"You talkin' to me playa?"

"Come on Ma, let's not play games a021ght? Ain't nobody in this joint but you, me, and the bartender. Let a nigga buy you a drink."

"Thanks, but I ain't finished with this one yet."

"Don't make no difference. I got the next one."

Chaz reached into his pocket and pulled out a wad of fifties and hundreds. Seeing the crispy greenbacks may have impressed some women but not Trish. Being associated with Sugar and Spice, she was used to being around large sums of cash. Although Chaz seemed to have a little paper, what Trish was really interested in was the bulge in his pants. She may have been a carpet muncher but unbeknownst to Sugar she loved to ride a stiff dick. While she was busy sizing up his dick through his pants, he was just as busy checking out her petite frame. Melony may have been his girl, but

Chaz was a cockhound in every sense of the word. The day he got out of prison he vowed to try to fuck anything in a skirt. He peeled off a fifty, laid it on the counter, and told the bartender to keep 'em coming. As soon as Trish would finish one drink, the bartender was placing another one in front of her. After four drinks and some serious macking by Chaz, Trish was on fire. With the bartender engrossed in a replay of the Cavs and Lakers game and the bar being empty this time of day Chaz made his move.

"Damn baby you look good as fuck," he said, placing his hand on her thigh and squeezing it gently. The second his hand touched her skin, heat surged through her body.

Her pussy became wet instantly as she let her hand travel down to his crotch. The liquor in her system told her to grab his dick and she didn't argue with it as she clutched his hard on. "Damn baby, it's like that," she purred.

The sensual way she touched him almost caused him to nut in his jeans. Chaz couldn't take it anymore. Grabbing her hand he pulled her toward the back of the bar and into the men's bathroom. Once inside, he turned around to face her only to find that she had fallen to her knees. Quickly, Trish undid his belt buckle and before Chaz knew what was going on, she had his dick in her mouth.

"Oooo....ohh shit baby," he moaned. It didn't take long for Chaz to send millions of swimmers down Trish's throat. Chaz was satisfied but Trish wasn't done.

After swallowing nearly all of Chaz's cum, she pushed him into a stall and told him to sit down. She was pleased to see that busting a nut didn't make his dick go down. He was still rock when she mounted him.

"Oh, fuck!" she yelled.

Although her pussy was wet, Trish hadn't had a dick up in her in a while so it took a minute to get all of Chaz's massive man inside of her. The pain soon turned to insatiable pleasure as she bounced up and down on Chaz's love tool. Chaz's face contorted as he grunted and moaned trying to push every inch further up inside Trish's vagina. He under hooked her shoulders and with one quick thrust emptied a second supply of seeds, this time deep inside her womb. The two of them sat there for a full five minutes before getting up and exiting the bathroom. The two eased back down on the bar stool and looked at the bartender who was enjoying an overtime thriller by the Cavs and Lakers. After getting Trish's cell phone number, Chaz told her that he had to run. On his way out the door, the bartender glanced at him, gave him a sly smile, and shook his head. Chaz got within a block of Melony's apartment and got pulled over by the police. The cop told Chaz that he was stopping him for failure to yield, which Chaz knew was some bullshit. He figured the flatfoot was just bored and was simply harassing him because he had nothing better to do. He was the most surprised person in the city of Cleveland when the cop arrested him for violation of parole. Chaz knew he'd done nothing to violate his parole, but went down to the station without a fight. But as luck would have it, for once the judicial system was on his side. With no witnesses the case was flimsy and Chaz was finally released.

Chapter 39

Dre sat back on his couch smoking a blunt and drinking a glass of Hennessey. Turning his head to the right, he stole a quick glance at CeCe as she slept in a recliner, snoring softly. He then picked up his Desert Eagle forty-five caliber handgun and pointed it at CeCe's head. Rage filled his heart as he cocked back the hammer. After closing his eyes and taking a deep breath, he uncocked his weapon and sat it back on the table. For the past six weeks Dre had tried to forget about the fact that his cousin had fucked his woman and just enjoy the large paper that was now coming his way but he couldn't do it. Every time he fucked CeCe he wondered if she was thinking of or comparing him to Ty.

Whenever he saw Ty, visions of him coming in CeCe's face or mouth played in his mind. He knew how kinky Ty was and he definitely knew what kind of freak his woman was. That alone made him want to blow Ty's brains out. He thought that Ty would've been in jail by now stemming from the time that he set him up, but Ty's slick ass lawyer kept getting the trial date pushed back and that was making Dre antsy. He didn't know how much longer he could keep associating with Ty without killing him.

CeCe on the other hand was liking the new Dre. In her eyes Dre had transformed from the lame, non-fucking half a man that was there before to the confident, pussy pounding, fuck machine who was blowing her back out on a regular. The fact that he wasn't talking as much as he used to didn't bother her one bit. She just chalked that up to him turning into the strong silent type. Looking at CeCe one last time, Dre grabs his gun off the table and stood up to leave. He stuck his gun into his waistband and walked toward the door, accidently bumping into the recliner and waking CeCe up.

"You going somewhere baby?" she asked groggily. "You know we got that meeting in less than an hour."

"I know that. I'm going to pick Ty up," he said, slowly walking toward the door.

"Shit baby, he can't drive his self?"

"You gotta problem with me goin' ta pickup Ty?"

"What? Dre go 'head on with that shit. I don't give a fuck about you pickin' that punk ass nigga up."

Dre stopped dead in his tracks. He turned and glared at CeCe, who had laid back and closed her eyes. "Was he a punk ass nigga when you was fuckin' the shit out of him?"

CeCe opened her eyes and sat straight up. "Huh? Nigga what the fuck you talkin' 'bout?"

"Don't play stupid with me CeCe! You know what the fuck I'm talkin''bout! What? You thought I wasn't gonna find out about that shit?"

CeCe was speechless. She had no idea that Dre even knew about the affair.

"What's wrong? Cat got ya fuckin' tongue?"

"CeCe took a deep breath and held up her hands. "Ok, look Dre. That shit happened a long time ago. I ain't fucked wit that nigga since then."

She walked up to Dre and tried to wrap her arms around him but he pushed her arms away and before he could stop himself, he backhanded her to the floor. CeCe fell right beside the end table that had her Nine millimeter resting on it.

"Nigga no the fuck you didn't!" she screamed.

Seeing her reach for her gun, Dre made a dash for the door. He could have gotten his gun out before she got to hers but in truth, he didn't want to shoot her. Dre opened the door and ran out of the house. The bullet whistled past his head just as he jumped off of the porch.

✟✟✟

Chaz hadn't been out of jail a full two days and was already having a bad week. Melony was seven weeks pregnant and he didn't have a dime to his name. Mo wasn't answering his house or cell phone, so he couldn't hit his big brother up for a loan. The large sum of cash that he'd stashed in the back of Melony's car had mysteriously disappeared while the car was in the Police impound lot and Chaz was pissed. He knew beyond a shadow of a doubt that the crooked ass Police had divided up his dough and there wasn't shit that he could do about it. He needed money, fast. After getting tired of hearing Melony bitch about morning sickness for the past hour, Chaz walked out of the house on a mission for liquor. After purchasing a fifth of Jack Daniels, Chaz walked out of the local state store and ran right into Bennie.

"Damn, if it ain't my nigga Bennie! What's been up wit chu fam?"

"Ain't shit poppin' playboy! What's good wit chu?" asked Bennie as the two exchanged a manly hug and a fist pound. "I heard yo' ass got out over a month and a half ago dawg! Where the fuck you been hidin?"

"Man it's a long ass, depressin' ass story. But yo man, where the fuck is my brother? He ain't answering his house phone or his cell phone. Him and that broad Stacy on vacation or something?"

"Man you know how that nigga do. He outta town handling some business." Bennie decided to keep his mouth closed on not hearing from Mo in over six weeks for the time being. He wanted to find out from Stacy what was really going on before he jumped the gun. But one thing was for sure. Someone was going to tell him something about Mo's whereabouts at this meeting.

"Damn nigga," Chaz said. "Let a muthafucka take a look at you dawg." Chaz stepped back and looked Bennie up and down. Bennie was g'd up. His wrist held one hundred and thirty diamonds and the equally iced out chain around his neck had a price tag of around forty thousand dollars.

"Damn nigga, you must be gettin' it to be blinged up like that," Chaz said, with dollar signs in his eyes.

"Nigga listen. The Chedda Boys get the job done son," he said as he held up his chain. "Man speaking of jobs dawg, I need one like a crackhead need a rock. I'm broke as a joke man. Plus, I just found out that my girl is pregnant. Y'all got room for another stallion in y'all stable."

"You Mo's brother nigga. Hell yeah we got room for you." "We got a meeting in about..."

"Daaammnn dawg," Chaz marveled as he eyed the rocked up thirty thousand dollar Rolex.

"Oh, yeah nigga, we the shit. Them other nigga are just a piece of it. Let's roll out. I'ma let them otha niggas know what time it is."

Bennie hit the chirp on his flossed out Bentley GT that he hardly ever drove. It was silver with charcoal tinted windows, Lorenzo rims, and yokohuna tires. The total cost of tricking his ride out was somewhere around sixty thousand. Chaz's day had just got a hell of a lot better. He hopped in the passenger's seat in search of a come up. And he planned to get it by any means necessary.

$$$

Dre walked in Ty's living room and handed him a double deuce bottle of Corona beer. "You ready to go to this meeting cuz?" Ty asked, lacing up his pearly white air force one's.

"In a minute dawg. Let's drink one first while a nigga get some rest."

"Rest? Nigga what the fuck you need rest for?"

"Shit nigga, I just got finished banging my girl dawg. She wore a muthafucka out."

"Oh, yeah?" Ty said, avoiding Dre's gaze.

"Hell yeah. Man CeCe got some good ass pussy. Matter of fact," Dre bragged as he leaned down to whisper in Ty's ear, "if she was just anotha bitch instead of my woman I would let you test drive that shit nigga."

Ty tensed up, but continued to play it off. "Fuck outta here man. I don't wanna fuck yo' girl dawg."

"If she was just anotha bitch, she wouldn't be my girl nigga."

The two looked at each other in awkward silence for a minute. "Look at us though dawg," Dre said, breaking the silence. "Since them two hoes Sugar and Spice stepped on the scene, we been making mad loot."

"Hell yeah," Ty co-signed. "That's what the fuck I'm talkin' 'bout."

"Let's toast to that shit," Dre replied. They clicked their bottle of beer together. "Last one finished is a bitch," Dre challenged as he turned his bottle up.

"Then I guess you gon' be a bitch then nigga," Ty said, turning his bottle up and accepting the challenge. Dre purposely let Ty finish his beer first as he pretended like he needed a break. "Hell yeah nigga!" Ty shouted. "I told yo' bitch ass! Nigga you know I'm the king of drink."

Dre shrugged it off and continued to drink his beer slowly. After about ten minutes of shooting the shit with each other, Ty grabbed his stomach.

"You ahight dawg?" Dre asked.

"Man I gotta go to the bathroom," Ty said, as he half walked, half limped to the bathroom doubled over.

Dre smiled a sinister smile. The extra strength laxative that he gave Ty was starting to take effect. He waited three minutes and then went to the bathroom door. Pushing the door open, he stared at a grunting and moaning Ty sitting on the stool.

"Damn nigga, where the fuck did you buy that beer from? That shit got me all fucked up."

Ignoring Ty's complaints, Dre pulled out his gun. "You didn't think that I would find out about you fuckin' my woman Ty?" Dre asked.

"What? Man what the fuck you talkin'…"

"Ty she just got finished admitting the shit man! Don't

make the shit worse by lying to me man! You my fuckin' cousin!"
Dre yelled, pointing the gun in and out of Ty's face like it was a
finger. "How the fuck you gon' play me like that man?"

"Dre, I'm sorry man. That shit was a big ass mistake. We
didn't mean for that shit ta happen cuz. We ain't done nothing
since and I swear that shit ain't never gon' happen again."

"I know it won't."

With tears stinging his pupils Dre pointed the gun at Ty's
head. He then closed his eyes, pulled the trigger and exposed his
cousin's brains to daylight. As his final act of revenge, Dre took
out his dick and pissed in Ty's face. After that he closed the bathroom door and walked out of the house.

Chapter 40

Sugar and Spice pulled up in Gordon Park driving a cherry red 2009 Maserati. Both were iced out with platinum diamond bracelets and chains. Sugar stepped tall in a pair of Prada Boots while Spice slid gracefully in Jimmy Choo open toes. They sat in the car and awaited the rest of the crew. Ten minutes later, Stacy pulled up in a white 2009 Lamborghini Murcielago. She too was iced out with diamonds. The platinum "S" hanging around her neck cost a small fortune. Before she could get out of her car, Bennie's Bentley pulled up beside her. Chaz was riding shotgun sitting right next to him.

"What it do pimpstress!" Bennie yelled around Chaz.

"Who's your friend Bennie?" she asked, not recognizing Chaz from the photos sent from jail.

"Yo' this Chaz. Mo's brother."

Stacy squinted her eyes and looked a little harder. "Oh, shit nigga, it is you. Damn you done got big as fuck!" She got out of the car, walked over to the window, and gave Chaz a hug.

"Shit, all a nigga could do was work out. Hey, Bennie told me that my brother was outta town handling some business. When you talk to him, give him my cell number and tell him to call me."

"Ah...Ok, I can do that," Stacy said as Bennie gauged her reaction carefully.

Just then CeCe pulled up in her gold 2009 Mercedes Benz CL class, looking mad as fuck. She quickly jumped out of her car and head straight for Stacy's car. "Yo where the fuck is Dre?"

    Seeing the look on her face, Stacy motioned for her to get in the car as Bennie and Chaz looked at each other in confusion. After getting CeCe in the car and rolling up the windows for some privacy, Stacy asked her what was wrong. CeCe finally confessed that she had slept with Ty behind Dre's back and that Dre had found out about it, confronted her, and then slapped her.

    "Let me ask you somethin' sis," Stacy said. "If me and Dre was sleeping together and you found out about it, what would you do?"

    CeCe slowly shook her head from side to side. "I don't think I could let that shit ride sis. Somebody would have to die."

    "Well if you feel that way, then take it like a woman. Dre didn't kill you. He slapped you out of hurt and anger. Put yo' self in his shoes. His woman slept with his cousin."

    CeCe took a deep breath. "I guess you got a point."

    CeCe took out her droid cell phone and texted Dre, telling him that since she was in the wrong, she was gonna woman up and take the slap, but told him that he'd better not make that shit a habit. Two minutes after she got finished texting him, Dre pulled up in his blue tricked out Yukon Denali. Thinking that everyone had arrived, Stacy got out of her car and walked toward Sugar and Spice's car, motioning for the rest of the crew to do the same.

    "What the fuck was that all about?" Chaz asked Bennie in reference to CeCe.

    "Man I'll explain that shit to you later,' Bennie replied. "Oh, you strapped?"

    "Yeah I got my girls twenty-five on me, why? Ain't we amongst friends?"

    "Supposedly, but you never know," Bennie said mysteriously.

    Disregarding Bennie's comment, Chaz started thinking about all the money he was gonna make being down with the Chedda Boyz crew. He couldn't wait to start pocketing the dough. Once everyone gathered around Sugar's car, she began talking. "My friends. I wanna just start by sayin'... wait, where the hell is Ty?"

Dre quickly spoke up before CeCe had a chance to. "I don't know," he said. "I ain't seen him all day." CeCe cut her eyes at Dre. She tried to get his attention but he ignored her.

"Well, I guess somebody can fill his ass in later," Stacy said.

Sugar then looked at Chaz. "And who the hell is this?"

"Oh, my bad," Bennie said. This is Mo's Brother Chaz. He gon' be part of the crew from now on.

Sugar didn't like it but preferred not to make a scene. She didn't know Chaz so she didn't trust him. She decided to talk to Bennie and Stacy about it later.

"Anyway," Sugar said, "I called this meeting because our business associate likes the way that we been getting the dope off and bringin' the dough in. He likes it so much in fact that he wants to double our product. I know I don't have to tell y'all what kinda money we talkin' about if he does that." Ever so slowly smiles crept across the faces of the rest of the crew as they did the math in their heads.

Bennie however had his mind elsewhere. "So, once again, we gon make a major move without Mo knowing about it huh?"

"He'll know about it when I tell him," Stacy said.

"And just when the fuck is that gonna be?" Bennie asked. "I ain't heard from Mo in over six weeks. Correct me if I'm fuckin' wrong, but y'all don't think that shit is strange?" He was directing the question to Dre and Chaz. Ty wasn't there and he was convinced that whatever was going on, CeCe was a part of it.

"Look Bennie I don't know what the hell you are getting at but I told you…"

"Fuck that!" Bennie yelled. "The last time I checked, I was second in fuckin' command. We ain't gon' do a muthafuckin' thing else 'till I hear from Mo! I don't give a fuck how much money we stand to loose, I wanna get the fuckin' ok from Mo!"

Sugar, Spice, Stacy, and CeCe all looked at each other. They knew that wasn't going to happen.

"I ain't gotta wait for Mo to do a fuckin' thing!" CeCe boasted. "I'm a grown ass woman and I can make my own decisions with or without Mo!"

"Look," Sugar said, "either y'all take this deal or me and Spice will go somewhere else! We don't need y'all to make this shit happen!"

Chaz started to panic. He didn't know what was going on, but he desperately needed this deal to take place. Out of the blue, Bennie's cell rang. When the name of the hospital popped up on his phone, he instantly put everyone in the meeting on pause.

"Hello," he answered quickly.

Mr. Bennie Crayton, this is Nurse Payne. You left the hospital in the middle of the night. You weren't supposed to release yourself."

"What do you need?" Bennie asked in an irritated tone.

"We got your test results back. The doctors really need you to come back in for consultation."

Beads up sweat instantly formed on Bennie's forehead. "Yeah, I will," he said, knowing his life was about to change. He hung up with glassy eyes and refocused on the deal at hand.

"We ain't doing shit without Mo and that's fuckin' final!" Bennie shouted.

"Mo ain't coming back!" Spice yelled. "The muthafucka dead!"

An eerie silence washed over the park. For a few seconds, no one said a word. Then Bennie broke the silence. "What did you say?" he asked.

"You heard me," Spice said. "That nigga killed Stacy and CeCe's mother so while they were in the Bahamas, she blew his fuckin' brains out! So like I said, that nigga ain't coming.... " Before she could finish her sentence, Bennie and Chaz had drawn their guns. Bennie had his pointed at the four women, who were standing side by side. Chaz had his turned on Dre, who was still shocked at the revelation that his brother was dead.

Bennie spoke slowly, "First of all, y'all got the shit wrong. Mo didn't kill yo' fuckin' mother, I did! Mo killed your father," he said, pointing at Sugar and Spice. "And like I said, ain't no fuckin' deal without Mo, and sense he ain't here no more then the deal is fuckin' terminated! I don't give a fuck if I have to start from the ground, we ain't doing shit without Mo! As far as I'm concerned, all you muthafuckas died with Mo!"

Bennie cocked the hammer.

Pow!!

A loud shot echoed throughout the park. One body hit the cement. Chaz then lowered his gun and walked over to Bennie. A large hole took up residence where Bennie's ear used to live. Chaz just couldn't afford for this deal to collapse. As much as he loved his brother Mo and Bennie, he loved himself more.

Stay tuned for Mo Chedda
Coming Soon

CHECK OUT THESE LCB SEQUELS

 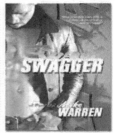

K'WAN
Presents

NATURAL BORN KILLAZ

Terry L. Wroten

K'wan Presents   Natural Born Killaz   Terry L. Wroten

ORDER FORM

Date:	Phone:
Email:	

MAIL TO:
PO Box 423
Brandywine, MD 20613
301-362-6508

FAX TO:
301-856-4116

Ship to:	
Address:	
City & State:	Zip:

Make all money orders and cashiers checks payable to: **Life Changing Books**

Qty.	ISBN	Title	Release Date	Price
	0-9741394-5-9	Nothin Personal by Tyrone Wallace	Jul-06	$ 15.00
	0-9741394-2-4	Bruised by Azarel	Jul-05	$ 15.00
	0-9741394-7-5	Bruised 2: The Ultimate Revenge by Azarel	Oct-06	$ 15.00
	0-9741394-3-2	Secrets of a Housewife by J. Tremble	Feb-06	$ 15.00
	0-9724003-5-4	I Shoulda Seen It Comin by Danette Majette	Jan-06	$ 15.00
	0-9741394-4-0	The Take Over by Tonya Ridley	Apr-06	$ 15.00
	0-9741394-6-7	The Millionaire Mistress by Tiphani	Nov-06	$ 15.00
	1-934230-99-5	More Secrets More Lies by J. Tremble	Feb-07	$ 15.00
	1-934230-98-7	Young Assassin by Mike G.	Mar-07	$ 15.00
	1-934230-95-2	A Private Affair by Mike Warren	May-07	$ 15.00
	1-934230-94-4	All That Glitters by Ericka M. Williams	Jul-07	$ 15.00
	1-934230-93-6	Deep by Danette Majette	Jul-07	$ 15.00
	1-934230-96-0	Flexin & Sexin Volume 1	Jun-07	$ 15.00
	1-934230-92-8	Talk of the Town by Tonya Ridley	Jul-07	$ 15.00
	1-934230-89-8	Still a Mistress by Tiphani	Nov-07	$ 15.00
	1-934230-91-X	Daddy's House by Azarel	Nov-07	$ 15.00
	1-934230-87-1-	Reign of a Hustler by Nissa A. Showell	Jan-08	$ 15.00
	1-934230-86-3	Something He Can Feel by Marissa Montelih	Feb-08	$ 15.00
	1-934230-88-X	Naughty Little Angel by J. Tremble	Feb-08	$ 15.00
	1-934230847	In Those Jeans by Chantel Jolie	Jun-08	$ 15.00
	1-934230855	Marked by Capone	Jul-08	$ 15.00
	1-934230820	Rich Girls by Kendall Banks	Oct-08	$ 15.00
	1-934230839	Expensive Taste by Tiphani	Nov-08	$ 15.00
	1-934230782	Brooklyn Brothel by C. Stecko	Jan-09	$ 15.00
	1-934230669	Good Girl Gone bad by Danette Majette	Mar-09	$ 15.00
	1-934230804	From Hood to Hollywood by Sasha Raye	Mar-09	$ 15.00
	1-934230707	Sweet Swagger by Mike Warren	Jun-09	$ 15.00
	1-934230677	Carbon Copy by Azarel	Jul-09	$ 15.00
	1-934230723	Millionaire Mistress 3 by Tiphani	Nov-09	$ 15.00
	1-934230715	A Woman Scorned by Ericka Williams	Nov-09	$ 15.00
	1-934230685	My Man Her Son by J. Tremble	Feb-10	$ 15.00
	1-924230731	Love Heist by Jackie D.	Mar-10	$ 15.00
	1-934230812	Flexin & Sexin Volume 2	Apr-10	$ 15.00
	1-934230748	The Dirty Divorce by Miss KP	May-10	$ 15.00

Total for Books	$	
Shipping Charges (add $4.25 for 1-4 books*)	$	
Total Enclosed (add lines)	$	

* Prison Orders- Please allow up to three (3) weeks for delivery.

Please Note: We are not held responsible for returned prison orders. Make sure the facility will receive books before ordering.

*Shipping and Handling of 5-10 books is $6.25, please contact us if your order is more than 10 books. (301)362-6508